FOGBOUND MANOR

· A NOVEL ·

FOGBOUND MANOR

MEG NORTH

BLACK ROSE PRESS
PORTLAND ME

Fogbound Manor, by Meg North

ISBN: 978-1-944384-01-2

For John and Valerie Atkin –
your kindness and support makes
me want to be a better writer.

* * *

And for Emily,
whose work inspired this story.

one

AT MY FATHER'S FUNERAL, there was no coffin. Cold and stiff, I sat in the Tate pew in the front row of the Kennebunkport church. My family's name was engraved in the wood on the side of the pew, and it was the same name that would have been carved into my father's coffin. But his body would never be brought back home to the place where he grew up. He rested a hundred miles away and a hundred fathoms down, spending eternity at the bottom of the Atlantic beneath the Isles of Shoals.

"Miss Harriet Tate will now speak on behalf of her father, Captain Sumner Francis Tate."

The minister stepped aside, and I rose from the pew. My eulogy folded and crinkled in my hands. With my skirts rustling and footsteps softly clicking on the wooden floor, I made my way to the pulpit. Black mourning bunting draped along the ends of the pews, black curtains shadowing the paned windows. The walls gleamed white and the pulpit before me was dark and polished mahogany. I couldn't look up at everyone - not yet. I couldn't have them all staring at me. My audience was not merely here for a funeral. They wanted to hear what I would do about my father's loss.

I smoothed the wrinkled eulogy on the pulpit, my fingers smearing the ink a little. I took a deep breath and allowed myself to look up and face those sitting, waiting. Not a sound. Not a cough, not a whimper. Nobody wept for the captain, and neither did I. My grandmother sat next to the empty space on the pew I had just vacated, staring down at her hands. She would not look up at me.

"There –," a pause, then a plunge into it, "there was a great storm off the coast of the Isles of Shoals. A tempest of such ferocity and power it was a foe Captain Tate could not withstand. We should be celebrating the return of another successful voyage. Yet, it was not to be. His record was unequaled in the history of Kennebunkport. No captain before him could match his success."

A success that I attest to, I thought. The Tate Mansion on Pleasant Street, the daily comforts I'd grown up with. I took a deep breath and continued.

"Captain Tate was a stellar example of his name, one deeply etched into the lives of those here in Kennebunkport. With his shipping company, he left a legacy that his family will forever attempt to uphold."

That I will uphold, I wanted to say. There was none other to assume the helm he had vacated.

"A town mourns this loss," I said. "Its effect will be felt the rest of your lives, and certainly the remainder of mine. My grandmother has said farewell to her only son, and I remain as his single child. May God watch over my father's everlasting soul, and may the Tate legacy live on."

I folded my eulogy and quietly returned to my seat. Grandmother clasped my hand so firmly it felt she was drawing from my stalwart energy. I will make sure, I promised silently. I will make sure the Tate legacy lives on. What other course in life is there? None will keep me from this aim, and damn those who want to try. They have yet to realize how strong I am.

A town did, indeed, mourn. There were no coffins to represent the crew onboard the *Phoenix*, no graves to dig, no final memento from a loved one to remember them by. Every one knew someone and could not be comforted by their glaring absence. A storm swept the ship onto the rocks, and none had come home.

One by one, the minister called out the names onboard. Edmund Percy, the first mate and my father's lifelong friend. Lemuel Sanborn, the second mate and perhaps the kindest man I'd ever known. His younger brother, Leander, was the third mate. I sat numbly in the pew, hearing the names of the dead like church bells thronging in my ears. Endless numbers of the dead, everyone a widow to cope alone.

The minister could say no more and ended his final sermon for the *Phoenix*. I wanted to go to each person in the church and remind them of my own upstanding firmness in helping to run the shipping company. They were lucky enough to not have a shiftless character trying to put their lives back together. I wanted to smooth the choppy waters this storm had started, and set the Tate name on a better path.

Grandmother stood up from the pew. I rose by myself, though there was one member of our little family who decided not to follow suit.

"Are we heading back to the Tate Mansion?" Cousin Francis Scully wiped his nose and smirked at me. "I'd thought we could stop by the shipping company this afternoon."

"Certainly not," I said. "You only just arrived in town yesterday, cousin. Would you not like to rest from the journey before a plunge into work?"

He shrugged, spreading out his legs and folding his arms across his thick woolen coat.

"Weren't you just saying something about a legacy, Harriet? Seems the best way I can carve out my own legacy is to get right to it."

"All in good time," I muttered. As if to agree with me, the church bell began to toll the hour. "And, if you would, my name is Miss Tate."

"Aren't we proud to be so?"

He put his hands on his knees, rocked forward, and lunged his body upright until he was standing. In the process, he knocked against my shoulder and nearly pushed me aside. A crude creature. I took my little lady's watch out of my pocket and adjusted its dial to coincide with the church clock.

"Let's be off to the house, then," I said. "Grandmother, if you would."

I offered my arm, but she would not take it and walked past me down the church aisle. If any of the townspeople wished to offer condolences they did not, and she was allowed passage through the crowd. Cousin Francis sneered at me and ambled after her. My father had four sisters, and none of them bore any male children besides this specimen. He and he alone was to be the new overseer for the Tate Shipping Company - though he would be instructed properly if I had to etch it into his skin.

One figure held back from the crowd. I'd noticed her when I'd ascended the pulpit to speak my father's eulogy. She was so bent with grief she was no larger than a child, but upon lifting her black lace-edged veil, lines of age crisscrossed her pale forehead and crinkled her red eyes.

"Mrs. Percy," I acknowledged her. She was the widow of my father's first mate, Edmund Percy.

"Miss Tate." Her voice broke with bitterness and sorrow. She clenched a sodden handkerchief. "Fine words for a murdering captain."

"Many souls were lost upon the *Phoenix*," I said quietly. "Would that Captain Tate have been saved, without his crew? Could he show his face in town again?"

"It was his fault." She pressed her black gloved hand to her mouth. "My Edmund would have steered away from those rocks ... They were almost home."

"I know."

"What calm you have," she accused. "Oh, you will find extra coins to line your coffers soon enough. The rest of us lost more than husbands and sons and brothers. What, will you be setting up a charity for us?"

"If I am inclined to do so and have the funds," I replied. "Then I can allot a certain percentage of the Tate Shipping Company's holdings to that family member which was most connected with the deceased."

She shivered as if against a sharp wind. "A percentage! I was warned against asking you for generosity. I can see I was foolish to request it."

"Mrs. Percy -"

"No." She wrapped her veil about her face once more. "Let it be known throughout Kennebunkport that Harriet Tate carries on her father's legacy. To the exclusion of the rest of us."

She brushed past me, nearly stepping on my feet, and stomped down the church aisle. Mrs. Percy, you will get your fair share. But I will not stand by and watch my father's shipping company bankrupted just so I can allocate more money to your pocket. There were sixty men onboard the *Phoenix*. Sixty families in a town of two thousand. I don't create the numbers. I merely live by them.

"Harriet, are you all right?"

A soft voice, quiet and comforting on this most comfortless of days, came from an older gentleman standing in a back row. He extended a gloved hand and I shook it rather gratefully.

"Mr. Godwin," I greeted. "Sir, you could have seated yourself in the Tate pew. My father respected you as his accountant."

"No wish to disturb." He fitted his black silk hat upon his head and offered his arm, which I took. "I cannot imagine how you are handling this tragedy, though your eulogy delivery was strong."

"My name is emblazoned on the largest, most profitable company in town." We slowly made our way down the aisle towards the rear doors. "Now I am to ensure it remains that way."

"I have not had time to accurately assess the financial implications of this ship's loss," he admitted. "I am going out of town for a few days to visit an ill sister in Biddeford. I trust you can oversee the accounting while I am gone."

"Of course. I would not be a good apprentice if I could not do those kinds of sums."

He patted my hand. We stepped through the doors and onto the icy walkway outside the church. The bell ceased tolling, and funeral attendees began to disperse back to their homes. My grandmother had already ascended into the family carriage parked in the street, and my cousin stood sullenly by the open door. Mr. Godwin had yet to meet his new boss and approached Cousin Francis on his own.

"Mr. Scully," he said. "You are now appointed both owner and overseer of the Tate Shipping Company."

"I am." He almost didn't shake Mr. Godwin's hand, but decided at the last moment to do so. "And you are?"

"Mr. Godwin," came the reply. "The company's accountant and

primary bookkeeper."

"Ah." My cousin perked up. "The payroll accounts too, I wager?"

Mr. Godwin glanced at me, questioning. The last I'd seen my cousin, he was a mousy-haired pimply schoolboy with no interest in studies. Grandmother said his father got him into Bowdoin College purely based on the size of his purse and nothing his son could academically offer. This was what little I knew about my company's successor. Would that the captain had named a different heir, but what choice did he have?

"Yes," Mr. Godwin answered. "However, I am to be absent this week. So do speak to Miss Tate about those inquiries."

"I'll be at the company first thing in the morning, then." Cousin Francis yawned and cracked his knuckles. "Why'd you hold this funeral so early, Harriet? Cut into my Saturday night fun you did."

"Take that issue up with the minister," I said coldly. I turned to Mr. Godwin. "Thank you, sir, for your help. I shall see you upon your return."

"Indeed, Miss Tate."

He gave me a polite bow, then wrapped his muffler snuggly about his neck and headed up the street towards the apartments he rented half a block from here. Cousin Francis sneezed and held his mittened hand up to his red nose.

"Got yourself a nice old suitor don't you, Harriet? He must be well past forty."

He stepped in front of me and jogged up the steps into the carriage. I climbed up after him, seated myself, and shut the door. The carriage began to pull from the churchyard and down Main Street.

"It's Miss Tate," I corrected again. "Mr. Godwin is a fine teacher. He has instructed me in all manner of finance to run the company."

"A gentleman, too," Grandmother added. "He lost his wife some years ago, but he always had a fondness for Harriet."

Cousin Francis laughed. "Oh, good. Then she can marry, not be a Tate any longer, and that's the end of the family name."

"Nonsense," I said. "I have no intention of doing anything of the sort."

Grandmother looked at me with a strange sense of pity, while Cousin Francis leaned against the carriage window.

Nonsense, indeed. There was no chance I could marry Mr. Godwin, for he had not asked nor would I accept. My heart belonged to the company, to stand by its side and watch it prosper as greatly in the future as it had in my past. My father would not be around to see my success, but I could be proud of my accomplishments.

That's what it was like to be a Tate.

two

From across the carriage seat, I eyed my cousin as one would assess fish at a market. He slumped against the window, drawing circles on the foggy glass. Finally, he gave up from boredom and languidly addressed me.

"How long until we arrive at this mansion? I wish to see what will be mine."

I pulled out my lady's watch and consulted it. A grayish wintry sky and dim sunlight made it difficult to ascertain the accurate time.

"In approximately three minutes," I said. "We are turning on to Pleasant Street."

Indeed, the carriage made the shift as it bore left. My cousin perked up his stance, scooting down to peer out the fogged window. The Captain Tate Mansion promptly came into view, and it made me feel gladder than I imagined to see it. It was an enormous, grand home befitting its family name and generations who'd lived within it. I could recall the creak of each floorboard, the smoky scent of each fireplace, the taste of the sea-scented air breezing in each room. It was as if my skin were its clapboards and bricks, my bones its chimneys.

"My, my," Cousin Francis remarked as we pulled into the carriage-way. "It is beyond my understanding why Mother wouldn't bring me to her childhood home. We could have been playmates, Harriet."

How absurd. "I do not remember having much time to play."

At last, the carriage pulled to a stop and we all stepped down into the icy carriageway. My cousin couldn't help gawking up at my home, as if in front of a prize racehorse. He did not see clapboards and glass windowpanes and shutters - he saw how wealthy such a grand home would make him.

"You see?" I said to him. "This house you rarely visited and a company you know little about is to be yours. If you do heed any advice – "

But he neither heeded nor listened, and promptly left my side. Our butler let him in before either Grandmother or myself had the chance to catch up, and by the time we were in the foyer, he was darting through the rooms like a burglar inspecting things to steal.

Taking Grandmother's arm, I draped a warm shawl about her thin shoulders and led her at once into the parlor. A cheery fire dispelled the morning's cold gloom, and I had just seated her when the house's future owner popped into the room, quite out of breath.

"Will you kindly calm yourself?" I ordered. "Grandmother and I are both fatigued."

"When are you going to the company tomorrow?"

"I leave at seven o'clock each morning." I smoothed my skirts and took my customary chair by the fire. "Eager to begin the day's duties, are we?"

"Duty is for the dull-minded." He crossed the room and went over to the fireplace, poking it until tiny sparks leapt out and singed his trousers. "Indeed! I should think this house's architect wouldn't have made fireplaces so large and prone to injury."

"You should pay attention to the proper way of doing things."

He heaved a frustrated sigh, slammed the poker back onto the fireplace holder, and stomped over to a chair.

"If duty is for the dull-minded, then you will not find running a company very exciting." I leaned forward. "Perhaps you might let someone more accustomed to boring tasks oversee it."

"Clever, Harriet," he muttered. "Painting yourself to be the perfect person for such an occupation."

"I am," I said. "I have had years of practice."

"A company of that size doesn't need constant care. I attended business lectures at Bowdoin College. The right leader, and profits would triple. Each ship brings in thousands of dollars per annum. It can only do better with someone qualified, like myself."

"It is precisely due to constant care, as you put it, that the company has been so successful. What, you assume leadership equals absence?"

Grandmother sighed. "My dears, I must beg my own absence from this discussion for tonight. Good night, Harriet, and to you as well, Francis. Welcome to Kennebunkport."

She slowly rose from the sofa. I offered to help her upstairs, but she refused and soon parted. After she'd gone, I stared across the room at my cousin for some time while forming my next reply. A man so unlike myself, as if we were on opposite sides of the same moon. Yet, none of the great challenges I had faced in my young years crippled me in any way. In fact, I had become all the stronger for it. This Cousin Francis, heir and inheritor, would not deter me.

"If you are reluctant to turn the responsibilities of the company over to a woman, which is understandable, then I suggest appointing Mr. Godwin. He is more than apt for the position, and I can produce several references to vouch for the quality of his character."

"Including yourself, I suppose."

"Not just me," I said. "He also lives modestly and wouldn't require a salary increase."

"You're to marry a man of low means? I wouldn't have thought that given your propensity for finances."

"I'm not to marry any one presently," I retorted. "None have offered that I have not declined."

He laughed. "I read about a spinster in a fairy tale once, Harriet. But I little believed they existed in real life. You are determined to maintain a life without marriage, just so you may devote yourself to the company?"

"It is a valid reason."

"Valid, perhaps." He tapped a finger to his chin. "Though I cannot be convinced Captain Tate viewed such a situation as the best course. Tell me, cousin, did he want his daughter to run a company or bear sons?"

I bit my lip to keep from snapping back. I refused to insult him and cause a deep chasm in our brand-new acquaintance. The truth was that I needed him to appoint me as the one to run the company. The fact that I was an only daughter with no right to inherit that title could never be changed.

"Would you care for some dinner?" I asked abruptly. "Our cook is a good one, and there are leftover foodstuffs in the pantry."

He shrugged, already disinterested in continuing the conversation. But I had learned much from his character, and all of it was vexing. If he could just let me alone with my thoughts, I'd think of another solution.

"There is also plenty of wine," I added.

"Quite so."

Without another word, he vaulted his leggy, ungainly frame from the chair and popped out of the parlor as quickly as he'd popped in. Thank goodness. Bear sons, indeed. I would rather bear witness to a sustaining Tate Shipping Company.

Mr. Godwin possessed a kindness of character, but he did have practical sense and a diplomatic nature. Maybe he could persuade my cousin towards my point of view. It was not just the best for me. It was the best course for the company. Leadership did not require absence, it required diligence.

The clock struck seven, and I took my leave for the evening. I was not hungry and walked mechanically upstairs to my chambers. It was still a little light out, and a hearty fire warmed my cold room.

A copy of the February Portland newspaper lay upon my bed along with my tea tray. I picked up the newspaper and brought it over to the firelight. The headline announced in bold, black letters the loss of the *Phoenix* and all souls onboard.

"All souls," I read aloud. "The *Phoenix* was returning from a voyage to the East Indies. Its last message indicated that it stopped in South Carolina to outfit the ship with supplies. It traveled up the American coast and was ahead of its original schedule of March 1, 1855 to return to its berth in Kennebunkport. A horrific winter storm hailed the ship off course on the Isles of Shoals, where it was repeatedly dashed against the outlying rocks. Island onlookers could only watch in terror as the mighty ship splintered and sank, sending all of her crew heavenward."

I folded the paper and set it back on the bed. I turned and walked over to the window, looking out over the front lawn and to the rest of Kennebunkport.

"What a legacy," I muttered. "Which you left me, Father. You always left. I stayed, and now again, I am staying. Though at least I don't have to wonder when you'll come home and find me as unworthy as you did when you were here."

I returned to the bed, picked up the newspaper, and casually tossed it into the fireplace. The doomed, sunken *Phoenix* would not rise from her ashes, and neither would my father. Flames crackled and sputtered, blackening the edges of the newsprint and blotting out the headline. The account of Father's death disappeared like his body into the sea.

I smiled, a smile of relieved bitterness. He was gone, and he'd never find me inadequate again.

three

At breakfast the following morning, fifteen minutes before seven o'clock, I ate my bowl of hot porridge and steamed milk alone. I was used to Grandmother's absence, for elder complaints excused her. A servant informed me that my cousin had left late last night and not returned to the house.

"Fitting," I said. "Thank you."

The girl bowed and returned to her duties. What did I expect - that he would be the one to wake me with more enthusiasm than the rooster? I'd be a greater fool than he to assume such a thing.

Precisely as the foyer grandfather clock bonged seven times, I donned my woolen cloak and mittens. It was Monday, the nineteenth of February, 1855, and spring was as far off as could be imagined. I stepped gingerly down the icy walkway to the road, clutching my hood under my chin against the dry frigid air. My cold fingers gripped a small metal pail, with a hunk of wheat bread and a wrapped bowl of stew for my luncheon. As per my usual custom, I would forego the carriage and make the journey on foot.

Down past Kennebunkport's shops and to the docks area, where small stores and merchants gave way to fishing shacks, stacked lobster traps, and beached boats covered with winter canvas. My destination was soon in view. It was a long, low building that looked more like a warehouse than a shipping office. Snow clung to the black letters proclaiming the Tate Shipping Company upon her bland brick walls. As long as anyone knew, my family's company had been in Kennebunkport shipping. My ancestors were of true Puritan stock, and I could say with absolute fact that they were the first to proclaim these low tide waters and deep inlets a home. The Tates belonged here, and I, as a Tate daughter, would likewise remain.

An unfamiliar carriage was parked outside the main door, with a red-nosed bulky gentleman standing by his placid bay horse.

"Ah, Miss Tate," he said. "I presume, of course."

"You presume correctly, sir. What business can I entertain you with?"

"Business, indeed." He vigorously rubbed his gloved hands together and blew on them. "You might know of my father, Mr. Gideon Cressey. He is a primary investor in the company."

"I believe I have seen him, sir, though we are not acquainted. Mr. Godwin attends the monthly treasury meetings." I, of course, was not privy as a woman. My involvement was only with the payroll accounts. "Is something amiss with the purchasing?"

"No, miss. Father is stricken with a bad case of the rheumatism and wishes for me to examine the investments."

Reluctant to let him in, I offered a different solution. "Mr. Godwin will be out of town for the week, but I am sure he will see to you personally Monday next."

"Father does want to be sure of the dividends, you know. The company remains in good standing?"

Of course it did. "I beg pardon, sir –"

"There's been talk," he cut in. "To lose a ship of the size and cargo capacity as the *Phoenix* was no small loss."

"Folks are prone to speculate when such things happen," I reassured him. "Mr. Cressey, I shall see to the figures. Do leave me your card, and I will write to you directly."

"You will?" He glanced at me, a glance I had received hundreds of times before. Most folks couldn't comprehend how good I was with figures. "I had read a Mr. Scully was to take over those proceedings."

I reached into the pocket of my dress for the door keys. "He may be a Tate by blood, sir, but he is not one by name. I am extremely familiar with the figures, and I will be writing to you within twenty-four hours. Will that appease you?"

By the shocked expression on his face, he had never been spoken to by a female in such a way. He mumbled something about looking forward to hearing from me, then got into his carriage. A sleepy driver wrapped head to toe in blankets against the cold turned the horse about, and they slowly vacated the premises.

"In good standing," I muttered. "Oh, how I despise idle gossip."

I tried the door latch, surprised to find it had already been unlocked. Curious, I pushed the door open and stepped inside. The building's largest square footage was reserved for shipbuilding and its accoutrements, while a small room had been set aside for the purpose of serving as an office. It was within this chamber that I had spent five years working alongside Mr. Godwin. It was as familiar to me as my own parlor. I knew every knothole in the floor, every wave of the window glass panes.

Yet on this morning, something was different. Several oil hurricane lamps were lit, and a gangly, rather ungainly young man relaxed in his chair at my own position - the inside desk. To describe my fury was akin to an Isles of Shoals tempest. The foul rat was already determined to displace me.

"Cousin Francis," I began tersely, "you are early."

"Morning, Harriet." Once again, the usurper didn't address me respectfully. "I can't be late every day if I'm the new overseer."

"Which you will be," I forced myself to say. I removed my mittens and placed them in my cloak pocket, then began untying my bonnet. "And since you are to be the overseer, I will show you how to perform your duties. The most pressing task is to ascertain the extent of the *Phoenix's* financial loss, so on that note - "

He waved his hand, cutting me off. "I beg to differ. It seems the most pressing task is for you to show me where things are, and then be on your merry way, Harriet."

"Miss Tate," I corrected. "You may call me Miss Tate."

"I may, or I may not. We are cousins, you know. Doesn't that count as a reason to be less formal?"

I hung my bonnet and cloak on hooks by the door. "Not at all. Further, this position is far more complicated than any college lecture. I estimate it will take at least a fortnight to simply comprehend the basics."

"At the end of which, Miss Tate, will you leave."

It was not a question. I sucked in my breath, pursing my lips. A good boxing about the ears would cure him of such smug impertinence. I reached down and turned the key on the desk oil lamp, casting a wide circle of yellow light upon the warm wood surface. A giant ledger book, as large in width and breadth as a floor rug, lay closed. I grasped the edges of the green leather cover and slowly opened it to the last page where I'd recorded the previous ledger. I was a far different student than Francis and dutifully studied beneath Mr. Godwin for many years. I could keep track of the finances better than anyone besides him.

"When I do leave," I resumed, "I depart with the clear reassurance that my father's company will be attended to with the same exacting level of detail I have displayed. You are able to handle this obligation, I presume?"

"Of course. I can do better than a woman, to be sure. My education level and gentleman status in the community are all that is required for the position."

I ignored his snide comment. "Good. Like I said, the damage for the lost ship must be ascertained. To do that, you first assess the financial value of the ship itself. Then calculate the cargo obtained in the East Indies, and finally add the general compensation for each man onboard to obtain the total sum."

"Sounds delightful. Say, how much do you earn for your salary here?"

A sum so little it was laughable, and certainly not a figure I'd disclose to him. "You will receive ample compensation for your position. Shall I proceed?"

"Ample, hmmm? How much is ample?"

"Are your personal expenses so great they require a king's purse?"

"I certainly need more than a spinster," he retorted. "It's expensive to both oversee the company and take care of you and Grandmother, in case you hadn't considered that."

My face remained expressionless. In less than twenty-four hours, my entire financial circumstances had become beholden to this character. I'd rather have a husband provide for me than Cousin Francis, though my marriage prospects were as dim as the winter sun.

"Your salary," I finally answered, "will be two hundred dollars per month."

He grinned, as contented as a child with his favorite nursery meal. "Two hundred. My, my. Well, may I be so bold as to say this is the most fortuitous thing that has ever happened."

"I'm glad of it," I muttered.

Two hundred per month would keep Grandmother and I in the same circumstances we'd been accustomed. Provided my cousin did not squander his salary, I foresaw no change in prospects.

"Now," I continued, "let us resume the calculations."

His expression immediately altered from enthusiasm to pouting disappointment. "You may worry about numbers and monies, but now I have the responsibility of an overseer."

He suddenly stepped from the desk and over to the door, where he grabbed his hat. Puzzled, I followed him.

"Cousin, it is eight o'clock in the morning. Where, pray tell, are you going?"

He shoved his arm into his wool coat. "To the bank, of course. I have a few cheques to write, and I must meet with my financial manager. It will take up the rest of the day, I'm afraid. You're used to running this place, so I'm sure you'll be glad to get rid of me."

I would be relieved to be left to myself, but his reasons for leaving were more than a little suspicious.

"The bank will be open tomorrow. Without completely understanding how great a loss the ship was - "

"We can prattle on about that at a later time." He wrapped his scarf about his neck and took up his walking stick. "You didn't happen to bring the carriage?"

"I did not," I said flatly. "Good day."

I waited until he'd shut the door behind him and his clacking footsteps had ascended the beach slope before sitting back down in my chair. A sick, uneasy feeling had settled in my stomach, and I was suddenly nervous. I never should have given him the monthly salary figure. What cheques was he going to write? I chewed the inside of my lip, thinking intently.

The clock began to chime eight tones for the morning hour. Well, I must get back to work. If tasks were not completed to a high standard after my cousin took over, then I wouldn't be held responsible. I was only accountable for my own work ethic, and that was that.

With the ledger book before me and a quiet morning with no more visitors, I slowly made my way through the annual accounts. How at peace one feels when engaged in work that calls upon their most natural attributes! My burdens dropped from my shoulders, I forgot about Cousin Francis, and the hours folded into blissful working solitude.

Being both companion and friend, the clock alerted me to the noontime hour. I broke for luncheon and warmed my stew on the little stove in the corner. The fire was cheerful, the meal hearty, and I relaxed in relative warmth and comfort.

Was this such a dire situation after all? I had two full weeks to convince Cousin Francis of my right to remain in my position. Given rising profits for the next quarter, I could supply him with enough money to stay out of my way. Then Mr. Godwin and I would run the company together.

"Harriet, are you here?"

Startled, I leapt at once out of my chair. A shadowy figure I immediately recognized emerged from the doorway. I was both pleased and puzzled to see him.

"Mr. Godwin?" I smoothed my skirts and approached him. "I thought you were to be absent the rest of the week."

He closed the door and walked into the shipping office. He looked flushed despite the cold, and was breathing quite heavily.

"Won't you sit down, sir?" I said when he didn't speak. "I can boil a pot of coffee, if you need it."

"No, no." He indicated the huge ledger book. "Hard at work as ever. You did not even take one day off to commemorate your father's passing?"

An odd question, considering Mr. Godwin had only met my father twice and knew as little about the captain as I did.

"The best way, I believe, to honor the captain is to carry on the work he left. I saw no reason to delay."

"Of course."

He appeared so nervous and fidgety. Something about him greatly confused me. He hadn't even taken off his scarf nor did he seem at ease to be here. We stood silently facing one another for some time until I had to speak up.

"Sir, I should like to resume my work ... unless there is something you wish to say to me?"

He gripped the back of a chair, staring down at its caned seat rather than at me. "You do honor your family. I was waiting for your father to return to Kennebunkport, so that I might ask a private meeting with him."

I sighed. "Please, sir, do not listen to any rumors about the company not being in good standing."

"I beg pardon?"

"Mr. Cressey, an investor, visited me this morning with the purpose of examining his stock purchases and the dividend payments."

Mr. Godwin shrugged. "The loss of the *Phoenix* needs to be taken into account first."

"Of course. That's what I shall do."

He looked up at me, smiling in a friendly manner. Thank goodness I had eased his mind about that.

"What a fortunate man I am, to have such a reliable partner."

"I will continue in that capacity," I said. "I strive to be a good example of your teaching methods. My cousin is proving himself as inept at being overseer as a goose."

He chuckled. "Yes, you are a good example, Harriet. I have never known another woman to display your intelligence in such a mature fashion. It brings me great comfort - and companionship. I am not a wealthy man, but my frugality has rewarded me with a sizable savings."

How could I have felt such unease this morning? Mr. Godwin was truly the greatest asset in my life. With his savings we could buy off my cousin with a bribe for his share in the company. I could even provide him with a monthly stipend.

"Your father is not here now," Mr. Godwin continued, "so I cannot ask him what I wanted. As it stands, there are no impediments to prevent us from deepening our companionship. The sum I have saved will be a gift of security and ease for you and your grandmother."

He was halfway through this short speech when I realized what was occurring. A deeper companionship, of any marital or intimate manner, had never entered my thoughts. Mr. Godwin was a platonic ideal in my mind, best kept in that realm.

"Mr. Godwin," I said gently, "I hope you do not do Mrs. Godwin's memory a dishonor for speaking to me this way."

He shook his head, and I felt ill.

"She would wish for me to enjoy the remainder of my years, Harriet. Please do not think on the past, when there is our future to consider. A future I know would be best for both of us to share together."

He wanted to marry me, to provide me with a large dowry, and for us to be joined as man and wife.

"I cannot say I agree," I said softly. "The past has sculpted my current decisions in such a deep way I cannot forget it for one moment. We have a remarkable partnership within the business setting, but that is where it must remain."

"Harriet, you need to face what has happened. Mr. Scully has the full right to owning this company."

"His right to own takes precedent over my name and expertise?"

Mr. Godwin couldn't look upon me any longer. He folded his arms, planted his feet wide apart, and stared up at the ceiling.

"Yes. Perhaps you have had too much independence here. Like living upon your own island, where none can dissuade you or challenge you.

But it is the law, Harriet. Mr. Scully will take possession, and you cannot."

I scoffed. "Then why offer marriage, sir? What good is it to me?"

He didn't speak for a long while. I did feel like I was upon an island of my own. It was bequeathed to me to watch over, and what an ill mistress I was proving to be! I did not even have the rights to the floorboards I stood upon. I had attained the highest level of position within these walls that I could, but it was a false title. I'd have to pass it on to Cousin Francis. He was a son, and I was not.

"Harriet, I am trying to make the best of your disadvantaged position." Mr. Godwin finally looked at me. "There is good in it, but I know you and that is not the way you feel. I have delayed my trip for too long, so I shall take my leave."

What, was he going to depart without discussing the company?

"Mr. Godwin, what about your position here? Use your savings to provide my cousin with enough salary to - "

"No, I cannot," he interrupted. "The money would be for you and you alone, Harriet. I refuse to line that man's pockets."

"Then - am I to be a Tate in name only, with no company or home to own?"

He walked towards the door and lifted the latch. My question hung like fog in the air between us. At last, he said:

"You are intelligent enough to find your own way."

He slipped out the door into the cold. Silence replaced him as a companion, and my rational thought processes lined up like clockwork in my mind.

My inept cousin would take over the position, gorge himself with fat monthly salaries, not leave a penny to the widows of the *Phoenix*, and then I'd have to marry somebody - anybody - merely to support a regular lifestyle. Mr. Godwin, despite our seventeen-year age difference, was a worthy candidate. Though, could I see my arm upon his, our hearts entwined? Or would his personal habits grate upon me, his insistence on acting with authority infuriate me, his rights to my property and body make me long for freedom?

The clock on the mantel had stopped. I opened the case and re-wound it, listening for the reassuring ticking. If only men could be like clocks! Steady and reliable, as regular in their habits as a ticking sphere of numerals.

Mr. Godwin's proposal had reminded me just how alone I preferred to be.

four

On my walk to the company the following morning, I kicked every insignificant dirty patch of snow. Furious at Mr. Godwin for not helping my company with his money, angry with Cousin Francis for his ridiculous attitude, annoyed that Mr. Cressey had dared suggest my company wasn't in good standing. You want me to prove to all of you I'll be a better leader than Captain Tate ever was? That I'm the true successor?

No matter - I am up for the challenge.

I rounded the corner and descended down to the docks. Pale dawn light slipped over the low tidal waves, turning the soft waters a pearly shell pink. Waves gurgled around the dock pilings, and sleepy morning gulls lazily glided above the shore. I smelled the briny underbelly of the sea and the acidic tang of pine trees behind me.

I unlocked the door and slipped inside the dark office, then set to work lighting the fires and lamps. After winding the office clock, its familiar ticking set my thoughts at ease again. It was time to assess the *Phoenix*'s loss so that I might look into Mr. Cressey's investments.

I heaved open the giant ledger book and sharpened my pencil. Yet my anticipation at beginning my task was short-lived. For, within only a few moments, my calculations were returning figures to me that were so far below my expectations that at first I thought my years of financial apprenticeship had disappeared. Was it possible I was fatigued?

"No," I muttered aloud. I quickly redid the sum, but to no avail. "It - it just can't be."

Of course, I knew the *Phoenix*'s loss would be expensive ... but this was astronomical. It claimed so much of the company's annual budget that it was only February, and we'd be at a financial loss for the rest of the year! I blinked, shaking my head. My shoulders tightened. I knew I was right, and that was the horrible truth of it.

One by one, I added the figures. First was the ship herself, including the raw materials she'd used as part of the asset. Then the lost cargo and her crew - including her captain. With a grimace, I realized I didn't have to pay any salaries.

By the time I completed the sum, I was wiping my forehead with a handkerchief. Thousands of dollars sunk in a matter of hours. The company would suffer beneath this blow for years to come, and might not fully recover for the better part of a decade. If the *Phoenix* had returned with no cargo, then we might have been able to recoup the losses by means of other ships. But the staggering loss of both the ship and cargo combined ...

Tick. Tick. Tick.

"How in God's name?" I whispered to myself. Shaking, I re-sharpened my pencil. "I can do this."

The clock struck eleven, and Cousin Francis still had not arrived. His presence at this time would have been unbearable. I stood up from the desk and was about to add more coal to the stove when the front door nudged open and a woman stepped in, wrapped and bundled in heavy woolens against the cold. She hadn't even closed the door behind her when I recognized her at once as my closest childhood friend.

"Betsy," I greeted. "How kind of you to come by."

She didn't answer me at first, stomping her feet and blowing on her gloves. She'd married a fellow classmate of ours, a kind young man who worked in Kennebunk several miles up the road. I hadn't seen her since the wedding.

"Goodness," she mumbled through her scarf, removing it quickly from her throat. "If I'd known it was so cold out, I would have hailed a carriage."

"You walked here from Kennebunk?" I went to the stove, opened the grate, and began dumping coal onto the flickering embers. "Come and get warm."

"Thank you."

Her tone was stiff, and she headed straight to the fire. Something about her manner wasn't as friendly as I thought it could have been, given our lengthy absence from one another's company. I'd remembered to gift a card and basket of muffins for Christmas.

"I could have sent a carriage if you didn't have one - "

"Not necessary." She removed her gloves and splayed her fingers over the stove. "You're here by yourself?"

"Until the time my cousin arrives. Mr. Scully has been appointed as the new company overseer, so I shall not be here after next week."

"What a pity." Her tone edged in bitterness like a knife. "The Harriet Tate I used to know would be quite put out to be so displaced."

I sucked in my breath, more than a little curious as to her reason for arriving. Was it to utter statements such as this?

"I am still that way," I said evenly. "I have not changed, Betsy."

"Of course you haven't." She suddenly put a hand to her lips, and a stifled sob escaped. She turned from me, staring out through the window at the fogged landscape beyond. The cold brought an opaque mist over the gray sea, and the sky was as colorless as the water. Her shoulders rose and fell in a great sigh.

"He's gone, Harriet."

Ah, now her reasons were made clear. "You knew someone on the *Phoenix*."

"You've forgotten, haven't you? I had a feeling you would." She fished in her little wool bag for a handkerchief and held it to her eyes. "My brother, Harriet. Samuel was onboard."

I was quite at a loss for words, and for a moment couldn't breathe. Dearest Samuel was gone.

"I am sorry for this, Betsy. I hadn't known."

"That much is clear." She sighed. "I thought you cared for him."

I had, and felt mixed feelings upon hearing this news of his death. Dear sweet Samuel was such a good, upstanding young man. Better than most, certainly.

Betsy went on. "I received a note from Mrs. Percy yesterday, that you would be starting a fund for the widows. The Tates have never done anything so generous for this town. How much is to be raised? I now have to look after Samuel's children. I must know my portion."

Her arrival could not have been more ill-timed! My hesitation upon answering only heightened her anticipation.

"Harriet, tell me you have begun this fund."

"It has not yet been established," I said gently. I stopped and turned from her. I couldn't look at her, and I couldn't break the news any less harshly. "Just this morning I finished my calculations for the ship's loss, and the company is in danger of bankruptcy if drastic measures are not enforced."

She looked at me so oddly I felt like an alien from a distant planet. "The Tate Shipping Company in danger of bankruptcy?" she repeated. "Oh, Harriet, I never took you for one to tell grand tales, but I must have been wrong."

"I do not exaggerate. I wish I did."

I'd never been more serious in my life. The realization at last dawned upon her, and though her look of horror matched my own reaction, I couldn't help but feel relieved. The news was out.

"Just like you," she spat, her voice a nasty whisper. "Just like the Tates."

"You are pleased my family's company shall suffer?" I asked. "Betsy, this was not of my doing."

"I would be pleased to see my brother walk through my door again." She gathered her scarf and gloves. "I thought you were to help me. But I should have listened to Mrs. Percy."

"I can't revive the *Phoenix*," I said. "I lost my father as well. It is a tragedy we must recover from."

"Oh, you'll recover." She finished wrapping her scarf about her neck and yanked open the door. A frigid chill whirled into the office. "Though what I'm supposed to do, I do not know!"

She slammed the door and barreled up the slope towards the main road. I went to the stove, put on another lump of coal, and warmed my fingers over its heated iron. Anger sizzled on the back of my neck, made my shoulders cramp. Numbers brought clarity and peace to my life, yet they seemed to not be so comforting to others.

I was so peeved and frustrated after Betsy's visit that I restarted my calculations from the beginning, if only to have something to relieve my mind. My thoughts were like a blunt hammer on stone, pounding viciously away at circumstances I could not alter. I couldn't resurrect the *Phoenix*, I couldn't rewind the days. I couldn't squeeze more money out of the paltry figures I had to work with, and it was as if my dry veins attempted to bleed more liquid from parched skin.

My luncheon lay untouched and I worked feverishly for hours, only stopping to rewind the sluggish clocks or rekindle the sputtering fire. My cousin's absence was merely a reinforcement of my opinion about his idle, spendthrift character. Men could afford to be so lacking, for they had nothing inherent in their nature to prove to an opposite gender. Instead, they spent their time either improving or dishonoring the lives of those around them.

My work kept me so preoccupied that when the object of my consternation finally arrived, I didn't hear him enter and only noticed his presence when my ankles chilled from the cold gust. The door whooshed shut, and Cousin Francis loped into the room, ungainly as a colt, and staggered over to the chair by the fire, dropping into it and thrusting his face towards the heated cast iron. His cheeks were as red as September apples, his nose swollen, and his hair uncombed. What a specimen, I thought bitterly. I picked up my sharpening knife and whittled the edge of my pencil.

"I'm sure you enjoyed your first salary payment," I quipped.

He didn't say anything. His glassy eyes slowly blinked. Well, by this time tomorrow all of Kennebunkport would know about the Tate Shipping Company. I might as well inform him.

"Unfortunately, that will be the final time you are able to withdraw two-hundred dollars from the account. I am reducing it to a lower sum, which I will let you know tomorrow."

He slowly blinked again. Had he spent the entire day at the Wharf Tavern? I was about to ask him when he stretched back in the chair, splayed out his legs, and tucked his gloved hands behind his head.

"I'll need more by tomorrow," he mumbled.

"That is not possible." I held up my calculations sheet. "Inspect the numbers for yourself."

"Why would I?"

I closed the ledger book. All day, I'd tried to make the numbers from the *Phoenix*'s loss equal a greater sum than I could calculate, but to no avail.

"You're coming with me to the bank tomorrow," Francis slurred. He coughed, holding his hand to his forehead. "I insist."

"I cannot assist you in withdrawing more funds."

"Then deduct it from my salary for March."

"If only it were that simple."

"It is that simple, Harriet."

"Miss Tate," I corrected sharply. I slammed the pencil down so forcefully I cracked the tip I'd just sharpened. "I shall not be withdrawing more funds because there aren't any. The shipwreck negatively leveraged the company, and we are operating at a loss."

For the first time, he swiveled his head towards me. His watery eyes struggled to focus.

"One ship could do that?" he asked thickly. "You're lying."

"Of course I'm not. Why would I?"

"You want me out. You want to run this company yourself, and you would do anything to position yourself here."

I stood up from the desk and stepped deliberately towards him. He straightened in the chair, knees clacking together, and stared up at me. I pinched the fabric of my dress and held it out.

"I am surprised, with your Bowdoin College education, that you have not realized I am a woman," I said curtly. "I cannot run the shipping company. I only report the facts. If you take a salary, you will bankrupt this company in two months."

"That is utter nonsense."

"I never speak nonsense." I returned to the table, picked up the calculation sheet, and physically placed it on his lap. "Your salary is reduced."

He didn't look at the sheet. "You just want more pay for yourself."

"I'm eliminating my own salary entirely."

"What a hardship you face," he sneered.

He tossed the sheet to the floor, and stared at the fire, tapping his fingers together. I walked over to the clock on the wall shelf and opened the case to wind it.

"You'll find a reduction greater hardship than I do." I twirled my finger around the clock face. "The company lost a ship two summers ago while rounding Cape Horn, and that shipwreck combined with the *Phoenix* is the real cause for the situation we find ourselves in."

"We," he echoed.

He still didn't look at me, nor did he seem to comprehend what had transpired in the twenty-four hours he'd been appointed overseer. His mental anguish was like a child struggling to learn a simple concept.

"Yes, we," I said slowly. "As the company overseer - "

"Quiet."

I obeyed, curious to see what solution he would come up with. After several moments of silence, he suddenly lurched to his feet, as unsteady as a split tree, and tightened his scarf about his neck. I closed the clock face door.

"Where are you going?"

"To the Captain Tate Mansion. I want you removed from the company premises immediately, effective this hour."

Well, what did I expect? A convivial handshake and an attitude of togetherness?

"Removing me won't solve the problem," I pointed out.

He clomped to the door and flung it open so hard it crashed into the wall.

"Harriet, you've been nothing but a problem since I arrived."

He stepped out through the open doorway, his boots crunching heavily outside. Perhaps it was best to go home and inform Grandmother. I retrieved the calculations sheet from the floor, folded it, and placed it in my dress pocket. Then, I systematically doused the fires, put on my cloak, bonnet, and gloves, and locked the office behind me on my way out.

My thoughts, so ferocious and insistent all day, slowed to a numbness, and I walked home like a mechanical being, placing one foot after another on the icy, cold ground. How fast a future could change ... so fast. Like I was a victim of somebody else's bad news. Yet I kept receiving blame, anger, and disapproval for my actions. What would they do, given the same circumstances? Was I truly doing the right thing?

Part of me knew I was, and another part of me felt I wasn't.

The candles in the front windows of the Captain Tate Mansion were cheery this afternoon. Reflected on the glass panes, the golden glow warmed me. I was greeted by the butler as soon as I passed into the front hall, and after he'd taken my outerwear, I followed the sound of voices coming from the parlor.

"- don't know the situation I'm in, Grandmother. I - I'm not going to divulge every detail of my personal finances, but trust me. I need that salary."

Cousin Francis prattled on about my deplorable actions so he could evict me from my own company. I didn't wait to hear more before I pushed open the parlor door and entered, effectively cutting off the conversation. Cousin Francis perched by the fireplace, leaning on the mantel to prevent from toppling over in a drunken stupor, his face a brilliant scarlet. Grandmother sat on the sofa, her posture erect, her expression one of fatigue and depressed pity.

"Good evening, Grandmother." I walked over to her in greeting, but did not sit. She lifted her hand, and I squeezed her fingers.

"You are home early, dear. Francis has informed me that you shall, as he put it, chop his salary."

"He is right." I turned and faced him, my hands clasped at my waist. "It must be chopped, to a sum no greater than ten dollars per month."

"Two-hundred to ten?" he barked.

"Yes. And you are to move into the second-floor guest chamber tomorrow."

He had no words for that proclamation. Grandmother looked puzzled.

"Harriet, I confess I don't understand the meaning of this. What has happened to create such a drastic measure?"

"I've already told Cousin Francis. My news that I must share is neither pleasant nor expected, so for that I am sorry."

"You are not," Francis quipped.

I glared at him. "I am. This is my family. My name is on the company."

"Harriet?" Grandmother looked quite grave. "Tell me."

"I've spent all day doing my calculations." I reached into my dress pocket, brought out the sheet, and handed it to her. "But the loss of the *Phoenix* is far greater than I anticipated, and we are on the verge of bankruptcy."

I glimpsed a flicker of horror in her eyes, barely perceptible, but still enough to let me know how great an impact I'd delivered. Her fingers trembled like tiny sparrow's wings as she adjusted her glasses and peered at the figures on the sheet. I took my seat in an upholstered chair near the fireplace, tucking my legs under and smoothing my skirts. Cousin Francis threw up his hands in an exaggerated gesture, nearly knocking over the fireplace tools.

"Nothing but rubbish, Grandmother," he muttered. "You cannot trust one number on that paper."

"I may not know what I am looking at, but I do trust Harriet." Grandmother spoke to the calculations sheet before her, without lifting her chin. "I anticipated that the loss of the *Phoenix* would be a catastrophe, but not on this level."

"It's not merely due –" I began.

"Some other ship sank awhile back, or so Harriet says," Cousin Francis interrupted. "What kind of company is so unstable that it can't even lose two ships?"

Neither of us answered him. And, in that moment, with my cousin's watery unfocused gaze pinning me and my grandmother's shocked silence a cold space between us, I felt like I was a widow of the *Phoenix*. As if I had been married to not only the ship itself, but the company and everything it represented. Without them I was left to grieve. The floors and the icy walkways and the gravel paths disappeared, and I stepped unsteadily forward over black chasms.

I gently broke the silence. "I am prepared to make changes to offset the damage. I'll remove my own salary and am also cutting Mr. Godwin's pay. I can consult with the servants to reduce our house expenses. If we are diligent about this, then perhaps we can remain solvent for the rest of the year."

I didn't want to say what I must, after I'd spoken of it to Betsy and Mrs. Percy. But it simply had to be mentioned. I looked down at my hands.

"There can be no widow's fund, either."

Oh, how harsh it sounded. As if I was the one responsible for a financial calamity.

"What a pleasant lot you are," Cousin Francis said. He turned from the mantel and unsteadily walked across the parlor to the door. "I'm not moving in here."

"You can't afford your room and board at the hotel," I said. "I should think with a ten-dollar monthly salary that would be obvious."

"I'm not taking ten dollars. I need that two-hundred, Harriet."

It was time to abandon tact. "Then you will be solely responsible for the downfall of the company. If that occurs, I will ensure your reputation is so damaged no employer in the state will hire you. Everyone will know."

He stared at me. "You wouldn't do that. It's your family's reputation, too."

"What have I further to lose, if we come to that?" I demanded. "You don't understand the consequences of your desires. Forego the salary, move to the second floor, and assist us to recover in every way you can."

Grandmother gave a little smile, though it was not one of pleasure. She looked strangely proud of me.

Cousin Francis could not hide his shock at my assertive tone. After staring perplexedly at me for several moments, he vacated the parlor, stomped through the foyer, and slammed the front door behind him. No doubt he was returning to the Wharf Tavern for the evening, to spend what remained in his purse before he had to face reality tomorrow. As we all must.

"How like your father you are," Grandmother muttered. She folded up the calculations sheet. "You would have been quite the captain."

"Men need direction," I said. "All too often they let the wind take them off course."

"He has debts, Harriet."

I shrugged. "I assumed as such. I can also advise him on how to handle his creditors."

She pursed her lips. "First, you can advise me on how to budget our household expenses."

"I will," I said gently. "I seem to have the gift for finding money in unexpected places."

Grandmother sighed. I loved her more dearly and tenderly than I could ever say. I would not let her son's name vanish from the legacy he worked so hard to build. To watch my grandmother suffer would be a deep sorrow. It had been the two of us together since my mother died when I was ten years old. Her final years with me would not be spent in times of hardship.

"Grandmother, I ..." Oh, if I could do anything. "I am sorry. What is there to do, that I have not already considered?"

Her answer made me grimace. "You already know, Harriet. Encourage a suitor. A husband provides both an income and a successor to the company. Though, it is not the course you'd wish to take."

"That is nearly the exact thing Mr. Godwin told me, when he proposed yesterday," I said dully.

Her eyes widened. "Harriet, you must accept him. He might not have an exceptional fortune, but he would be overseer and owner of this house as well."

I buried my face in my hands. "He does have a large savings he offered to us, Grandmother. Yet, I cannot."

She put a hand on my shoulder, but I could not bear her kindness and pulled away.

"Should I marry, I would become obligated to his life. He does not incite romantic feelings in me, and never shall."

"My dear, marriage is not a passionate tryst, especially given the circumstances you face. Take advantage of it, and you will help your family."

She leaned over and kissed my forehead. Then she left my side and walked out of the parlor to go upstairs. I gazed into the fire, listening to the mantel clock tick. How like my father I am. Well, I cannot be the next captain of the *Phoenix* or the overseer of the Tate Shipping Company or the owner of this house.

But I can lead my family into a better future.

five

"You are not to join Francis at the company today."

Grandmother sat across from me at breakfast, and she delivered this command just as we were finishing. A glance at the clock revealed I would have to ready myself now if I were to leave exactly at seven o'clock. I put my spoon down and tried calmly to find out the reason.

"Why ever not?"

"He is now the overseer." She poured more tea into her cup. "I do not wish you to do his job for him."

I scoffed. "Grandmother, he cannot perform a single task as well as I can."

"I am aware of his shortcomings, my dear."

"Then I ask again. Why am I not to work at my own company?"

She set the tea pot down. "You are a bright and capable girl, but it is no longer your company. It belongs to Francis now."

Harriet, you need to face what has happened. Mr. Godwin's words were like a stone in my heart. What purpose must direct my life now, if not to be the daughter of Maine's finest sea captain and rule in his place?

"If I have been proven unfit to lead, then I gladly admit my defect of character and step aside." I took a deep breath, suddenly on the verge of weeping. "But you cannot take this from me. It ... it means so much."

She picked up her teacup and sipped quietly, not providing any hopeful words to buoy me on these cruel waters. A useless understudy was to play the role I had dominated for so long. Cousin Francis wouldn't put in the care or the proper attention. He wasn't even a Tate.

The front doorbell chimed, and on the other side of the dining room door, I heard muffled voices in the foyer. A man had arrived, his tone urgent. It sounded like Mr. Cressey, and I was about to rise from the table when the butler entered with a letter in hand.

"Miss," he addressed me, "a message of post-haste has arrived for you. The rider awaits your immediate reply."

"Then I will see to it at once."

He handed me the letter. The envelope had an odd appearance, far different than any other letter I'd received. It was a brittle old brownish square of parchment. Shaky brown ink trembled across its surface, as if written by one with the hand tremors. It was slightly damp, and scented of the sea.

"It's addressed from someplace called Herrick Island," I read with some difficulty. "I don't know anyone from that locale."

"Neither do I," Grandmother said. "Where is such a place?"

I opened the crinkled flap and removed its contents - a three-page letter written in the same rickety lettering. Grandmother peered over at it.

"Read it aloud, Harriet."

"If I can."

It was like holding an ancient map, and the paper was so fragile and translucent it glowed with a golden luster.

18th February, 1855

To Miss Harriet Tate,

What terrible news to greet my eyes on this saddest of days! The great cargo ship the Phoenix has sailed its final voyage and become one with the creatures of the deep. Oh, disastrous and vexing loss! Once, her mighty travels were the stuff of legend - and now, she shall never rise from her maritime grave. If you could but feel my incredible sorrow, it would comfort you to know her loss will not soon be forgotten, and certainly never in my own lifetime.

From my distress, you may suppose that I was a celebrated passenger, a passionate investor in her cargo, or a relative of one of her crew. Yet, in truth, I reveal that I am none of these things! Indeed, it was not the loss of so important a vessel that immediately caused me to put pen to paper in this letter, but the surname attached to its famous captain! This Captain Sumner Tate of the Phoenix holds a singular interest to me.

I must be allowed to convey my earnestness to its fullest, Miss Tate, in the hopes that you will grant me an audience - in person - to discuss a series of strange events that affect us both.

Yes, Miss Tate, we are oddly and intimately connected in a way that I guarantee you have not yet been made aware. The relationship between the Tates and the Herricks is a topic of such vast importance that your presence is required *at once. Whatever expense is accrued by means of your travels or lodging here at Fogbound Manor will be handsomely compensated. I only await your acquiescence for us to begin the adventure of a lifetime!*

Post your reply at once. I implore you, Miss Tate, to do this with the utmost haste. I eagerly wait for you to accompany me.

With best regards,

Jonah Herrick
Fogbound Manor
Herrick Island, Maine

"This is utterly ridiculous."

Grandmother was equally stumped. She reached for the pages, pressing a finger to her lips while she reread them silently to herself.

"What is this Mr. Herrick speaking about?" I asked, so confused my mind had snapped awake. "Do you know any connection between the Tates and the Herricks, as he claims?"

"Not at all. He sounds like a raving madman, better off on this remote island than amongst the civilized. Look at his letter! Far too forward and passionate for an educated writer. If I were you, I'd write a terse reply to let you kindly be."

"Well, of course." I had already made up my mind to reject his ludicrous offer. "I would never in my life take up his offer to journey to Fogbound Manor."

I immediately pardoned my absence and went into the parlor to pen a quick letter. The more I thought about it, the more convinced I became of this Mr. Herrick's imbalanced nature. Would I ever draft three pages of such babbling nonsense? His exuberant condolences appealed to my current circumstances, but I did not wish to become embroiled in some fanciful 'adventure.'

There would be no doubt in Mr. Herrick's mind that I had refused both him and his offer. My letter was stated such that I could recite the whole thing if he were in my presence:

21st February, 1855

Dear Mr. J. Herrick,

I received your letter. Thank you for offering your condolences on the loss of Captain Tate and his ship. As for your offer, I have come to the conclusion that I must decline.

Sincerely,

Miss Harriet Tate

Short and to the point, the exact opposite of Mr. Herrick's exuberant prose. I did not give a reason for declining his offer, for I did not see adequate cause to do so. Hopefully, he would not bother me again.

The rider was feeding his horse grain in our stables when I located him and handed him my reply.

"Thank you, sir," I said. "Please see that Mr. Herrick receives this at once."

"I will, miss." He stuck a foot in the stirrups and pulled himself up onto the stallion's back.

"One moment," I said. "Can you tell me where exactly is Herrick Island? I am unfamiliar with it."

"Off the coast of Rockland," came the answer.

But there was no further elaboration, and he had soon trotted down the carriageway and up Pleasant Street.

Upon returning to the house, I found Grandmother in the parlor still trying to make sense of Mr. Herrick's letter. She was about to toss it into the fireplace when something unexpectedly stopped her.

"I should destroy this," she said, "but I feel you should keep it."

I took it and placed it on the mantel. There was no need to read it again, and it served as a suitable example of all the odd occurrences that had appeared in the wake of my father's death. I helped Grandmother to sit and joined her on the sofa. The mantel clock was about to chime the eight tones, and I felt like I was one hour late for work. I should be at the company, not sitting aimless at home.

"The message rider said Herrick Island is off the coast of Rockland." I shook my head. "It is at least one hundred miles from here. I confess I have no idea why this Mr. Jonah Herrick thinks there is a connection to our family."

"My son never mentioned the Herrick name," Grandmother said, "nor did my own father. He was rarely at home, much the same as my husband. It takes a woman of great strength to love a man of the sea."

"And the ability to bear solitude."

"Yes."

Whatever sort of a future I envisioned had altered from infinity to a finite number of hours. Each tick of the clock another moment I spent away from my true self. Disconnected, shoreless. For the first time in my life, I faced the possibility of aimlessness. It could not be more unbearable. I abruptly stood up from the sofa.

"I cannot stay here, Grandmother. Let me at least have the pleasure of a walk."

She didn't look up at me. "Not if your destination is the company. But yes, you may depart if you wish."

"I shall be back in time for luncheon."

I made my way across the room, each step a stride away from a boring afternoon at home. But when I reached the doorway, my grandmother's voice halted me.

"Harriet."

I paused and briefly looked back at her. "I will not go there. You can trust my word on this."

"Enjoy your walk, then."

"I will, thank you."

She did not deter me any further, and with relief, I entered the foyer, closing the parlor door behind me. After putting on my cloak and mittens, I nudged the front door open and swept it shut before the frigid wind could chill the entry.

My walk down Pleasant Street was cold and biting. I clutched my scarf to my face in a poor attempt to shield my skin from the fierce gusts shaking bare-branched trees and whipping dead leaves across the sidewalk. Winter's icy grip had not yet left the town of Kennebunkport, nor was it likely to loosen its hold for many more weeks. I could only imagine how cold Herrick Island must be!

An adventure ...

"Nonsense," I muttered aloud.

Harriet, if you dare think longer on this, you will go halfway towards convincing yourself to accept his offer - which was so ludicrous I frowned. Leave Kennebunkport? Abandon inept Cousin Francis to his post and leave Grandmother to mourn for my father alone? Adventure, indeed. I wouldn't enjoy myself for one moment with such thoughts to haunt me.

I headed towards the center of town, which even on a cold Wednesday morning seemed too crowded, so I veered down a little neighborhood side street and sped quickly by the houses. At the end of the street, a wide section of pale dead grass spread out over a knoll overlooking gray Atlantic waves. I stepped from the road onto the grass, and followed the embankment. Fierce oceanic winds whipped my woolen scarf about my face and stung my cheeks like straight pins. I picked my way along the embankment, careful not to slip and tumble down to the rocky shore below.

At last, I came to the burial ground hill. Gently sloping above the tides, it afforded each of its ghostly patrons a seaside view. Iron gray stones as thin as clapboards, carved with chunky block lettering and stark images of willow trees and urns. Most of the graves were empty, for the greedy sea claimed more lives than the land.

I found my father's stone easily, for it was the youngest. Less than a month since his final breaths were drowned from his body. Crowning his domed headstone was a carved image of the *Phoenix* eternally sailing on calm waters. I'd given my instructions to the stonecarver for the epitaph:

Capt. Sumner Tate

OF THE BRIG PHOENIX
1805 - 1855
HE CAUSED THE STORM TO BE STILL,
SO THAT THE WAVES OF THE SEA WERE HUSHED.
- PSALMS 107:29

What I wouldn't give to cause my own storm to still and for the churning turmoiled waters to hush. I lived in the wake of a different tempest, bracing myself for more destruction and loss.

It wasn't enough, it was never enough. My father punished me as surely as if he was standing here, condemning me to remember I'd failed him. I wasn't what he wanted, and had never been since the moment I drew breath.

Beside my father's grave was that of my mother's, together with three tiny headstones for three tiny dead boys. Father was away at sea when I was born, and by the time I met him I was a toddling child. While he was away again, Mother gave birth to my first brother. Healthy, strong, and dead before the age of two. Another brother, another hope, another death. After the third boy, Mother never recovered. She lay ill and lingered, a living phantom, for two more years. I celebrated my eleventh birthday without her.

I am healthy, I am strong, and I lived. Now a woman, I was to be dutiful and obey my father's wishes. My body would someday produce the boy to carry on the Tate name. That was my path, as solid and assured in my father's mind as the cold stone he rested beneath.

Even from the grave, Father, you continue to define me. You berate me as unworthy of your perfect example. Well, though I may bear your surname, I am different and let no-one mistake me for you.

Let my own actions define the Tate legacy.

Struggling to hang onto her bags, the young housemaid trudged down the front walkway. I watched her shiver against the cold. As the bitter wind swirled about my ankles, I softly closed the door. For the past four days, I had become my home's ruthless factory foreman. This little maid was the fifth servant to pack her things and depart. *It's imperative we reduce household expenses.* My own hollow words could not soften the blow of what I had to tell them. Yes, you must pack your things and depart at once. I felt like every one of them was Betsy, looking to me and finding no solace.

So on a Monday morning, instead of going to the company, I was in charge of firing servants. With a headache plaguing my temples, I slipped down the hall and entered the kitchen in the back of the house. Grandmother conferred with the cook, taking my advice on reductions.

" - no longer purchase ten pounds of beef per week, I'm afraid," she said. "We'll take five pounds, though perhaps we should only buy three. Less sugar, of course. Less milk and eggs as well."

The cook would not look at me. No servant faced me any longer, for I was the one to summon them to the parlor to deliver the damning news.

"If only it were summer," the cook observed. "We'd be growin' half these things instead o' buying 'em."

I rubbed the back of my neck. "Grandmother, please don't forget to reduce our firewood and coal costs. Also, we can close off rooms we no longer need to heat."

Grandmother bit her lip, her mouth drawn. "We're to be chilled in our own home, Harriet? It could be three months."

"It could be longer," I said quietly, "but it cannot be helped."

The cook glared at me. "I suppose you'll be letting me go next, eh? I wish you much luck in trying to manage by yourselves in that fashion."

"No, that is out of the question." I opened a cupboard door and removed a tea tin. "I would greatly appreciate a hot pot of tea in the parlor. When I checked last night, there was enough flour for scones as well."

Grandmother tapped her pencil against the expense pad. "Less flour, too. As little as you can manage."

"Less, less, less." The cook snatched the tea tin from me and plunked it on the chopping table. "When are you going to tell me to buy more foodstuffs?"

Her tone irritated me. "When we are forced to sell the house, then I can readjust the budget accordingly."

"Harriet!" Grandmother admonished.

The cook turned her back and began heating water on the range. I could not bear to have either of them look at me the way they did and promptly left the kitchen. Instead of resurrecting my sinking company, I was forced to let servants go and become the target of the home's wrath.

The parlor was cold, and I could find no housemaid to heat it for me. With a reluctant grimace, I picked up a poker and jabbed at the dying embers in the fireplace. It reminded me of Cousin Francis, and I imagined it was his face in the ashes. Jab, jab. I snickered and felt a little better. He might as well not exist in my life at all, for all the good he was doing.

Only a man of the highest moral standing could help my family. Shame, then, that I should immediately think of Mr. Godwin. How considerable was the size of his savings? Large enough to ignore my absent feelings of love for him? It might come to that. To sacrifice my future heart's desire in favor of more firewood and flour seemed the most mundane of bargains. I did not even know if I could love deeply enough to submerge my oppressive reality ...

Ting. Ting.

Thanks to a dwindling salary the butler had received a rare day off, so it was I who answered the front door. Who should appear, but the same message rider who had so abruptly departed the Tate Mansion last Wednesday. He blew in from the cold and whooshed the door shut behind him. Whilst I regarded him with open-mouthed astonishment at his swift return, he reached in his long coat and drew out another letter.

"Miss Tate," he gasped from exertion. "I – personally am to give this to you. From – Mr. Herrick directly."

I stared at the envelope, hardly believing this nonsense should continue. It was an identical twin to the one propped on the mantel. I should toss them both into the flames.

"Sir, have you spoken to this Mr. Herrick?"

"He paid me double the wage to ride post-haste here."

"I see," I remarked. "So, he received my reply, yet did not acknowledge that I have rejected his offer to go to Fogbound Manor."

"He expected your refusal, miss." The rider shrugged and wagged the envelope at me. "I can't very well throw it in the sea."

"Of course you could. And I also assume Mr. Herrick wishes a reply?"

"He does, indeed."

What began as a meddling annoyance now irritated me greatly. My second letter would exactly mirror the sentiments of the first. Better to write back as quickly as possible and put it out of my mind.

"All right, then." I stepped aside to allow him passage. "You may wait in the parlor while I draft my reply."

He nodded, and as he passed from the foyer into the parlor, he tripped on the doorjamb and dropped the envelope. A clinking sound coming from within the wrinkled parchment caught my attention at once. He retrieved the letter, and I heard the sound again. A slight jingle, like the tinkle of a bell. I immediately reached out and took the envelope from him.

"On second thought, I shall read it. I will rejoin you momentarily."

"Certainly, miss."

He stepped into the parlor, and I quickly shut the door behind him, so I could enjoy the solitude of the foyer undisturbed. I held the letter up to my ear and gave it a little shake like a Christmas box. Sure enough, I heard the jingle again. It was the unmistakable sound of clanging coins.

Excited, I turned the envelope about and quickly lifted the sealed flap. I pushed the letter aside, not minding that I accidentally tore it a little, and could have wept with relief when I glimpsed the flash of gold.

I was right - they were coins! Two glittering golden coins, each as large and round as a biscuit cutter. How unlike they were from any other kind I'd ever seen. This was not modern currency, but money from an ancient time, decorated with square crosses and quatrefoils, rimmed with antiquated lettering I guessed must be Latin. The gold was thick and lustrous, and the coins weren't perfectly round or smooth but misshapen with a hammered surface. They were incredibly beautiful, like two ancient jewels.

An adventure …

"All right, Mr. Herrick," I murmured. "What have you to say?"

I carefully pocketed the gold coins and retrieved the letter, which was barely legible with its shaky hand:

24th February, 1855

Dear Miss Tate,

It was only moments after your letter arrived that I hastily put pen to paper to draft a suitable reply. I can scarcely imagine why you would refuse my proposal, as it will provide a much needed distraction from your current circumstances and allow you the inner satisfaction that derives from learning about your family.

I can see now that you will not be easily persuaded to launch on a quest without more knowledge of its background. I shall divulge a little of it to you now. To start, I have information about a particular ancestor of yours, with the same surname, that made a rather peculiar choice.

Around about the year 1720, Captain Francis Sumner Tate alighted upon my family's island and, true to his nickname of the Pirate of Shoals, decided to unload his winnings he'd gained from other ships and bury them in an unknown location somewhere below this rocky surface.

So, I have been researching exactly where this pirate has hidden his wealthy cargo, for I deem it to be a great sum – a very great sum indeed! Miss Tate, I implore you to have a care about the others involved with the Tate Shipping Company who stand to lose a great deal of their fortune if you refuse me again.

You must come to Herrick Island at once. I can be your patron for your meals and lodging here at Fogbound Manor.

There is a great adventure that awaits you, should you choose to accept - and you will be the recipient of a massive and substantial treasure. I desire your companionship as we embark on the search for it.

This treasure does belong to you and I, for we are the ones to represent our families - me as the Herricks and you as the Tates.

Write to me directly and say you will come.

Eagerly awaiting your reply,

Jonah Herrick
Fogbound Manor
Herrick Island, Maine

Again, his words bombarded me with childlike silliness. A Pirate of Shoals with the last name of Tate to bury treasure on a Maine island? I could not even think of it without shaking my head in disbelief. There could not be any pirates in Maine, especially none who buried treasure or were related to me. My family was involved in shipbuilding and cargo sailing, not nefarious actions. No true claim could validate this man's wild assumptions.

I folded the letter and put it back in the envelope. As soon as this message rider departed, both letters would find a grave in my fireplace, never to be thought of again. And what of the coins? A number of explanations came to mind. They could have been bequeathed to Mr. Herrick from a family member, purchased on a European voyage abroad, or perhaps custom-made by a skilled metalsmith. Just as fabricated and fanciful as Mr. Herrick himself.

"I don't need fancies," I said aloud. "I need real money to save my real company."

Suddenly, I heard the unmistakable sound of a carriage pulling up alongside the house. I cracked the front door open to take a peek and was immediately sorry I'd done so, for Mrs. Percy's black bonnet emerged from the halted vehicle.

Of all the visitors to come to the Tate Mansion today. Ever since Betsy's departure, I had half-expected her arrival, but it was still so ill-timed I felt agitated and nervous. Oh, and it was not just Mrs. Percy alone. She had also brought her two young daughters, dressed all in black like little mournful dolls.

Well, the town's most ardent gossiper was about to hear directly from me that the Tate legacy was as hollow as Mr. Herrick's treasure promises. There was nothing to do but greet them cordially and carry on in as polite and formal a fashion as I could.

Once I heard the bell's ring, I opened the front door and, servant-like, nodded my greeting.

"Good afternoon, ma'am. Welcome to the Captain Tate Mansion. May I take your cloak?"

Neither she nor her children said a word, but merely swept past me into the foyer. It was only after Mrs. Percy turned about that she realized who had greeted her.

"Harriet! I took you to be a housemaid."

The little girls snickered. I opened the parlor door and gestured for her to enter.

"My cook is preparing fresh scones and tea. Do join me in the parlor."

"I have come on a business errand, Harriet. It must commence immediately."

"Then our meeting shall be brief," I said. "I would not want to intrude too greatly on your time."

She sniffed, put her hands on the backs of her daughters, and the three of them marched into the parlor. Once I had entered as well, the message rider quickly rose from the sofa in greeting. He looked a bit un-comfortable, until I quietly reassured him that Mrs. Percy and her lovely girls were paying a short call.

"We are, indeed," Mrs. Percy said. The rider moved aside so her daughters could seat themselves on the sofa, but she herself remained standing, as did I. "And you are, sir?"

"Oh, I'm here delivering a message to Miss Tate."

"I see."

And that was the end of her regard and attention upon him. Mrs. Percy removed her gloves, and I noticed her wedding ring was still upon her left hand. She wanted me to know it remained there, for she displayed her hand several times as she spoke to me.

"You are an intelligent young lady, Harriet, so what I have to say I'm sure you will immediately comprehend. I was at the bank this morning, conferring with Mr. Redmond about my account, when I noticed Mr. Scully had also arrived. I'm not sure I would have noticed him, except for the fact he smelled like a tavern."

Her girls giggled. I stood where I was and did not smile. Without me at the company, Cousin Francis had continued to display his poor character habits. I hadn't expected anything less.

"Mr. Cressey stepped in shortly thereafter, and approached your cousin about some sort of investments he had made in the Tate Shipping Company. And do you know what Mr. Scully said to him?"

I could wager two gold coins I knew what he said.

"He told Mr. Cressey that his investment payments were no longer a concern, for the company was bankrupt and he wouldn't be bothered with the figures any longer." Mrs. Percy scoffed. "What can you make of that?"

I wanted to feign stupidity and ask what she was talking about, but we both knew that wasn't the truth. Nothing would revive her husband from his watery grave and nothing would revive the company, either. Her eyes bore into me, fierce and proud, like a bird of prey. No use saying anything other than exactly what I was thinking.

"He spoke the truth," I said. "The Tate Shipping Company will be declaring bankruptcy before the first of April."

"This – this is true?"

"Yes." I was not about to reveal any further details that I could help.

Now she had to seat herself, for her face was ashen. The daughters stared at me, stone-faced and glaring. Before my guest could speak anything else, Grandmother entered the parlor with the tray of scones and tea.

"Thank you, Grandmother," I said. "Mrs. Percy has informed me that Cousin Francis was at the bank again this morning."

"What a family you have," Mrs. Percy muttered. "And you know why he was there? To withdraw more funds from his account! None for Mr. Cressey, you see. When I inquired, he said it was because he had to take what he could before he lost the company. I have never seen such an attitude from a gentleman in my life."

Cousin Francis was no gentleman, and his actions at the company truly reflected that. It was sinking due to the ill choices of its ridiculous captain, and there was nothing I could do.

"Mr. Scully knows of our situation," I said, "yet it seems, as overseer, he is uninterested in saving the company."

"Your father would never have let this happen," Mrs. Percy said. "I suspect there is to be no widows' fund, either."

"There will not."

She sat back on the sofa. "How Christian of you, Harriet."

"These are the actions of my cousin, ma'am. I would not be a good example of piousness if I were to lead my father's legacy into ruin."

She folded her arms and turned her head, looking past me to the fireplace. "What are we to do," she said softly, as if she were speaking to herself. "Thanks to this, you have led others into ruin."

"I know. I am not proud of this choice."

She looked directly at me. "It's not a choice you should have made."

I could sit here and disagree with her all day. But she had already been here thirty minutes, and a hundred hours of discussion could not relieve any of us of what had happened. Mrs. Percy was not to blame for her bitter anger. She struggled, along with Betsy and Mr. Cressey and everyone else in the town, and saw me as the cause of their struggle.

As I put my hand into my dress pocket, I felt the coins. I closed my fingers around their solid round forms and took them from my pocket. As soon as the firelight gleamed on them, a rush of excited feeling sped from my heart. It was like holding a golden future in my hands.

"Harriet – what have you got there?" Grandmother was the first to ask.

"They arrived in a second letter of Mr. Herrick's," I explained, indicating the message rider.

He sat quietly in the chair opposite me. Upon being acknowledged, he stood and approached, peering intently at the treasure in my hand. Mrs. Percy gave the coins half a glance, then scoffed yet again. If I had an entire chest of money waiting to give her, she could not be pleased. Her daughters, however, each leaned forward with tiny open hands.

"Don't touch," their mother snapped. "They're not for you."

I opened my fingers, allowing the full firelight glow to illuminate the coins so brightly they shone like lamps. "Mrs. Percy, these can be the first coins added to a widows' fund."

"Oh, Mama," one of the girls piped up. "They're so pretty!"

"Like pirate gold," added the second girl.

"Absolutely correct," I said. Anything to placate their mother's grief. "I give them to you freely."

Mrs. Percy softly slapped each of the little girls' hands away. "We do not accept them, Harriet. Further, I am severely disappointed that you would bribe us with such paltry tokens. I see now that any business to discuss will be met with frivolity. Please ready yourselves, my girls. We are leaving."

I abruptly stood up and walked over to her. She did not shrink from me, but as I approached, I watched every last tiny grain of respect disappear from her eyes. The Tate legacy, indeed. She'd never alter her opinion of me again.

"Mrs. Percy," I said softly, "you may depart if you wish. You may speak to everyone in this town about how I have ruined the company and damaged my family's name. I can take that responsibility and not shy from it. But madam, the pride you have displayed in rejecting this money has altered my opinion of your character. I make the choices I do to save my company and help those who need it. What is the reason behind your choices?"

She stared at me. Her eyes like the gray slate of my father's gravestone. Carved with years of loss, hardship, waiting, raising her daughters alone while Edmund Percy sailed the seas. Well, she chose to stay alone. That was not my decision.

She heaved herself to her feet, yanking her daughters up as well. There was no need to announce her departure or bid me any polite farewells, so she was more than able to see herself out. Before she left, she made sure to give me one last disappointed look. But it was a dull attempt to hurt me, and my armor was too strong.

The front door thudded behind her, and its echo resounded through the parlor. My grandmother had stayed silent through this whole ordeal, but she could not bear another moment in my company any longer. I wished her a good evening, and she softly left the room.

Clink. Clink.

I turned the gold coins over and over in my hand. Firelight caught the glint of Latin words circling the rims:

Tempus Rerum Imperator

It reminded me of an incantation spoken for awakening powers. Yet the magic was for me alone, since none other in the room could see the potential. Like a gifted orphan not given the opportunity for their genius to radiate.

The message rider and I were the only ones now remaining in the parlor. He balanced his elbows on his knees, fingers pressed against his lips while deep in thought. I slowly got up and went to the little writing desk in the corner to draft my reply. My energy spent, I couldn't find the stamina to even pick up the pen.

"Miss Tate, if I may say, you have quite the obligation to uphold."

His observation hung in the air between us, then dissipated like fog.

The mantel clock began to strike the hour, and I silently counted four tones before replying.

"I do, sir. And it will take more than two coins to save my company."

"Let me see them, if you would."

"Of course."

He took them from my hand and examined them. He turned them over and over, touching the rough surfaces, muttering to himself. He might know Latin, I thought.

"What do they say?"

"Oh, I can't read them. But they are real gold, I can inform you of that much."

I hadn't suspected them to be so, and I was quite surprised by this statement. Perhaps I might be able to offer them to a seller. The money would purchase more firewood and flour, to start. I put the pen down and stood up from the desk.

"Sir, you do not need a reply from me in order to convey to Mr. Herrick my dire situation. Please tell him I appreciate his offer and the kind gift, but my family's company needs me. There is more to be done here, and I must do what I can to save it."

He nodded. "I will return the coins to him, then."

I was about to agree, but something stopped me. I held out my hand, and he reluctantly placed the two coins on my palm.

"I shall need to look into these further," I said. "Thank you for delivering them to me."

"I do what is required of me." He rose from the sofa. "As you do as well, Miss Tate. I was to advise you not to come to the island, but now I see you are too intelligent to become caught up in Mr. Herrick's ridiculous fancies."

I smiled. "Thank you, sir. I am absolutely certain I will not."

"Indeed. You have quite the monumental task facing you here. Good luck, Miss Tate, and farewell."

He reached forward and took my hand, then shook it with a somewhat relieved expression on his face. Then he said he would see himself out and quietly departed from the house.

I returned to the fireplace in the parlor, looking at the coins once more. Why would Mr. Herrick go to such great lengths to prove to me I should journey to Fogbound Manor? Oh, what did it matter? I put the coins in my pocket, leaned down, and doused the embers. The little mantel clock had ceased ticking, so I opened the case to unwind it, and the last flickering flames shone upon an etched motto within the case that I recognized immediately.

Tempus Rerum Imperator.

And beneath it was the inscription in English – "Time is sovereign over all things."

Indeed it is, I thought. Time is the captain I serve, and my company is sinking. I am running out of time to save it.

I may not be able to, but I don't know how to face those inevitable hours.

seven

"Harriet?"

The tiny candle flame flickered above its beeswax taper. It danced to one side, like a petticoat blown by a breeze. I passed my hand over it and felt a whisper of warmth.

"Harriet, are you all right?"

Every second slowed to the length of my breathing. In and out, passing through my lips. I could not feel the clock's steady ticking.

"Yes." My voice sounded like a woman dying. I licked my lips and said louder: "Yes, Grandmother, do come in."

My bedchamber door creaked open, and Grandmother softly stepped in. Her shadow made a dark shape on the wall, pale winter light outlining it like charcoal. I sat back in the chair, my hands clasped. I had risen early this morning, made my bed, and attempted to read before giving up and coming to sit at this little tea table by the window. The dancing candle flame was the only lively being in the room.

"You did not join me at breakfast. I was told you also refused the tea tray."

"I am not hungry."

She leaned against my white bedspread, half-sitting upon it, tracing her finger along the stitched whorls and spirals. The veins on the back of her hand gently curved and criscrossed beneath her skin.

"I made this for you, when you were born." She touched it like she might have touched my infant cheek. "Just as well I decided not to make any for your poor brothers. They didn't live long enough to sleep beneath a child's blanket." She paused, her hand flat and taut upon the bedspread. When she spoke again, her voice wavered, though her eyes upon me were steely. "You have had a life denied to so many, Harriet. One of privilege, comfort, and social standing within this town. By a divine hand, you were gifted all a girl could wish to have."

All? I thought tiredly. So much, and yet so little. If I was truly blessed, then the title of overseer would be mine. I made ready to add to her observation when she cocked her head at me, and I silenced.

"Yet, none of these gifts have been met with an outlook resembling humility or gratitude. I love you deeply, but Harriet - you are as cold a woman as I have ever known."

Grandmother turned from me and faced the wall, arms clasped over her cotton chemise. How could she understand?

"It's not fair. If I'd been a man, my qualities would be exonerated and revered, not slander against my own gender. I've only ever sought to be what I was supposed to be in the first place - a son."

My declaration fired from my mouth like a bullet. She surprised me by smiling, though it was not an expression of happiness.

"Yet, you are not. Have you ever just wanted to be what you are - a daughter?"

What good would that do? A son wouldn't have been forced to stay at home while my father left. A son wouldn't have been discouraged from pursuing a worthwhile occupation, whether at sea under the captain or running the shipping company. A son wouldn't be forced into marriage merely to gain money or birth another in the family line. A son would have been everything a daughter couldn't be - a daughter like me.

"No," I said simply. "I have not wanted that."

She slowly raised herself from the bed, clinging to a counterpane to steady her frail weight. Ghostlike, she seemed to hover between two worlds, her white chemise and white hair ethereal in the light.

"Then I, too, wish you had been born a son, Harriet. That's the only thing that would have made you happy." She sighed and looked at the candle flickering beside me. Her stare was vacant, as if clouded by fog. "I bid you return to the company today. We must salvage what we can."

"I will try."

She reached for the doorknob, turned it, and paused in the doorway before departing.

"Perhaps you should take Mr. Herrick up on his offer. If he is able to financially compensate you, then you cannot delay."

"Perhaps," I echoed.

Though I had no intention of departing Kennebunkport while Cousin Francis still occupied my office. He needed a stern educator, not an absent mistress.

"Thank you, Grandmother. For letting me return."

She gave a little shrug, as if it did not matter what I said at all, and slipped out of the room. I abruptly stood up, leaned over and blew out the little candle flame. My exhaustion vanished at once. The coins jingled softly in my dress pocket, an audible reminder of the task before me.

You're right, Grandmother, I cannot delay. I must away to the company at once.

A darkened bank of clouds had rolled in off the ocean and split the sky into alternating wavy lines of deep charcoal and flat gray. It would rain soon, and I hurried as best as I could through the cold streets. Fearful urgency crashed through me, and I was nearly at a full run by the time I reached the top of the slope.

As I paused, gasping, a low thunderous growl resounded above me and it began to rain. I could barely see the washed brick of the Tate Shipping Company, for all the black carriages and crowd swarmed before it. I could hear their tumultuous shouts and angered cries, and none noticed as I picked my way down the slope.

Icy stinging raindrops splattered on my cheeks and shoulders just as I reached the outer circle of the crowd. It only took one familiar face, a young girl with blondish hair whose father was the postmaster, to recognize me.

"Miss Tate!" she announced with a happy flourish, simultaneously pointing at me and tugging on her father's jacket. "Daddy, look who it is!"

Daddy did look at me, as did half the town. Disbelief, shock, dismay. Then a consuming tide of furious anger, more fierce and mighty than the stormy Atlantic rumbled from the crowd and poured forth upon me.

"How dare you show yourself!"

"I want my investments back!"

"Run the Tates out of here!"

Were they to pull out pitchforks or tar and feather me? I endured their spewing wrath, feeling surprisingly wearied by it all. I stood quietly before them, not saying a word, rain pelting my bonnet and dribbling down my cheeks. The afternoon storm only served to whip my onlookers into a frenzy, though it drove many of them to seek the shelter of their carriages. I remained where I was, sodden and staring. I answered none of their pleas, I offered no consolation for their grief, and I certainly didn't match their anger with a display of my own. Though I could never name a time in my life I was more furious.

How dare *you*, I silently accused. How dare you judge me. How dare you blame me for a storm whilst another rages above us. You see that I am powerless in the face of this natural tempest! How dare you -

"Harriet!"

A single cry of kindness, shooting through the air like an arrow of comfort. I recognized the voice immediately, and marched right through the crowd towards it. I caught a glimpse of warmth, a golden beacon slicing through the gray rain and black-clad townspeople. Then a strong arm grappled with me and swept me out of my soaked hell.

The heavy door thudded behind me, and I collapsed to my hands and knees. It took me a second to notice I was indoors, back in my own company, and it was Mr. Godwin who assisted me to rise.

"Let's get you to the fire," he said hurriedly, and almost before the words were spoken I was thrust into the chair before the stove. Its smoky heat thawed my skin. I fumbled for the tangled ribbons at my neck and removed my bonnet, feeling like a drowned rat.

"Mr. ... Mr. Godwin," I breathed. "Oh goodness, thank you."

He picked up the stove grate and jammed more coals within, then stood next to it, glancing worriedly between me and the feeble fire.

"It's all right," I reassured him. "I'm all right."

"I had no idea you were out there," he admitted. "Mrs. Percy arrived an hour ago, she had brought Mr. Cressey, your school-friend Betsy showed up, and before I know it, I'm barricading the door against the whole damn town. I was gone five days, Harriet. No one will tell me what the hell has happened."

"I already told you," sneered a familiar voice.

I sighed in disgust. Cousin Francis sat in my chair at my desk, peering in the huge ledger book at numbers he couldn't possibly comprehend. He shoved the pen in the inkwell and stood up, moving his long legs awkwardly across the floor until he'd carried himself over to me. He loomed like a foolish brown goose.

"Harriet knows, too. Don't you?"

Rain thwacked the bricks outside. A strange calm loosened my tightened chest.

"Then let me be the one to inform you, Mr. Godwin. My father's glaring error in appointing Cousin Francis as overseer has resulted in, quite simply, a financial catastrophe. By the first of April, I will be declaring bankruptcy and closing the company doors. If you would assist me with the paperwork, sir, I'd be much obliged."

He didn't say a word. I had stunned him to speechlessness, and he looked as grim as at my father's funeral. Five days you were gone, Mr. Godwin. In those five days, I could have righted the ship and kept it afloat.

"I should have you run out of town," Cousin Francis threatened. "What a pack of lies you spread."

"I do not lie, nor have I ever. I believe Mr. Redmond at the bank would vouch for my accuracy. Were you not there yesterday withdrawing more funds from a depleted account?"

Mr. Godwin stared at my cousin.

"Further," I continued, "did you not also inform Mr. Cressey his dividend payments were no longer a concern due to the bankruptcy? Mrs. Percy was kind enough to enlighten me."

"You're not privy to such gossip, Harriet," Cousin Francis muttered. "You haven't been here in days. What would you know?"

"Then I implore Mr. Godwin to call upon Mrs. Percy. She can attest to these truths." I turned to Mr. Godwin. "After the *Phoenix* sank, the company was in danger of insolvency. If I had been able to reduce at least thirty percent of our expenses, then we would have managed the remainder of the year. But Cousin Francis withdrew more than two hundred dollars this week, and thus - I have no choice."

The poor accountant could not comprehend all that had transpired in his absence, so he collapsed into a seat beside me and stared at the fire for a long time. The clock had stopped ticking. I rose from my chair and walked in my wet skirts over to wind it. Time is sovereign over all things, I thought gloomily.

"I agree with your judgment, Harriet," Mr. Godwin said at last, "but not your final decision. To save the company, would a sum of ten thousand dollars be adequate?"

"Yes!" Cousin Francis exclaimed. "Do let me know how quickly I can obtain this sum. It shall be put to use at once!"

Tick. Tick. I closed the mantel clock case.

"Where?" I asked dryly. "The Wharf Tavern? That is where your salary went."

"Out of the question, Mr. Scully," Mr. Godwin snapped. "It is my own personal savings, and nothing on this earth would convince me to bequeath it to you."

Cousin Francis smirked. "Indeed. A man with a savings that large has a distinct purpose in mind. Perhaps as a wedding present for Harriet? Not that she'd acquiesce, for she is a spinster through and through."

"I'd rather be a spinster than a spender and a tippler." I scoffed. "Call me what you will, Cousin Francis."

"Same to you," he shot back. "For I am the overseer, and you cannot dethrone me."

Mr. Godwin vaulted to his feet and marched right up to Cousin Francis. His physical presence made my relative so agitated he took several steps backwards until he eventually reached the desk, where he plopped down nervously. It was just like a child being put in the corner. I'd never seen Mr. Godwin so infuriated. He shook his finger at my cousin like a sword.

"Enjoy your throne, Mr. Scully, for you will not sit long upon it. As I can readily afford it, the first thing I will do is hire a lawyer. I can easily prove your inadequacy and install myself as the company's owner."

How could it be possible to feel both relief and protest at the same time? A Tate would not own my family's business? Oh, how I needed this opportunity, and yet I could not ... No, I could never accept it.

Mr. Godwin returned to the fire, though he did not sit down again. When he addressed me, his tone was grave.

"I know, Harriet. I wouldn't change the name, if that comforts you."

Cousin Francis guffawed from his chair. "Means that much to you, eh?"

Yes, it means that much. For those possessing neither a name nor legacy to live up to, they could never comprehend my responsibility. I sighed and stuck my hands in my pockets. I heard a soft jingle, like a distant sleighbell.

The moment I drew out the treasure coins from Herrick Island, they received a strong reaction. Cousin Francis leapt up from his seat and darted over, as excited as a child at a shiny tin toy. Mr. Godwin marveled at their beautiful lettering and faraway whisper of antiquity.

"Mr. Godwin, hold out your hands."

I clinked the two coins into his palm. He circled his finger around and around them, as if tracing their outline into his skin. I felt at last I had found a rightful home for them.

"A gift of my own," I said.

"Harriet, I cannot possibly accept."

"Yes you can, and you will. Please use them to start the widows' fund. That is the most valuable thing I can give to help those in this town."

He cocked his head, and I could tell he was about to refuse me again.

But he'd known me for many years and decided to acquiesce.

"Thank you, Harriet." He placed his hand over the coins, concealing the stunning gold from sight. "I know you will do what you can to help your company."

His kind words were the first I'd received from anyone about this matter. My cousin, however, looked as sour as could be.

"That's a mighty fine dowry you have there, Harriet. Too bad you don't have anything else to offer your lover."

"I can get more," I suddenly promised. "I will get more."

Both men regarded me with blank skepticism. Neither had ever heard a statement from me that sounded so nonsensical.

"Harriet, these are 17th-century Spanish coins," Mr. Godwin pointed out. "You do not have anything like this."

"Told you she was a liar," Cousin Francis quipped.

"I do not lie, and I make no false promises," I countered. "I have been expressly invited by a Mr. Jonah Herrick to visit his island and reclaim my rightful Tate inheritance, which consists of these coins."

"I beg pardon?" said Mr. Godwin. "Harriet, you cannot be serious. We can work something out with a lawyer - "

"I do not want to," I said firmly. "It would not change my mind, either."

Oh, from the hurt look in his eyes he knew exactly what I meant. His kindness and willingness to help me were more admirable than any other in my life. But to admire someone's character was far different than joining my heart with his. I had one last chance to preserve my name, save my company, and ensure I wouldn't have to accept any proposal, marital or otherwise, I did not wish to.

"I have decided to depart from Kennebunkport tomorrow. I shall return before the first of April, at which time I will bring a great sum of money for the company."

Neither could find the words to reply to what I'd said. Cousin Francis gaped at me as if I was an asylum inmate. Mr. Godwin shook his head in disappointment like a father bemoaning his child's decision. Let them feel however they wanted to feel. I must take this chance. It was more drastic than any choice available and my last option. All I had to do was say yes.

"Well, my mind is made up. You must excuse me. I'm returning home to pack my things. I will see you gentlemen in a month's time. I bid you both a good night."

"Harriet – "

Mr. Godwin tried to stop me. I waited, but he said nothing further. Good luck, I thought silently. Do what you can to save my company while I am gone.

I picked up my bonnet and was out the door before my own doubts could deter me. My head was held high despite the rain, and I marched home like a captain set upon a purposeful journey. I would go to this Mr. Herrick and accompany him, though I needed more luck than Mr. Godwin to find more of those coins.

Maybe on a place as distant as Herrick Island, I could truly fulfill my Tate legacy.

eight

✷

I was so infuriated by my argument with Cousin Francis and the disappointing way Mr. Godwin had looked at me, that when Grandmother asked why I was home so early, I could only reply that I had nothing to say.

"Harriet, please. Will you not come sit with me by the fire?"

I pressed my lips together. "Thank you, but no. I informed both Mr. Godwin and Cousin Francis at the company that I shall be leaving in the morning."

"Where are you going?" But in the next sentence, she answered her own query. "To the island. You're accepting that mad Mr. Herrick's offer."

"I gave the coins to Mr. Godwin, and I must get more. Grandmother, I cannot marry him to save the company, and I cannot stay here and watch Cousin Francis run it aground."

"So, you have made your choice."

"This morning, you encouraged me. Do you prevent me from leaving now?"

She suddenly stepped forward, right up close to me, and grabbed my hands, clasping them within hers.

"I lost my son, Harriet. My beloved boy. He was my only companion whilst his father sailed away. I had my daughters as well, whom I deeply loved. But Sumner was special to me. He always knew what to do, and every time he made a decision, it was the right one. He was guided by an inner compass that never failed him. He was born to lead, born to be a captain. How could this storm have taken such a man? How could his own nephew refuse to be as good as he?"

Her sorrow unearthed me. Bending something inside which I had never realized was fragile enough to snap. If it should break, we'd both tumble into a chasm I couldn't save us from. I could only take the character my father instilled in me and do what he would have done, given my situation.

"I've spent my whole life doing what he would approve." I smiled tenderly and bent to kiss her cheek. "Do not be frightened. We will keep what Father built. I will see to it."

"Harriet ... " she whispered softly.

"I am going." I lifted our clasped hands. "And upon my father's life - everything he was - I will bring home money to save our home and our company."

She leaned forward, her little white head upon my shoulder, and softly wept upon me. I was like a ship's mast and she the gentlest of breezes fanning the sails. Yes, Grandmother, be comforted by my strength. It shall not falter. I gently helped her upstairs to bed, and by the time I reached my own bedchamber, her fears and sadness had carved my convictions so deeply as to never be shaken.

I slept as well as could be expected, and in the morning I resolutely packed my carpet-bag full of dresses and warm underthings to make my journey. I didn't feel as if I'd miss the house as it was now. I would miss Grandmother, though. My final instructions were to the remaining four servants - the cook, the butler, a housemaid, and a lady's maid. I summoned them into the parlor whilst I waited for the driver to bring the carriage around to the front.

"Please see to it that Mrs. Tate is kept comfortable. You will have the added benefit of a reduction in work, since she will not have many callers, no need for elaborate meals, and her personal needs are few. Those rooms besides the kitchen, parlor, and her bedchamber should be closed off and unheated. If you are in need of any assistance, please contact Mr. Godwin at the company."

"So, he's in charge of the sacking now?" the cook quipped.

"He is, if I made the decision."

The butler stepped forward and took my carpet-bag from my hands. "If you would, miss."

"Thank you, sir." I smiled gratefully at him. "I journey up to Rockland now. I bid you each farewell."

"Miss, you're going alone?" my housemaid inquired, her eyes huge.

I nodded. "I am. I appreciate your concern, but I shall be quite well. I plan on returning before the first of April, for that is when I must declare bankruptcy for the company."

This somber declaration made all four of them gape at me. I had no doubt they would have also been part of the crowd outside the shipping company. Just before I left the parlor, I addressed the cook.

"There is one dear favor I must ask, if my grandmother is forgetful of it."

"Oh?" Her tone was surly.

"Yes." I pointed at the mantel clock. "Please keep the parlor clock wound. It costs nothing to keep the time, and I would be ever so grateful if you would."

Her arms folded, she turned and glanced at it, then back at me, with a puzzled expression. Finally, she shrugged and gave me a nod.

"Very well, then," I said. "I thank you. Good day to you all."

It wasn't the way I wanted to leave, without Grandmother, but the carriage had pulled up. It was time, so I turned and swept from the parlor. The butler opened the door for me, then followed me as I swiftly walked out the door, down the steps to the walkway, and up to the carriage. The butler handed me my carpet-bag, smiled sadly at me before I left his side and climbed up onto the carriage seat. The driver clicked the door shut, and I sat straight, staring ahead at the empty seat before me. When the driver assumed his perch and the carriage jerked ahead, I kept staring.

I did not look back at my home, and felt better as soon as we'd pulled from its vicinity.

The journey was short, just a quick ride across the river to the neighboring town of Kennebunk. I had barely time to warm myself in the cold carriage before we'd arrived at the depot. I departed and thanked my driver, bidding him to return at once should Grandmother desire his services that day.

The carriage depot was a busy, chaotic place even on a chilly Wednesday morning. Many conveyances and passengers booked passage to various places both northern and southern along coastal and inland routes. At the ticket office, I slid my pay across the counter while remembering the odd gold coins in Mr. Godwin's hand. Would that I possessed more of those! Were it not for the widows' fund, those rare pieces would be in my possession ...

But my thoughts had no other time to linger on such matters, for my carpet-bag had been hoisted onto the back of a departing stage. I joined the small noisy throng of passengers jostling and bumping one another as they filed up the steps and into the coach. It was a tight squeeze, and I pulled my woolen skirts closer to my legs, avoiding an uncouth gentleman, if he could be called as such, who took up temporary residence on my left. Upon my right was an elderly woman in an old-fashioned Spencer high-waisted jacket and poke bonnet, the brim of which entirely obscured her face from view. I tucked my hair into my cloak hood and settled uncomfortably in the seat as best I could.

As soon as the stage rolled from the depot, a welcome lightness replaced the taut nerves along my shoulders. Be gone with you, Cousin Francis and Betsy and Mrs. Percy and Mr. Godwin and Mr. Cressey and all the rest. Your sneers shall no longer haunt me, nor your accusations grate my ears.

Cold woman am I! Yet, I feel nothing but warmth. For I am leaving, and that cheers me as surely as a hearth fire. A smile spread over my lips, and I enjoyed the gentle rocking of the large carriage as we drove away from Kennebunk.

Be gone with you all.

nine

My prayers for solitude must have been answered by a higher power, for I met no uncouth persons nor was subject to prying questions from the other passengers. Perhaps I wasn't recognized, for I certainly didn't know any of them. They jovially laughed amongst one another, spitting out the windows and cracking jokes that were not funny in the slightest.

Once we reached Portland, I followed the posted signs and changed coaches. I showed my ticket to the carriage driver when he announced departures, and took my seat. The elderly lady also joined me, and it was just the two of us. She promptly fell asleep before the wheels pulled from the depot.

As soon as I was on my way again, I leaned into the velvet cushioned seat and relaxed. My companion's hands were folded on her lap, and her poke bonnet provided an effective pillow to support her neck as she snoozed against the window. A wave of numb exhaustion crested over me, and I stared blankly out through the carriage glass at the passing winter February scenery. A cold blanket of grayed snow covered the gently rolling farmlands. Black bare tree branches were silhouetted against the colorless sky, and only a few blots of color, in the form of glowing orange windows, emerged through the dimming light. It grew dark, and the carriage still drove on.

At last, after many hours of the gently rocking wheels, I glimpsed a lively town on the horizon. Tiny yellow lights flickered, and the homes became more crowded together. The driver pulled down the main street of the town, passing over a bridge under which churned a rushing dark blue river brimming with chunked ice. I shivered and drew my cloak about my shoulders. The carriage finally pulled into a small carriage depot, and I swiftly stepped down. The elderly lady said not a word, but tottered off into the snow.

I had arrived in Brunswick, the very town where awful Cousin Francis had received what he thought was a good education at Bowdoin College. I had a couple of dollars I'd reserved for lodgings along the voyage, and I reluctantly parted with my money at a local inn. I slept restlessly and woke an hour before the carriage was to depart, so I dutifully dressed, ate a simple meal, and arrived in plenty of time.

This time, I was the sole passenger. My former relaxed state had disappeared in the night, and for the first time on my short journey, doubts crept into my mind. I prided myself on not fearing hardly any circumstance, and certainly not this one, but I couldn't shake the general feelings of unease. It seemed the further I journeyed from home, the more exposed I felt, as if my clothes were slowly being stripped from me and I'd be forced to face the bracing chill in nothing but a chemise. No matter how much I entertained other thoughts, that feeling would not completely subside. These minor terrors had me at their mercy.

Reflecting my turmoil, the weather steadily worsened. From the dim carriage window, I anxiously watched the sky's pale gray hue darken into an ominous shade of dirtied charcoal, and snowflakes began to dip and blow all about. By the time I'd journeyed to my final mainland destination late that evening, a true and forceful winter storm had descended upon Rockland. My fears escalated to annoying anger, and I slammed the carriage seat in frustration.

The last few miles painfully crawled beneath the carriage wheels, and the horses' strained grunts grated on my ears. I curled in a ball in the corner of the carriage seat, trying to doze while the horses' hooves clopped and the carriage rocked like a ship. My face was buried in my wool mittens, and my warm breath eased the aching cold in my fingers. Chills ran up and down my spine. I hadn't eaten anything in hours. I didn't feel hungry, either.

Then, amidst the scattered horse whinnies, I heard the sound of sloshing water against wharves. I raised an eyebrow and peeked out the thick carriage window glass. Had I at last come upon Rockland? I caught the saltied scent of the sea and guessed that yes, I had. A frenzied winter tempest blew flakes about and obscured my view, but I could glimpse glowing orange lights from different houses and buildings. I took my little lady's watch out of my dress pocket and noted the time to be seven o'clock in the evening. Twelve hours since I'd left Brunswick, and twenty-four hours since I'd last stood on familiar shores.

Abruptly, the carriage stopped. My watch flew from my hands like a silvery bird and landed on the opposite seat. I frantically scooped it up and tucked it back in my pocket. No good to lose my most prized possession, and I clamped my cold fingers around it. I grasped my carpet-bag, and, once the driver had opened the door, stiffly vacated the carriage and stepped down into the snowy sidewalk.

He held out his mitten, expecting some sort of tip for his services, but I had none to give. My newfound poverty combined with my lack of sleep and being forced to sit in one position for two days produced a snappish temperament, and I stomped by him over to the other side of the street.

"Miss!" he called into the wind, but I ignored him.

I have three dollars on my person, which I must spend on lodgings this evening. Where to stay, I hardly knew, but a few yards down the street I spied an inn sign swinging in the gale gusts. I bunched my cloak hood about my face, muttering unladylike curses at the snowflakes stinging my cheeks, and lumbered down the sidewalk.

I could feel the heat coming from within as soon as I approached the door, and my cold fingers grasped the stiff doorknob. I at last got it open and entered in a whoosh of swirling snow and gasping breathing. My first thought? I'd have rather performed a parlor trick for wages than enter this roughshod place. As if I had a choice.

Wide rustic boards crinkled under my feet, and the blasting tavern hearth was as large as a Medieval fireplace, stretching all the way across the side wall. Local riffraff, far from proper ladies and gentlemen, sat hunched over pewter ale mugs and steaming chowder bowls, laughing and conversing amongst one another as the evening's storm raged outside. After spending an entire lifetime by the sea, I correctly guessed them to be local sailors and dockworkers. I ignored their curious stares and the occasional frown, and walked across the rickety boarded floor over to the barkeep.

"A room," I said flatly. "How much?"

He finished mopping up an ale spill, tossed the dirty towel over his shoulder and leaned on the bar with both hands, his shoulders bent, and his large bearded face thrust towards me. There was a firelight glint in his dark eyes.

"Your name?" he inquired, loud enough for half the room to hear.

Instead of answering, I thrust my hand into my cloak pocket and brought out three crisp folded dollars.

"Will this be enough for one night? I'm to journey to Herrick Island in the morning."

"Herrick Island?" His bushy eyebrows jolted and he straightened, clasping his large hands together. "You, ah, don't resemble the fishing type, miss."

"What I do at Herrick Island is my business." I pushed the dollar bills across the sticky bar and glanced around the room. "Are the upstairs rooms through that far door?"

"No," said a quiet man's voice behind me.

I'd not noticed someone had approached me from behind, and considering the loud floorboards, that was quite a feat. Frowning, I turned and saw a young man standing just beyond my shoulder. Snow dusted his thick woollen coat and hat, and clumped around his boots. His arms were folded across his chest, and he regarded me with an intrigued, though rather surly look.

"Excuse me, sir," I said, though why I referred to him as 'sir' was out of habit and not because he was a gentleman. "I'm conducting a private business to secure a room. Can you point me in the direction of the stairs, for I have paid for my lodgings."

"You won't find a place here tonight," the man said. "What do you want to go to Herrick Island for?"

Obviously, the phrase 'private business' was lost upon him. But I was more than peeved I wouldn't be able to get a room. Before the barkeep could scoop up my precious dollars, I retrieved them from the bar.

"And you can find me such a place, I assume." I held up the money. "These are yours, if you will take me to a comfortable room in which to spend the night."

He reached forward to take the money, but I folded my arms.

"Not until I see the room."

He glanced at the barkeep, who shrugged and went back to filling up pewter mugs. I couldn't guess where this young man would take me at night during a storm, and it occurred to me for the hundredth time how ludicrous my situation had become. I should be at home, in my bed, looking forward to the next morning's dealings at the office, with Mr. Godwin by my side, and nary a lazy cousin in sight. I didn't want this new circumstance, and now I was forced to deal with this impertinent fellow.

"Well," I demanded, "am I to see the room, or spend the night standing in an inn?"

"You're better off staying on the mainland, in any rate," the young man said. "I'd not be so eager to go to Herrick Island, if I were you."

"I was invited," I said, which was more than the truth.

"I suppose you're wantin' me to believe you," the man muttered. He sighed and pushed up his cap, revealing dark hair. "I guess anyone, even a girl, who wants to go to Herrick Island is serious about it. But you really should keep your damn money and leave - before you realize you can't."

I should have expected him to speak to me in an uncouth manner, but for some reason, it still shocked me. Then my feelings hardened, and, as had happened many times before with Cousin Francis, I was quick to reply.

"I am as serious a lady as any you'll meet. I do not believe in nonsense, and I would like to leave, if it were not for circumstances I'd rather not disclose. So, if you have a room for me to stay, I shall gladly do so. Otherwise, have a good evening and do not presume to tell me what I should do with my money."

This speech was delivered as forcefully as I could manage, and once I'd finished, I really didn't care whether he thought highly of my feminine character or not. If there was one true thing I'd learned through years of experience, it was that to be a woman of perseverance and fortitude, I had to reject traditional views on how I should behave and instead meet men on their own ground. I was rarely listened to otherwise.

As expected, I received his surprised look. But it only passed over his features for a second before disappearing. His eyes narrowed and he contemplated me, perhaps wondering if I was serious. My convictions didn't falter and I returned his gaze with one equally as penetrating. He seemed satisfied that I meant what I said.

"Follow me."

He turned and headed towards the door back out into the snowstorm.

I gritted my teeth and was about to protest against returning to the cold weather, when I shut my lips tight and followed him without a word. It made sense that he would take me to a different location than this inn. Just before I stepped from the open doorway, I turned back - and noticed that the clock on the tavern wall had stopped.

I rolled my eyes. Someone should always ensure that clocks were wound and promptly ticking.

ten

Not even ten feet out onto the sidewalk, it occurred to me that I neither knew my companion's name nor had accurately assessed his true character before joining him. His general appearance and uncouth manner both gave me insight into a fellow of low birth and rank. He didn't seem to be a sailor, for I hadn't detected an odor of the sea or fish about him. Who was he, and why was he interested in my journey to Herrick Island?

Unfortunately, the strength of the storm made it difficult to breathe, let alone keep up a walking pace and converse at the same time. The wind was far more furious than it had been upon first arriving in Rockland, and it slapped across my face with astonishing force. Blowing snow sprayed us both in a torrent of chilled flurries that numbed my cheeks. I wiped my face with cold snowy mittens and clutched my carpet-bag to my chest as I followed this man down the length of the deserted sidewalk. There was no carriage or cab to hail, nor would I be able to afford one should it appear. None other seemed to be out this blasted night.

We finally reached the end of the main street and came upon a beautiful but foreboding scene. It was a harbor, shrouded in the darkness of a night-time winter blizzard. Dark waves crashed up around pier pilings and sloshed over wharves. Boats tied down with canvas shrouds rocked precariously in the wind. Snow scampered up from the vast expanse of ocean, and with few blockages to halt its path, hurled at us with tremendous speed.

The man turned back around and gestured for me to follow. Yet the force of the gusts kept me pinned at the edge of the final building, unwilling to walk along the harbor in view of those tremendous flurries. He stomped through the crusty snow over to my side.

"We're almost there!" he shouted above the roaring wind. "Follow me!"

What low level of ridiculousness I'd ever gotten myself into before tonight was made insignificant in comparison. Yet something within me had hardened through the years of constant diligent dutifulness, and I was no tender spring lamb. I left the shelter of the building and entered the full force of the oceanic winds. Petticoats bunched around my legs, and my feet were frozen cold lead weights. Yet I hauled the strength from deep within me, like drawing up a full bucket of tipping water, and pressed on. My legs were so tired my hips ached and bones trembled from the enormous force needed to overcome nature's wintry fury.

The young man turned about and made a wide swooping arc with his arm. I understood and slogged through the snow behind him. We were almost there.

Out of the foggy darkness emerged a building that looked so alike to the Tate Shipping Company I thought two days had suddenly vanished. It was a dock warehouse, perched at the mouth of a wide jutting wharf. Snow had whitened its roof, and its brown clapboards were dotted with tiny dark windows. My companion was a mere dockworker? I'd have rather taken up lodgings with a sailor.

He led me to the side of the building, under a small eave that afforded a surprising amount of shelter against the fierce snowy winds. I gasped, clutching my hands to my aching hips. The young man produced a black key from somewhere on his person, and unlocked the giant padlock on the side door. I couldn't breathe and I certainly couldn't speak, so I merely followed him into the warehouse. It was so dark I immediately stopped just inside the closed door, staring wildly about and seeing nothing.

A flicker of gold sprang up in the darkness. The young man had lit an oil lamp. He brought it over to me, the heat warming my freezing hands.

"We'll stay here tonight," he explained in a quiet but serious tone. "The storm will be over by the morning."

I squeezed my numb fingers and said nothing. We were standing in a warehouse, no more luxurious than a shed. Piles of rope, half-carved chunks of wood, carpenter's tools, and heaping sail canvas surrounded us. My breathing gradually slowed as I warmed, but I was so confounded as to why he'd brought me here, I spoke as soon as I was able.

"I should have stayed at the inn," I muttered. "What kind of lodgings are these?"

"Safe," he retorted. "If I'd have left you there, you would have met a worse fate than a nor'easter and a warehouse. Believe me."

"No man would dare lay a hand upon me, in any indecent manner," I said. "I would only have to speak my surname and they would know who I am."

"It wouldn't matter," the young man said. "Even the daughter of Captain Sumner Tate has no claim to safety here."

My mouth dropped open, and I had to take a moment to figure out how this fellow knew me. Was my father renowned amongst these rustic coastal folk? Without waiting for a reply, the young man left my side and disappeared into the blackness of the warehouse. He lit another oil lamp, then gestured for me to follow.

No claim to safety indeed, I thought as I picked my way past the ropes and sailcloth. I followed the bobbing oil light around a huge dark structure, which I soon realized was an overturned ship's hull. The young man brought me to what appeared to be the captain's quarters, though they were only half-constructed. A berth was built into the side of the hull, featuring a mattress dressed with bedclothes and a pillow. A second mattress lay on the wood floor. A little ship's stove and coal-hod with a shovel sat beside a small round tea table and pair of chairs.

The young man set his oil lamp on the table and went about scoop-ing coal into the stove and lighting it. He reached into a cupboard and brought out a pie, then set it on the table with plates and forks. I curiously watched him take a dipper off a wall and ladle beer from a small barrel into a mug. He pulled up a chair and sat down heavily at the table, then began cutting into the pie.

"Are you going to eat or not?" he asked.

I wasn't hungry enough to share a meal with him. "How did you know I was Harriet Tate?"

He stuck a forkful into his mouth and chewed, staring at me with a scowl. I didn't feel at all that I was safer with him than I would have been back at the inn. The pie smelled good, though. I cautiously approached the second chair at the table and put a hand on its back, but I did not sit down.

"Were you acquainted with my father?"

He swallowed noisily. "You don't let up, do you?"

"No one would ever accuse me of indifference."

"I can see why." He ate another bite. "Jonah sent me to bring you to the island."

Jonah ... Jonah Herrick. The letter-writer. He'd sent this man to fetch me? I pulled out the chair.

"Hungry, I take it."

"I am," I declared and sat down. "I was unaware that you were his servant."

"Servant," he growled, staring at me. "I am the Herrick family's car-riage driver."

"Indeed." I had been waiting for him to cut a piece of pie for me, but when he did not I helped myself and dished a slice onto my plate. "You are employed by this Jonah Herrick, yet you do not think you are a serv-ant? I had it in mind you were merely a dockworker. At least a driver is far above that station."

He grunted and focused on his eating. I did the same, and found to my delight the fish pie was delicious. After two satisfying slices, I placed my silverware on my plate.

"So, as you know my name by way of this Mr. Herrick, what is your name?"

"Boy," came the reply. "Is what Jonah calls me, so's I'm that."

"How unfortunate," I said. "Yet you did not answer my question, and besides, I do not care how Mr. Herrick refers to you. Can you tell me your name or not?"

He put down his fork and touched his chin thoughtfully, as if deciding how to answer me. Then he shrugged and wiped his mouth with the back of his hand.

"Lucas," he answered. "Lucas Penley."

"A fine acquaintance we have made, Mr. Penley," I said. "I do not fail to appreciate the supper tonight, so I thank you for that. I also assume that these accommodations are for the both of us?"

I indicated the captain's berth bed and the mattress on the floor. Mr. Penley nodded.

"Not my home," he explained. "I'll even be nice and give you the berth."

An odd feeling of queasiness overcame me as I thought about sleeping in a captain's berth. If I had been a son, the son my father so desperately longed for, then I'd have been spending the vast majority of my life resting in such a berth.

"Fitting," I remarked with a sniff, "to be a captain's daughter and sleep in such a place. My father sleeps at the bottom of the ocean now."

"Mine is also in the grave," Mr. Penley said. Oh, and the way he uttered it made my heart ache for him. A few simple words cupped a lifetime of sorrow.

I didn't know what else to say, nor did the exhaustion I felt allow me to continue on for lengthy conversation. I bid Mr. Penley a good night, which was hardly a statement I could utter with truthfulness on such a stormy strange evening, and retired to the berth. I climbed up into the wooden cocoon and drew the curtains about me to undress in private. By the time I got under the covers, darkness closed about me. My last thoughts before I drifted into a cold, restful sleep were about the time.

I'd be sure to check my little watch in the morning.

eleven

Smoky bacon and eggs sizzling in a skillet roused me from bed the following morning. After a surprisingly deep sleep my disposition had greatly improved, and so it was with a renewed sense of vigor that I dressed hastily in the private captain's berth.

When I drew back the curtains and emerged, I found Mr. Penley balancing a cast iron skillet on the tiny stove. He reached for a plain ironstone plate and carefully lifted the skillet. He tilted it like a listing boat, and a perfectly fried egg speckled with black pepper and salt crystals slid from the dark cast iron. In a practiced motion he replaced the skillet upon the stove, cracked a fresh brown egg, and splattered it onto the iron surface. Gradually, the runny edges turned opaque. Watching Mr. Penley cook was fascinating, with his careful temperature control and attention to the smallest detail.

Presently, a second egg slid onto an ironstone plate and was passed across the table to me. A plate of bacon strips and a thick jug of syrup sat on the table. Before sitting down himself, Mr. Penley helped himself to a mug of beer. He heartily drank and noisily smacked his lips together before diving into the feast.

"Has the storm left us?" I asked.

"I've been outside," he said between bites. "It's not snowing."

"Very good to hear."

I drizzled syrup on the bacon, then picked up my knife and fork. Mr. Penley used his bacon like an oar to scoop through the runny egg yolk and drip it into his mouth.

"Perhaps you've not had the chance to observe proper table manners," I remarked. "Eating with one's hands is never a viable option in company."

"I ain't a lady, ya see."

"I do see, Mr. Penley. I shall take this matter up with Mr. Herrick as soon as I am able to get the chance."

He stared at me, beer foam flecking his lips. "You don't talk to Jonah about me. You hear?"

"And why, pray tell, am I not to speak about you? Surely he must take some sort of interest in your well-being. I prided myself on providing fair wages and excellent references to all my servants."

"Well, aren't you the perfect mistress," he said sarcastically.

I was before financial circumstances forced me to let go of my favorite household help, a fact I decided to withhold from him. Instead, I answered:

"Perfection is an easily obtainable goal with the right amount of attention and perseverance. You displayed quite the aptitude for cooking this breakfast. Can you not apply the same attention to other things, such as personal habits and your decorum?"

He wiped his mouth and tossed a dirty napkin on his empty plate. Then he clamped his hands under his arms and leaned back in the chair, chin thrust down into his chest and dark eyes scanning every detail of my person.

"If you are wondering," I continued, "then yes, Mr. Penley, I complimented you. I believe everyone has talents, no matter how simple or rudimental, that may be of use to somebody."

"You don't have the talent for lettin' be what's needin' to let be," he growled.

I couldn't argue with that assessment. He pushed back his chair and rose from the table. After I finished my breakfast, he extinguished the stove, dumped our empty plates into a large metal tub, and grabbed his green coat and knit hat. He bundled up into his boots as I also donned my outer cloak and bonnet. I took up my carpet-bag, squeezing it close to me. From my pocket, I could hear my little watch ticking, and retrieved it to check the time. Twelve minutes past nine o'clock in the morning.

Mr. Penley paused at the door, and from beneath it I felt winter's icicle breath, causing goosebumps along my ankles and arms. It was the second day of March, and spring was many weeks in the future. Mr. Penley held the door open for me, and I stepped from the dry warmth of the warehouse into an astonishing and beautiful winter wonderland.

Blinding bright sunlight bounced off the stark white surfaces and careened about the tippling snowdrifts. A child laughed merrily as he ran by us, chased by a trio of playmates with arms full of snowballs. My boots crunched on the crusty snow at my feet, and the sky was a lovely periwinkle blue. Beyond the warehouse the vast sun-glistened ocean lapped gently at the bobbing boats. Fishermen at the shoreline unlashed their vessels from wharves, ready to cast off into the unknown. Since it was the same general atmosphere of Kennebunkport, it felt so familiar I reminded myself I was in Rockland, more than one hundred miles from home.

Mr. Penley picked his way down to the harbor shoreline at the back of the warehouse. I followed past snow-covered piles of hastily thrown rope and rounded net structures. I was about to inquire as to their purpose, when I saw a painted lobster on a boat and deduced they must be catching apparatus for that particular creature.

"I booked passage for us both," Mr. Penley said abruptly. He stepped onto a dock, kicking snow off its rickety boards.

"Passage onboard what type of vessel?" I asked.

"The mail boat," came the reply.

We approached a small sailboat, of no longer length than a railway car, tied up at the end of the dock. A skinny elderly man with his face obscured by gray whiskers had one foot on the skiff and another on the dock, tossing thick canvas bags into the boat. Thud! Thud! They hit the deck and shook the boat. With each thud he grunted, sweating despite the cold.

"Let's go," Mr. Penley grumbled. "He's been paid already."

"Up to t' island. Two passengers," the mail boat captain said. "She don't look like the sea-farin' type, Lucas."

He shrugged. "Don't care if you are or not. Get in, Miss Tate."

"I had it in mind that a larger vessel would ferry us across," I admitted. "Can not a sloop or a windjammer of some kind perform the task?"

"Does it look like there's one here?" Mr. Penley asked.

He plucked my carpet-bag from my half-frozen fingers. It landed on the deck with a similar thud as the mail.

"Get. In."

A brusque thing he was. And surly as well. I gingerly stepped to one side of the captain and plunked my black lace-up boot into the boat. A sudden and fierce desire to prove my independence to Mr. Penley caused me to grab handfuls of my woolen skirts and petticoats and haul the rest of my weight into the boat. Yet I was not prepared for the force to tip the boat sideways. A slosh of seawater hiked up over the edge and splattered my cloak. Luckily, I didn't also tip over.

"See?" Mr. Penley stepped into the boat with all the ease of a seasoned sailor. "Knew you could."

"It was not a matter of whether I was capable or not, Mr. Penley," I said. "You won't find me to be a lady of limited capacity."

He entered the small shelter up by the captain's wheel and sat down on a wooden bench. I copied his movements and sat across from him, in exactly the same way if we were in a carriage. The captain finished packing the boat, tossed off the ropes, and took the wheel. He turned the boat about, and we headed off away from shore.

I could not help looking back at the dock warehouse, wishing I had stayed within its sheltered walls. Snow piled in great jagged drifts against the sides. The sunny morning started to cloud, bare-branched trees along the shoreline clustered together against the cold.

Mr. Penley stretched out, propping a snowy boot on his knee. He yawned and pulled his knit cap down over his eyes, attempting to nap. When he wasn't growling at me or staring at me with a surly look, his face was rather handsome. Thank goodness he hadn't caught me looking. I jammed my hand into my pocket and drew out my watch. Its cold form quickly warmed in my fingers, and its steady ticking provided a means by which to measure these moments at sea. Why in God's name I'd chosen to journey a hundred miles from home, then take this rickety old vessel out across the untamed Atlantic Ocean, all in the name of pirate's treasure ...

I couldn't believe I was doing this. Harriet, you should have said no.

The weather began to worsen. A thick, dense fog descended, slowly and hungrily swallowing up the sunlight. Nature had put on a coat as woolly as sheepskin, yet made of nothing more substantial than airborne water vapor. It was a clammy, briny-scented substance that, unlike an artist, made everything colorless.

"Fitting," I said aloud. Mr. Penley might have heard me, though it was likely he did not. "Fogbound. Of course."

As if it played audience to my utterance, the fog swished from the front of the boat like a downy gray curtain and parted to reveal a new obstacle. A jagged tumble of black wet rocks, each larger than the boat, provided an impenetrable wall guarding a circular landmass. The rocks loomed ominously in the gray air, wearing thick brackish masses of seaweed. The mail boat captain jerked the wheel and expertly guided us around to the right, pulling the vessel up alongside the island so that I had a clear view up the craggy exterior.

"Ah," grunted Mr. Penley. "Home sweet home."

"Do you live at Fogbound Manor?" I inquired.

"Of course," he muttered. "Hopefully, not much longer."

He folded his arms so tightly over his chest they seemed to meld with his form. He resembled an escaped prisoner ferried to gaol. His eyes were open and staring straight ahead, glowing with an intensity that burned through the fog.

The boat slowed, gliding over the slight cresting waves lapping against the bottoms of the rocks. I peered through the fog, trying to distinguish any noticeable shapes or forms, but it was like clouded glass. I didn't know how the mail boat captain could see a thing in such weather.

Thank goodness he could, for he came around the rocks' edge, and a sandy shoreline about fifty feet in width provided a smooth entrance to the island. Waves from the boat's wake jostled against this gravelly beach. An old crooked dock jutted out into the water, and the captain wheeled up to it.

"Right, then, girl," he muttered to his boat, or perhaps to me, I couldn't tell which.

As soon as the captain had dropped anchor, Mr. Penley sprang to his feet with a vigorous energy and grabbed my carpet-bag. In two quick steps he'd headed to the back of the boat and jumped up onto the dock.

"Mr. Penley?" I called after him.

He'd either forgotten how to escort a lady out of a boat or never been taught. In any case, he disappeared into the fog as if it had reached out and engulfed him. Meanwhile, the mail boat captain cheerfully reached for the large mail sacks and began heaving them up onto the rickety boards, singing an old ditty as he did so.

Leave her Jonah, leave her
Oh, leave her Jonah, leave her
I know that she'd sail on without ye
Leave her Jonah, leave her

Thud. Thud. The mail sacks careened onto the dock. How entertaining, I thought, standing upright in the ridiculous tipping mail boat. Surrounded by fog, lost in a strange mist of my own silly decisions.

I pulled out my watch again, but the hands had stopped ticking. I started to wind it, but who could tell the exact minute or hour? No use trying to determine it by the sun, for the sky was a shifting colorless mass of gray. I frowned, straining to hear Mr. Penley's footsteps through the gloom. Oh, if I could only know the time!

Grumbling, I gripped my little watch in one hand, yanked up my skirts with the other, and approached the boat's edge. A canvas bag sailed right by my head and thudded on the dock. With the mail boat captain's strange shanty echoing behind me, I grasped the edge of the boat and lifted my weight up onto the rim. An oily black sludge of ocean water pooled between the boat and the dock. It smelled briny and salty. I was able to catch my balance and stand on the edge long enough to hoist myself up onto the dock. Thud! The last of the mailbags plunked down right next to me.

"Ah!" The captain lit a cigar, its tiny flame the only light in the flat gray. "Got yourself up on dry land, have ye."

"Without any assistance, it seems," I muttered, though he didn't hear me.

"I don't dock at Herrick Island for long." He took a drag on his cigar and the smoke blended into the fog. "Back in a week, missy."

"A week?" I cried.

He hauled up the anchor, grabbed the rope, and careened the wheel around. The little boat drifted from the dock. It presently vanished into the fog and could not be seen or heard from at all.

"A week," I repeated aloud.

Spending seven minutes upon such a dreary, foreboding place seemed ill conducive to my general sense of contentment, let alone seven days. How far from home I was. Far from the parlor at the Captain Tate Mansion, from the shipping company, even from the cozy dock warehouse on Rockland's shores. The captain might as well have dropped me on Neptune.

I don't know how long I stayed alone on the dock, for I had no sense of the time. I tried to count to sixty, but the lonely silence jarred my counting. I walked to the end of the dock and stared down into the black shifting waters. A breeze played with my hair, and I tucked the strands into my cloak's hood. I felt hungry, tired, and longed for a hearth fire to curl up in front of. Perhaps I should venture up the dock? Yet something within me seized my limbs and I could not move from my position. It was like standing on a precipice with the great expanse of the ocean beneath me as a bottomless tidal floor. No place to stand, no place to find comfort or refuge. I could not even see the great black rocks surrounding the island. Their craggy appearance would give a little sense of the earth beneath me.

Some solidity to cling to. I had nothing but the ever-pressing water vapor surrounding me, seeping into me, chilling me.

"Miss Tate?"

His voice cut through the fog and, though it was not spoken in a tone of friendliness, eased my nerves. Mr. Penley at last appeared, emerging from the fog like a spirit passing between worlds. He didn't seem to notice my distress at being left alone, and instead reached down and slung a mail-bag up onto his back.

"I've brought the carriage 'round," he said over his shoulder.

He started down the dock and disappeared again. I hadn't heard a carriage pull up, which was unsettling. I gripped my silent watch and walked unsteadily over the rickety boards across the black waters and to the shores of Herrick Island.

twelve

A great black shape darker than the brackish water emerged from the gloom. Four horses stood before the carriage. Breath curling like the fog, mixing and mingling with the vaporous air. The familiar scents of horse sweat and leather. Something recognizable in this desolation.

Mr. Penley opened the carriage door and swung the steps down. I thought he might offer me a hand, but he didn't and instead went around to the front, by the horses. He greeted each in a soft voice. His shoulder muscles moved beneath his shirt, and he curled his fingers to stroke their necks. How they succumbed to his tenderness, enjoying his touch, nuzzling for more. He caught me looking at him, and his eyes were dark and husky. I felt heated and my stomach dropped a bit. He gave the horses one final pat and clomped over to me. Any trace of gentleness in the moment vanished.

"You can't get in?" he asked gruffly. "Yer bag's already in there."

I scowled at him and climbed up inside. At once, a sense of exhaustion stole over me and produced a headache behind my eyes. I yawned and slumped in the seat, curled against the carriage window like a cat. Mr. Penley clomped up the dock again, disappeared into the fog, and soon reappeared dragging the mail sacks.

The carriage door creaked open. I sleepily opened my eyes. Mr. Penley had produced a white cloth wrapped about something round. He laid it on the seat, grunted that it was for me, and slammed the door. The carriage tilted as he climbed up to his perch. I unwrapped the cloth to find a wheel of smooth yellow cheese, a bit of cold corned beef, and a bread roll still soft on the inside. Not much more glamorous than the fish pie, but I ate with heartiness.

A whip crack startled me, and horses whinnied eerily in the fog. The carriage jolted forward into a bumpy, swaying rhythm. Outside my window I glimpsed the ground beneath me and some strange unintelligible shapes. That's all that exists on Herrick Island, I thought gloomily. Amorphous shapes waiting within the fog.

Soon, I started to feel the strangest sensation that we were climbing, and indeed my ears exuded the pressure from it. I could not have told where the fog ended and the clouds began, like some old master's painting of Mount Olympus, with the gods cavorting amongst a heavenly scene. Finally, we had climbed high enough so that I could take in a bit of my surroundings.

The island was as colorless as one could imagine. No vivid hue or spot of brightness could be seen in the landscape. It was as if someone had dumped dirty laundry water over the scene. Grays, browns, the blue-black expanse of the Atlantic, and the darkest of pine green fir trees. Patchy snow splayed over mounds of dead brown leaves. Matte gray rocks of various textured surfaces and sculpted shapes stuck out of the ground at odd angles. Pale and sea-scented, the cloud-like fog kissed every surface.

If I'd been writing a sketch on the area, I'd call it the land of gray for that was the predominant color. Whether it was a light misting gray spraying off the ocean waves at the base of the island, a medium foggy gray as the ever-present airy water vapor, or the flat shale gray of the thick, jagged rocks lining the carriage path. An artist would have a difficult time selecting another hue to describe the landscape.

Mr. Penley drove along a narrow carriage road, weaving in and around the great rocks so that I could only catch glimpses of the larger view for a couple of seconds at a time. Of course, I had no idea how big the island was or how far we were from Fogbound Manor. I'd not thought to ask normal, obvious questions such as these, and the fact that I didn't was enough to make me frown. I sat back from the window, pushed the curtain in front of it, and bathed myself in darkness. Nothing to see out there anyway. I might as well be color-blind.

In the dark, my highly-strung mental state plagued me. I could not still my mind, and my thoughts buzzed like flies. I felt a strange growing sense of panic. The rocks surrounding the island felt like heavy chains about my neck, trapping me on this gray colorless land like a prison. What other place besides a gaol could be so cheerless and monotone? I sat up straight and violently pulled the window curtain away from the panes.

The carriage swayed and horses' hooves clopped over the ground sand. The sky had darkened, and evening drew upon the island. I clutched my watch. We traveled deeper into an unknown I had no wish to be in. My bleak surroundings offered nothing but their bare skeletal forms to entertain the eye. Out here in the middle of nowhere, with nothing to see and no way in which to see it. I was not in hell, for I'd know the flames. I was in a vast purgatory, caught between worlds, no foot on a solid shore.

Wait, did the carriage begin to slow? I held my breath, fingers gripping the carriage seat. Yes, I was right. Mr. Penley had eased up on the reins. The scent in the air was also changing. No longer the constant briny oceanic odor, but something much more comforting. Oh, thank goodness. I smelled the smoky underbelly of a hearth fire. At last, some glint of warmth.

I scooted to the window and stared out through the gloom, ready to glimpse anything in the darkness. Ah, there it was. Faint, at first, hidden by the fog. Then growing ever brighter, ringed by a smoky aura. It was so high I felt I was peering up the side of a mountain. It was a lit window, mullioned diamond panes flickering with yellow light. It took me a few seconds to realize I was seeing Fogbound Manor. For there could be no doubt that this was it. It was slowly coming into view, the fog only allowing me to see a few more windows, dark and sunken into the thick stone walls.

Sandy gravel gave way to a hardened carriageway of packed dirt, and Mr. Penley drove up alongside the manor before abruptly stopping. The carriage creaked as he vacated his perch, and I heard a thud as his hard boots landed on the packed dirt. All nervousness within me had vanished, leaving a strange numb exhaustion that sapped my more tormented feelings and reduced me to mere mechanical motions. I made no protest when he opened the carriage door, and I slowly descended. A foggy breeze played with wisps of my hair. I breathed in the distant smell of a hearth fire, the salty twang of the ocean.

Fogbound Manor rose up before me. Its whole appearance was one of blocky massiveness and remarkable monstrosity, as if it was not a product of human hands but had erupted out of the shoals around it. Like a gigantic sleeping sea creature. A trio of thick round turrets topped with brick triangular caps created the feeling of a castle, while the high stone walls were a formidable fortress. Enormous double front doors stood atop the widest stairs I'd ever seen, flanked by carved stone railings and lichen-crusted urns trailing ivy leaves. The insistent tidal murmuring of the sea sounded from somewhere behind the manor. Its own personal orchestra.

Mr. Penley dropped my carpet-bag on the gravel. He gestured towards the front door, made a small grunt, then began to climb back onto the carriage.

"Where are you heading?" I asked abruptly. My voice sounded strange in the foggy night air.

"Where do you think?" he grumbled. "The stables."

"I see," I said, feeling quite foolish. "Thank you for the . . . assistance."

He shrugged, as if it was common to bring ladies to the underworld's remote entrance. Before I could stall him further, he'd climbed up, resumed his position, and started the carriage again. It rolled off into the distance, following the carriageway around the side of the manor and disappearing as completely as if it had never been here at all.

"Infernal fog," I muttered aloud to myself.

Mr. Penley was no great company, but I did not bear his absence well. If there had been anywhere else to go on this God-forsaken island, I would have gladly chosen it rather than approach this foreboding place. Left on Hades's doorstep, I had nothing but my own fortitude to convince me to walk forward.

I lifted my carpet-bag and climbed up the front steps, approaching the manor as if heading straight for a stone dragon's jaws. No face peeped in the window, no kind greeting from anyone. As soon as I'd reached the top stair, the mist gave way to a light rain. It pattered the stone beneath my feet, slid along the damp walls, and cascaded down my cloak. The huge front doors dwarfed me, smelling of wet wood and old iron. I reached up a tentative hand and pounded fiercely on the rusting door knocker. My gesture echoed throughout the interior of the manor.

I had not long to wait before a latch clicked on the other side of the door. It was shoved open by a sleepy-looking butler with a face that drooped like an old hound dog. He peered at me from underneath heavy eyelids, then it registered in his ancient mind that I must have been a person of enough importance to allow entry. I set my jaw, determined not to reveal the anxiety knotting my stomach, and stepped past him. He closed the enormous door behind me with a low whomping sound.

An incredibly dark and gloomy dimness permeated the hushed interior. I gathered that I was standing in a huge entrance hall, three times larger than my own foyer at home. Cold stone columns supported its high arching ceiling. Small sparks of light emitted from deep within the manor, like stars on a winter night sky. As my eyes grew adjusted to the lack of light, I could make out furnishings as dark and ancient as the manor itself. Gothic wooden benches that resembled Medieval church pews, ancient faded tapestries covering the thick stone walls. An enormous mahogany staircase wide enough for five people to stand side-by-side on its red carpeted steps. Some room close by exuded a smoky smell.

"Stokes!" a hearty voice cried. "Bring her in here."

The butler took the carpet-bag from my cold fingers and shuffled over the flagstone floor towards a doorway as large as a carriage-entrance. Upon passing beneath it, I entered a cavernous room that must be the main parlor. It reminded me of a cathedral with its vaulted ceiling, gray stone walls, and tall mullioned windows. An assortment of upholstered sofas and chaise lounges provided comfortable seating in front of the impressively carved marble fireplace. A hearth fire crackled with such cheerful vitality I felt renewed.

The master of the manor sat before this fire, wrapped in snuggly blankets. His tapestry chair was as large as a throne, with carved lion's paw feet. His long skinny legs propped up on a small velvety footstool. He turned his face to greet me, but he was bathed in shadow, and all I could make out was more darkness.

"Hello, Miss Tate."

"Good evening, Mr. Herrick."

I let down my cloak hood from my hair and walked forward. As I approached, I could see more of him, and any vague guesses I'd previously entertained about his appearance vanished when I saw his entire personage.

His skin was a sickly yellow, like a clouded moon. Dark hair, as brackish and mussed as seaweed, curled haphazardly on his shoulders, as if he'd told it to behave and it did not. His eyes were unusually bright, with black centers like pools of deepest ocean. His fingers were so thin and his arms so skeletal he could have easily passed for a corpse. I felt little but revulsion, and it required every last ounce of my composure to stand before him and appear quite unaffected by what I beheld.

"I am glad you have come." He set down the mug of tea he had been sipping and leaned forward, extending yellow fingers. "Let us shake hands, that we should be friends. You are to be my companion in this exciting adventure. Together, we shall discover wonders!"

His voice was surprisingly strong, and the force of his greeting seemed to be coming from a more physically robust man. He was such a contrast of health and illness, of life and death, that I felt peculiar.

"Sit, Miss Tate. Draw up the parlor chair there."

I did as he wished, seating myself at a reasonable distance. In the firelight my skin glowed with a healthy orange, while Mr. Herrick's featured a mottled tone.

"My illness does not prevent me from wanting to stay up all hours of the night discussing our mutual ancestry with you."

"But I am tired, sir," I said. "The journey was fatiguing, and I wish to be shown my room for a night of rest. We may begin our discussion at first light, if you so desire."

He flung himself against the back of the chair and rubbed his forehead vigorously. Then he snapped his fingers.

"Stokes! Stokes, at once."

The butler emerged from somewhere in the darkness behind us.

"Your room is prepared, miss," he said. "Please follow me."

I stood, a gesture that caused Mr. Herrick to roll his eyes.

"You would leave me so soon," he demanded. "I know I am ill, and my presence may be taxing to your senses, accustomed to seeing healthy men."

"I am," I admitted. "None other I have ever met outside of a hospital has had your pallor. I implore you not to overexert yourself. I will be here until the end of March. There is time to do everything you wish. But I must be allowed to rest."

"My goodness," he said with a degree of awe, "you are quite determined. I fear I may find an obstinacy in you that contrasts with my own enthusiasm."

"Call it what you will," I said.

My head was beginning to ache. What he thought of as stubbornness was common sense. Why unduly tire and wear out your guest when she had just arrived after a three-day harrowing journey? I got to my feet and bowed to Mr. Herrick.

"I bid you good-night, sir. I will come down to breakfast at first light."

He waved me away, dismissing me off-handedly. "We must get started at once!"

"We will."

That was the last thing I would say, for exhaustion threatened to pull me into the depths of the floor. I gave him a quick curtsy and slipped out of the parlor back into the entrance hall. A dim glow alighted next to the staircase. Mr. Stokes had lit a small chamberstick. Above, a crooked iron chandelier with three tiny candles cast little light on the steps.

"Miss Tate," the butler said.

He turned and began ascending the steps. Curious, I carefully lifted my skirts and approached the massive balustrade. I tentatively began to climb, keeping an eye on the butler's weak candlelight. The stairs were so massive and steep I could hear my heavy breathing and felt tightness in my lower legs. About twenty steps up we came to a large landing, turned, and kept climbing.

We reached a crooked hallway that disappeared into a dark and dizzying angle. I didn't dare pause for fear of losing Mr. Stokes and abandoning all hope of finding my way back to the parlor again. At length, we ascended to what I believed to be the third floor, though I could not be sure. I felt like we had been climbing stairs for quite some time, yet I sensed we were not even halfway up inside the manor. He turned off into a narrow hallway lined with cream painted doors and wallpaper of an old-fashioned style. I had barely time to think if one of these quarters would be mine before he entered a side passage, where he revealed a second staircase. We ventured even deeper into the manor's belly.

This second staircase was quite drafty and exposed to the elements. A single circular window built into the old wooden wall planks revealed little beyond the dark misting clouds. My skin felt clammy from the moisture in the air, and my nose filled with the relentless briny scent of the sea. I was glad I'd selected an extra petticoat to warm my ankles, for the air grew colder and damper with each rising step.

Another hallway, less formal and more crudely designed than the one below, greeted me. Low candles along small wall pockets cast milky light on the plaster walls and low doors. Mr. Stokes had to stoop beneath the low beamed ceiling, and I was glad of my small frame, for I would not hit my head. Just when I thought this hallway would be our final destination, he turned down the narrowest, darkest passage of all. It looked like we were descending into an old cellar. A prickle of fear brushed across my neck, causing me to shiver. I paused at the threshold, then took a gulp of foggy air and slowly crept after him.

"Here," he uttered.

We'd come at last to the end of the narrow passage. A large, thick door made of ancient oak planks was shoved into the crumbling plaster. Braced by flat iron bands and featuring a huge black chained latch, it was like the entrance to a Medieval church.

Mr. Stokes reached for a single skeleton key in his trouser pocket and twisted it into the padlock. He lifted the creaky old latch with a loud click, and pushed open the door. A warm golden glow, more comforting than I'd expected, emitted from within. He stepped aside to allow me entry into my new quarters.

From the door's appearance, I'd assumed Mr. Herrick would have me stay in a moldy dungeon. Actually, he'd given me an impressive chamber. It was papered in a strange deep pine green pattern with striking orange and red damask markings. A steeply slanted wall hovered over a low, wide bed with carved pineapple finials. Each item of furniture was at least a century old, but so solidly built I'd no doubt they'd last several more centuries. A large faded tapestry hung from a thick metal bar on one wall. The crooked sitting area featured an old button-tufted leather chair and antique side table. Two tall narrow mullioned windows looked out over the ocean beyond. Between the two windows was a wide, low chest with a flat top, upon which sat a folded wool blanket.

Mr. Stokes set my carpet-bag on the bed, bade me a good night, and shuffled off. I felt like a queen of olde England, ensconced in her Renaissance-styled quarters. Yet, this was only a temporary arrangement. I was leaving in less than four weeks and certainly had no intention of staying one day longer than necessary.

"Treasure," I muttered aloud. "Nonsense."

Once undressed to my chemise, I drew a bed-jacket about my shoulders and went to the windows. My view overlooked the back of the manor above the churning waves. Sheeting mist slapped the glass, and I inhaled the sea's salty fragrance. Up four stories above its somber expanse, I felt closer to these bottomless fathoms than upon the shoreline at Kennebunkport. As if my skin had vaporized into fog, and my soul swooshed along with the tides.

Abruptly, I stepped back from the windows. Thank goodness the glass was between me and that infernal wet hell. How could I have guessed that a place named Fogbound Manor would be anything but welcoming.

I turned away from the windows and went over to the bed. Heaped with ten layers of blankets and pillows, it seemed to swallow my small form. With the sheets pulled up to my chin and my body slowly warming, I lay prone, far too exhausted to feel anything but the most acute wakefulness. It reminded me of the first few weeks after Mother's death, when sleep seemed the state furthest from her. I clung to my insomnia until I'd faint from overtiredness - only to wake trembling with the fear that after every rest she drifted further from my memories.

Yet, there was one figure who could never depart from my mind. He loomed in a larger and more fearsome form than he had in life.

It felt like Father was here, and I hated him for following me.

thirteen

In the morning, the sky had cleared of the night's gale. Clustering gray clouds hung about much of the manor, and the ever-present wind whistled against the diamond panes. My first thought was of the time, but I could locate no clock within my chamber.

Shortly after arising, a laden breakfast tray was delivered by a sallow housemaid. She paid no heed to my informal attire of a chemise and bed-jacket, set the tray on the round tea table by the bed, and left without a word or gesture of civility. I tended to my personal toilette, putting on a warm woolen day dress of dark plaid and pinning up my hair. Once I'd finished my meal, a polite knock sounded on the door.

Upon opening it, I discovered a shriveled and bent old woman no larger than a child. She emitted an aura of willed strength, as if her bones were made of tempered steel. She eyed me curiously, peering up from beneath an old-fashioned mob cap. Her dress was of plain, dark cotton and she wore a stained apron.

"Miss Tate?" she queried.

"Yes."

"Mrs. Quinn the housekeeper. You're wanted in the parlor."

"I see. Do you happen to have the time?"

"Time?" She shrugged, as if I'd asked for something that could never be found upon an island. "Methinks a tick after nine o'clock."

"Nine!" I was horrified at how late it was. "How late. Tell Mr. Herrick I'll be down directly."

She shuffled out of the doorway down the narrow passage. Goodness, I would have to rewind my watch and make sure never to rise so late again. I couldn't even remember the last time I slept past five-thirty. It made me feel as if the day was already half over.

I quietly closed my bedchamber door and started making my way through the manor. Other passages slipped off from the main hallway, dim and foggy as tunnels. Tiny winding staircases no wider than my waist abruptly appeared along the walls as if a magical hand constantly moved them. This manor's size was unbelievably huge. Three of my houses could fit inside this great blocky castle. I guessed the square footage to be somewhere in the vicinity of seven to nine thousand, making it larger than any other single dwelling I'd ever seen. And always, its wispy hand on my shoulder like a guide, was the fog.

Finally, I found the main staircase. As I descended, I thought of my first meeting with Mr. Herrick. What to make of it, I had no idea. His state of health was so alarming as to be quite taxing to my senses. My first impression of his sickly being left no doubt in my mind his contributions to a treasure quest would be minimal. He was so eager to get started. What sort of mad delusions would grip a man in such fervor? Nothing of the sort could induce such feelings in me. Enthusiasm was best handled with a proper adherence to reality.

Upon reaching the entrance hall, I slipped my hand inside my dress pocket. I had remembered to bring my lady's watch with me, useless though it was. As soon as my fingers closed about the cold round form, I felt more at ease. Curiously, there was no clock to be found in the entrance hall. I'd no sooner made my way into the parlor when the master greeted me heartily.

"Ah! Good morning, Miss Tate."

Perched in his fireside chair, Mr. Herrick looked as vigorous as last night, and the wan light of day gave his skin a less greenish cast. A painter would need a varied palette to capture the various dull yellow shades present in his thin hands and sunken cheeks. Even the orange firelight glow couldn't mask his illness.

"Mrs. Quinn asked that I join you."

I took the chair I'd occupied last night and glanced at the fireplace mantel, but could find no clock there, either. What started as a curiosity was turning into quite the mystery.

"You seem to have no timepieces in your home, sir." I indicated the mantel. "Not a clock there, nor one in my chamber or the entrance hall. Mrs. Quinn was kind enough to enlighten me it was past nine o'clock, but I cannot determine the exact hour at all."

At this, Mr. Herrick scoffed. The glint of a watch-chain flashed from his waistcoat and I pointed at it.

"Ah, there. Please tell me the time, so that I might wind my own watch."

"The time is the same as time always has been and always will be on Herrick Island. The time is now."

"Why, yes. That is certainly true." He sounded as loopy as his letters. "If you wish to wax philosophical about living in the present versus living in the future, I would be up for that discussion. However, first I need to know the time. If you would, sir."

I opened my fingers and showed him my dearly prized watch. It was a lady's timepiece two inches in diameter, its silvered surface worn smooth as a beach pebble. I expressly required that each of my dresses contain a pocket for it, as I did not wish to wear it upon a chain. Without its soothing ticking, I might as well be in a skiff with no anchor.

"That is quite the useless little object you have there," he said carelessly. "You will find nary a clock at Fogbound Manor. I have no need or desire for one."

He must be joking. Had I met a man of such insolent temperament that he would play a prank on his guest hours after arriving? I bristled at the thought.

"The Tate Shipping Company, of my own family's making, would not have thrived for so many years without living by a clock. I'd be hard-pressed to guess how you do it!"

He chuckled. Suddenly, he reached down and snatched the watch from me. Panicked, I at once got to my feet.

"Sir, return it to me," I ordered. "If you say you have no need or desire for a clock, then so be it. But do not deny its necessity to its owner."

"My, my. Getting yourself whipped into a frenzy, when you have only just arrived. Please, do sit down."

He cocked his head at me like an inquisitive bird. How could I trust a man of such ill countenance, exuberant outbursts, and sarcastic observations? Each of his emotions flitted across his face, each holding no more weight than the fog.

"I would like my watch back."

"That is obviously plain. I do not think I could have made a more lasting impression of my character than if I'd dunked you in the sea. To meet a clockless man! Why, that is quite the puzzle, isn't it?"

I folded my arms. The fire hissed behind me.

"Sir, you will find my companionship upon your treasure hunt to be invaluable. I have a keen interest in finding it, for it will be put to a use that will benefit not only myself, but my family and successive generations. But regardless of the promise of financial gain, I will forsake this quest if a mutual quality of respect for each other's differing natures is not acknowledged."

"Ah, yes. I now recall the contents of your first letter to me. No boyish heart ever received so cutting a rejection." He leaned forward in the chair, dangling the watch like bait before a fish. "I absolutely acknowledge your different nature, Miss Tate. I also have a great deal of information to share and not much time in which to share it. Alas, the Fates shorten my life thread. Perhaps to a week or a month? Who knows? Allow me to repeat myself - the time is now."

He held the watch out and at last allowed me to take it. I clicked open the lid and gazed fondly upon the perfectly spaced Roman numerals encircling the central black hands. Mr. Herrick still hadn't told me what time it was. I must take it upon myself to find a clock within this behemoth of a mansion, and I shall do it the first chance I get.

"Thank you, Mr. Herrick." I slipped the watch back into my pocket and took my seat across from him. "It is a curious thing that you have become so interested in my family, when I know nothing of yours."

"What is there to know? Fogbound Manor is over one hundred years old, built by my Herrick ancestors." He sat back in his chair, grinning as widely as could be. "And what a home it is, eh? I should dearly like to know your thoughts on it, Harriet."

He startled me by mentioning my first name, and I corrected him at once.

"It's Miss Tate, sir. I do admire this manor's size, but I confess I have had too short a visit to form a more full opinion."

"Is that so? You are obviously a lady of more elevated thinking. Your viewpoints are accurate, and your observations startling in their cutting detail." He gestured to a mahogany bookcase on the far wall. "Tell me you have not been educated. Perhaps not at Harvard College like myself, but does one really need academia to prove intelligence?"

"I wouldn't know, sir," I said ruefully. "I received private tutoring until my sixteenth year, after which I formed my own course of study in advanced mathematics and finance."

He leaned over to a side table and picked up a mug of tea. "Though we have been acquainted less than twenty-four hours, I can already presuppose an accurate observance upon your true nature, Miss Tate. Was this course of advanced study pursued in order to benefit your family's company?"

"It was," I replied. "I confess I should have dearly enjoyed an academic experience at Harvard College. If I had such an opportunity, of course."

"Rather than apprentice to become a captain?" He sipped his tea. "Interesting. I would have assumed Captain Sumner Tate's daughter to be drawn to his profession, not one of a different path. However I do see why, as it seems it would have been a better use of your innate talents."

Accurate, indeed. For the first time in my life, I was engaged in a conversation with a gentleman who spoke to me on an equal level. As if we both stood on the same floor of a building, rather than me forever trapped in the cellar and men enjoying a loftier view. Mr. Herrick stepped down from his higher station to not only converse with me, but appreciate my personal contributions from my own point of view. Not even Mr. Godwin afforded me such an intellectual luxury.

No man ever had.

"I appreciate the ability to speculate upon a life I could have had," I admitted, "but those education options were completely unavailable. Within my limited sphere as a lady, I have exercised every choice."

"It's obvious you have and done well given the circumstances. We share quite a bit of common ground to begin our acquaintance."

If he was speaking of the similarities between ladies and gentlemen, then I couldn't disagree more.

"Common ground? I hardly think so."

He tapped the arm of his chair with his forefinger. "We are both the last of our lines. I am the last Herrick and you are the last Tate. Surely you must find something meaningful in that fact?"

"Only if I was the last son, as you are," I pointed out. "Then my choice would have been clear from birth - to assume the position of overseer at the company."

He surprised me by laughing. It was a more pleasant sound than I would have guessed from his ailing appearance.

"So, as you are a woman, you cannot assume any authority in the company?"

"Not necessarily," I said. "Thanks to my mathematical study, I track and process the payroll with the head accountant."

"My goodness, what a shared trait I have at last found in our natures!" he cried. "I, too, pride myself on my numerical calculations and how quickly I can deduce them."

I highly doubted this declaration, and decided to test him upon it. He was not the first man to display his factual prowess before me, only to be made to look like a braggart and fool.

"All right," I said. "Perhaps I can take advantage of your aptitude."

His dark eyes crackled like the fire. "Oh, please do."

"Very well." I took a deep breath. "When the *Phoenix* sank on February 1st, she lost onboard sixty souls not including Captain Tate. Each of these sixty men had at least three family members requiring financial assistance. The Tate Shipping Company suffered a loss calculation of approximately six thousand and five hundred dollars per annum - "

"Wait, stop!" Mr. Herrick clattered his tea mug on the table and threw up his hands. "I cannot continue with this discussion."

"Of course you cannot," I returned. "For your numerical aptitude is, quite frankly, nothing to speak of."

He tucked a finger inside his cravat, loosening it. "I see you are not one to fool, Miss Tate. You immediately saw my bluff, yet still decided to test me. Well done."

"Well done?" I frowned. "I mistake your meaning, sir."

"Come now, Miss Tate. Why would I, a man with no head or passion for figures, desire a companion accustomed to staring at ridiculous numbers in a ledger?"

I folded my arms over my chest, and he cocked his head, eying me. He'd counted on me rising to his bluffed challenge to prove himself right about our compatibility. I couldn't decide if it made me more peeved that I didn't foresee his bluff or that he had been toying with my intellect all morning.

"I hardly know," I finally said.

"On this treasure quest, I need my opposite," he confessed. "A companion to perfectly complement my faults and virtues. Why would I desire somebody exactly like myself?"

"A lack of common ground between two dissimilar persons creates absence rather than kinship."

"Oh?" He grinned. "And how many souls in Kennebunkport, a shipping village of fishermen and boat-builders, shared common ground with you, Miss Tate?"

Before I could think of a suitable answer, since an immediate reply didn't come to mind, he pressed on.

"I'd say very few, if any. It is curious you hide yourself amongst rustic folk. You should be sharing that mind with similar intellects in a broader sphere."

I stared at him. His conversation was so informal as to be absurd. Never had I been spoken to this way. A tiny but persistent sense that he was right was quickly brushed off in favor of recounting his observations.

"Mr. Herrick," I began, "while you may not have a head for figures, you also cannot claim an aptitude in tact. I assume there have been few ladies in your company, for not one of them would enjoy being spoken to in so frank a manner."

"Not many ladies," he admitted. "Perhaps if I were to address you as a fellow gentleman? Would that better suit your temperament? I think it would."

"It would not, sir," I disagreed. "I am no gentleman."

"I beg to differ."

He leaned forward and hoisted himself up out of the chair. His movements were faster than I anticipated, and in half a blink he was suddenly on his feet. He headed over to the fireplace and retrieved the long whiplike saber from above the mantel. He jabbed it in the air, dangerously close to me.

"Gentlemen learn fencing," he said. "Lunge right. Parry left."

"Mr. Herrick - "

"Not an appealing hobby?" He replaced the saber and took a box of cigars off the mantel. He opened the lid and flourished it before me, the cigars neatly wrapped and laid out like boxed fish. I sighed.

"Smoking is not - "

"My goodness, no cigar?" He feigned mock surprise. Then he returned the cigar box and retrieved a glistening clear bottle of golden liquid from a cabinet by the fireplace. "Every gentleman I've ever met enjoys a spot of cognac in the evening. Served room temperature in cut crystal. Allow me to pour one for you. Perhaps it is before luncheon, but - "

"Mr. Herrick," I interrupted. "I do not fence, smoke, or drink. I am no gentleman."

"So it would seem." He replaced the bottle in the cabinet. "Well, Miss Tate, you are as much of an anomaly as a backwards-running clock. A woman - yes, a woman - with the mind of a man."

He planted himself back in his chair and leaned forward, face in hands, like a child about to hear a captivating story. This character mockery had gone on long enough.

"If that is indeed your final analysis of me," I said evenly, "then in return, Mr. Herrick, I call you a gentleman with the mind of a child."

He sighed. "Of course I am."

"Of course?" I echoed.

"Oh, yes." He leaned back in his chair and draped one skinny leg over the arm, slouching down into the tapestry cushions. "Miss Tate, you do miss out on an incredible variety of experiences by denouncing a more youthful perspective."

"Is that what this entire treasure search is about?" I asked. "A boyish adventure through a youthful perspective?"

"I do not care for most adult things," he admitted. "When I learned in January that I was dying, I resolved to turn my back upon the responsible world and enjoy whatever fancies flitted across my mind's eye. I spent weeks exploring and indulging in any pursuit I found exciting."

"So now you live with no clocks," I said, realizing. "Pursuing a treasure hunt."

"Your logical reasoning does not fail," he said with a smile. "My beginning research has excited me to a degree I have never felt, since it gives me a glimpse into our shared heritage."

"What you call heritage I call simply another of these fancies." I shook my head. "Until the treasure is located, if it exists, then it is nothing more than a whimsical distraction from looking after your own health."

"Of course you doubt it exists!" he exclaimed. "Every one does. So, the great question I pose to you, Miss Tate, before we even begin is - are you willing to suspend your innate disbelief in order to join me?"

Innate disbelief did not even come close to describing how I felt about this whole ordeal. I now saw exactly what my situation was. Fogbound Manor served as the bleak, imaginative playground for a sick and dying man. I had to find the money before I lost everything, but could I overcome my own strong reasons for resisting it? Was there really treasure buried on this island, or was it as fake as one of Mr. Herrick's fanciful conjurings?

I leaned forward in my chair, balancing my elbows on my knees, and addressed him in a serious tone. I needed that treasure more than I'd ever needed anything in my life.

"Yes. I will join you, Mr. Herrick. I carry on my family's legacy in the best possible capacity, and the treasure is the single greatest asset in doing so. However, I do not operate by fanciful means, so I require tangible proof and evidence. The first step is to ascertain the research you have already done."

"You see?" He smiled, happy as a child ready to go off berry-picking. "I knew with your sensible guidance we would embark on this in a smart way."

"Smart is the only way to pursue something of this nature. I also have a schedule to keep, sir. It is imperative that I not tarry one moment longer than planned."

"Clocks, plans, schedules." He shrugged, playing with his watch-chain. "Give yourself permission to abandon such busy, pointless activity. What adventurer needs a clock?"

"I do." I scowled at him. "I still have not wound my own watch."

"Oh, you may wind it." He giggled like a mischievous school boy. "Pick a time, any time. Let the ticking tap through the house. Did you ever consider how little time we have? How little time any of us have."

"We each have the same amount of seconds in a minute and minutes in an hour," I said. "Time is equal for us all."

"Until the clock stops ticking."

"Every clock requires someone to wind it again."

"Which I am sure the lovely Miss Tate will do." He bounded up to his feet as quickly as before. "Stokes and Mrs. Quinn prepare my meals according to whenever I wish to eat. I assume you are accustomed to more regular meal-times?"

"I have breakfast at half-past six every morning, luncheon at twelve o'clock, and dinner at seven."

"You and your numbers, Miss Tate." He shook his head. "Who knows if it is noon or not? I never can tell."

I rose to my feet. He offered his arm, and I hesitated. His skinny elbow jutted through his jacket like a sharp stone. He shrugged.

"I merely wish to accompany you - but it seems my health is off-putting. Forgive me."

He bowed graciously, appearing every bit the well-mannered gentleman. I couldn't say I was hungry, for my mind needed to process all that he had said. His conversation today was no less curious than his exuberant outbursts in his letters or his petulant greeting last night.

"Shall we?" He gestured for me to walk before him. "The dining room is on the other side of the entrance hall, my dear. After you."

"I thank you, sir."

"It's Jonah, if you please. I can address you with formality, but as for myself, I claim none."

How odd, I thought. All part of his childlike mannerisms. As I headed to the parlor doorway, I couldn't help but feel the strangest mixture of emotions. Astonishment at being spoken to as an individual and not merely as a female, perplexity at his varied emotions and declarations, extreme reluctance to proceed forward with such a changeable man, and the utmost urgency to find the money and be on the next mail boat home.

But first, for heaven's sake, I needed to find a clock!

fourteen

✳

No sooner had I left the parlor and set foot in the drafty entrance hall when a familiar clopping set of footsteps could be heard from outside. The front door whooshed open. Mr. Stokes's white head emerged from the dining room doorway, shrugged when he realized it was only the carriage driver, and disappeared once more.

Mr. Penley appeared much the same as last night, old green coat pulled up under his chin, and a brown knit cap obscuring his brow. His cheeks and nose were red from the cold, but his eyes held a surprising warmth. He smelled of the stables, warm dry hay and saddle leather. Slung upon his back was a mail bag of various letters and packages.

"Good morning, Mr. Penley," I greeted, though I couldn't be sure it was even still morning.

His return greeting to me was nothing but his usual scowl. But when his gaze alighted upon Mr. Herrick, he regarded him with such a black glower I was instantly on edge. Thud! He slammed the mail bag to the floor, the echo bouncing about the cavernous hall. Mr. Herrick abruptly side-stepped the mail bag and plucked a letter from a hall table. His scrawly handwriting looped across the front.

"Boy," he began with a condescending smirk, "how kind to drop off my mail. If you would deliver this to the Wenthams post-haste. I want them to join us for dinner tomorrow night."

Mr. Penley didn't take the letter. From the way he was standing and staring suspiciously at his master, he wanted to turn right back around and head outside. Mr. Herrick wagged the envelope in front of him like a steak before a dog.

"I'd be much obliged if you'd also read it," Mr. Herrick urged in a sing-song voice. "There will be an extra setting at dinner for you as well."

"I decline," Mr. Penley grumbled.

He balled his hands into fists by his side and marched right past Mr. Herrick on his way to the front door. He had nearly reached his destination when the sound of his name stopped him cold.

"Lucas."

Startled, I looked to Mr. Herrick, for it was he who had uttered his servant's name. He had not called him 'boy' as before. Though what he said next was even more surprising.

"Your presence at the dinner will affect the rest of your life. Will you not be witness to your own inheritance?"

Brimming with hatred and deep, bitter pain, Mr. Penley's eyes were like those of an animal bleeding to death. Weakened by injury, longing for release. I'd never seen a grown man suffer so greatly.

"Please, Mr. Penley," I said softly. "I expressly wish it."

I took the letter from Mr. Herrick. Mr. Penley reached behind and gripped the front doorknob, poised on the threshold between the manor and his escape. He eyed me suspiciously, pressing himself against the door as I drew nearer.

"I will accompany you, if you like," I offered.

A half-smile, one more grim than grinning, played at his lips. Then he tenderly plucked the letter from my fingers. His touch was like that rare moment with his horses, stroking their long, soft necks.

"No need, Miss Tate. I'll deliver it."

"Then you will come tomorrow night?" I couldn't help asking.

He shuddered, as if I'd asked him to slaughter a beloved pet. Even though his reply was to me, his gaze flicked back to Mr. Herrick, skewering him with ferocity.

"I will."

"Thank you."

I stepped back, allowing him the space to open the front door and depart from the manor. Misting cold wind stirred my petticoats and caused a chill to shiver across my shoulders. The door quietly closed. Mr. Herrick jutted his chin at me, as petulant as could be.

"After our morning conversation, I had assumed you to be the last person to show such generosity to a servant. Accompanying him on his errand?"

"He was reluctant to follow his master's orders," I said simply. "A much more pertinent question is why the reluctance exists in the first place. He is obviously quite incensed with you. Did you recently lower his wages?"

Mr. Herrick laughed bitterly. "Believe me, Miss Tate, that boy has no financial concerns whatsoever."

"You did mention an inheritance," I pointed out. "I assume each of your servants will receive their fair share."

"Such a smart lady thou art." Mr. Herrick headed to the dining room doorway on the other side of the entrance hall. "Come. Let us have our luncheon."

I crossed over the threshold into the dining room, a chamber as vast and spacious as a Medieval banquet hall. A claw-footed trestle table with a dozen seats stretched before a long, low marble fireplace. Three enormous stained glass Gothic windows along the outside wall let in what little the selfish fog allowed for daylight, rendering a dim, grayish cast to the room. Were we to dine on suckling pig or some other Dark Ages dish? I felt I'd entered a time period two centuries hence.

Mr. Herrick limped over to one of the large armed chairs and scraped it back across the stone floor. He gestured for me to sit.

"Perhaps not as fancy as you are used to, coming from such a renowned family," he admitted, "but I assure you, the coastal delicacies will delight. Please sit."

I did as he wished, though could boast no appetite to share with him.

He seated himself across from me. A door opened at the far end of the room, and Mrs. Quinn ushered in several servants, each bearing a large silver chafing dish. A maid stoked the hearth fire, producing a cheerful crackling blaze as a cozy background. Between bites of my oyster stew, I stole glances across the table at my companion. He ate as heartily as a child, glugging back his drink and making little grunts and groans from the pleasure of eating. His yellow-green skin took on a flushed hue, making him look less like a corpse.

The stew satisfied my hunger, but my emotions were anything but satiated. My morning with the master had roused far more questions than could be answered. And what to make of his exchange with Mr. Penley in the entrance hall? I felt incredibly agitated and hemmed in, as if the thick stone walls bore immense weight down upon me.

"Mr. Herrick, I do wish to finish our meal as soon as possible. I really cannot delay even one hour."

He ignored me for several moments, thoughtfully chewing his food. At last, he wiped his mouth, cleared his throat, and addressed me.

"Eager to begin our quest, are you? Or rather, methinks you are eager to get the money. Not to worry. Stokes will take the mail bag up to the map room, and after luncheon we shall go to that chamber as well."

A map room? "I confess, and can hardly believe I'm doing so, that I am eager to accompany you there. I am not sure if you have read up on my family's current circumstances, but I can offer an explanation as to why I have come."

"Oh, I know why." He sipped from his water goblet. "A Mr. Francis Scully, your only living male relation and heir to the Tate Shipping Company, has assumed the position of overseer. The newspaper mentioned he was an educated man, but I can only assume his education was either thrust upon him or he did poorly. Since the lovely Miss Tate would never accept a far-fetched adventure to some remote island in the middle of nowhere if this cousin of hers proved to be a worthy successor. Sound about correct?"

That about was. In less than five minutes, he had accurately deduced the reason for my coming.

"It is, sir," I said with a pert nod. "One hundred percent, as far as that assumption. Cousin Francis's financial ineptitude has forced me to take drastic action."

He swirled the water in his goblet. "Both you and your pirate ancestor possess the same attraction to great financial sums. I do not wonder that you would go to extreme lengths for money."

Heavens, he did it again. Twisting my words and feelings into their most base meanings. Was this a game he'd play the entire time I remained here?

"It will be announced shortly, so I can speak of it here," I said at last. "Thanks to Cousin Francis, the company cannot survive too long without filing for bankruptcy. I am going to extreme lengths for the treasure, as you put it, in order to retain my family's livelihood. The town of Kennebunkport relies upon it."

"Quite the responsibility for your family's business. Though you are a hundred miles from Kennebunkport, you cannot forget its troubles."

"Nor would I wish to," I admitted. "I am here for a purpose, which remains in the forefront of my mind."

"Ah." He didn't have much to say after that, other than a single utterance which encapsulated all his understanding.

Silence descended upon us, though it was not altogether unpleasant. I felt such urgency to begin our quest I rose from my seat. Mr. Herrick followed suit, though got up a lot more stiffly. He wobbled on his feet, his knuckles turning white from gripping the chair so tightly. Without thinking, I stepped forward and abruptly took his arm to steady him. I couldn't help my gasp, for beneath his coat fabric was the thinnest, most scrawny bony arm. It was like holding a twig, fearful to snap.

"Mr. Herrick ... "

He yanked his arm from my grasp. "I cannot have you pitying me, Miss Tate. Neither you or any other. Listen to my voice and behold how quick my mind remains. Let my unhealthy appearance be but a strange companion to my natural vitality."

"You should be in bed, sir."

"And you should be in the kitchen, my dear. But our proper places do not suit us, do they?"

"No," I said with a little smile. "They certainly do not."

"Then I say to hell with propriety, and if I be damned for saying so, then I am sure to meet many alike fellows in purgatory." He moved away from the chair and limped over to the hearth fire, where a cane balanced against the bricks like a bellows. He grabbed it and tucked it beneath his weight. "We have six days before the mail boat returns. I do not think you want this Cousin Francis to run your entire fortune aground, so let us to the map room!"

Click, step. Click, step. He set off across the stone floor back towards the dining room doorway.

What choice did I have but to follow?

fifteen

✳

Outside an old door on the second floor, Mr. Herrick took a beribboned key from a curved nail. He inserted it into the escutcheon beneath the knob, but before opening, he turned to me, lowering his voice:

"Have a care with what you find within this chamber, Miss Tate. It is liable to spark an interest in a fanciful quest you never wished to be a part of."

I smirked. "Let me decide that for myself, sir."

"Jonah," he insisted. "Please do call me that."

"I am afraid I cannot."

He took the key out and dangled it before me, just like my watch earlier this morning.

"And why will you not call a man by his name, hmm? Especially when he wishes it."

"I was raised to be a lady, Mr. Herrick. I would not be a very good example of proper breeding should I be so informal."

"Ah, but you are a good example. The finest. Yet, I still insist you call me Jonah."

I sighed, already tired of this teasing. "Then, I shall have to postpone my visit to the map room."

"Nonsense!" He jammed the key into the lock. It clicked, and he gripped the doorknob with his skinny fingers. "I admit defeat in this case, Miss Tate. Though, allow me to be a fortune-teller for one moment and predict that before you depart my island, you will call me Jonah."

"If I desire to do so, then I will."

"Desire." His eyes, as black as Fogbound Manor's dim passages, seemed darker still. "What of Harriet Tate's desires? If she wants something, she will have it."

I didn't like the way he was looking at me, as he appeared half in shadow from the dark hall, pressed against the door. He gazed at me as if he was seeking something, though what, I hardly knew. At last, he tore his gaze from mine and slowly opened the door to the map room.

The interior astonished me. How far Mr. Herrick's obsession had progressed! I felt like a traveler passing from drab sand into an Egyptian treasure room. Scarcely a hint of wallpaper could be seen, and all four walls were absolutely covered in ancient maps and fading documents. The antique parchment gave the room a golden aura. Swinging lanterns with brass shades added to the jeweled warmth. A massive wide round table dominated the center of the room, strewn with globes, telescopes, and ancient astronomical instruments. Mr. Penley's mail bag had been dumped on top of the table, letters and packages piled haphazardly. A huge old orange cat rested on a tapestry chair, peeking one yellow eye open to regard me with disgust before snoozing off again.

"I call him Mr. Quinn," Mr. Herrick explained in a joking manner, "for he is a feline of such sour nature he must be married to my housekeeper."

I laughed. Mr. Herrick folded his arms, looking like a man quite pleased with himself. I'd not had occasion to laugh in a while.

"After you, my dear." He gestured to the table. "Go take a look."

I approached the table, then curled my fingers around its thick top and leaned over, surveying the incredible assortment of letters and envelopes. I could smell the cloying, vanilla-like scent of old paper, curling and peeling from age.

"Where ever did you find those two gold coins you sent me?" I asked. "I confess I assumed them to be fake. Only at first, though."

"They did not belong to me, but were from Reverend Gravitch," Mr. Herrick explained. He came over to the table, balancing his cane against its wide girth. "You see, here?"

He pushed aside the table clutter to reveal a well-drawn map of Herrick Island. It was irregularly shaped, like a cookie that hadn't risen on one side. The manor was located in the exact northern point of the island, in the center of a scooped cove. A curving line, which I took to be a road, led from the manor across to the island's eastern edge and up to a little church.

"The island chapel," Mr. Herrick said. "Reverend Gravitch and I are the sole permanent inhabitants upon my island, though he is at present hosting guests. He surprised me with a small sack of coins after my late brother died. Two of those coins ended up traveling to Kennebunkport, where I assume they went to help the company?"

"Indirectly." I thought regretfully of Mr. Godwin. "I wanted to set up a fund to help the widows affected by the loss of the *Phoenix*."

"Indeed."

Mr. Herrick reached behind the mail pile and pulled a burlap sack towards him. He untied the top and reached in. The flash of gold cheered me more than I ever thought it would. The coins were like the sun's eye captured in flaming disks that burned through all the cold and the fog.

"Let this be an additional compensation, ready to join its two brethren as part of the widows' fund."

"Mr. Herrick . . . these are so beautiful."

He smiled. "When I inquired as to where Reverend Gravitch obtained this astonishing little fortune, he said it was left to him at the church. Alas, this treasure was not buried - but it does hint at the riches to come!"

"They were left by the Tate Pirate of Shoals?" I could not believe my ancestor had gifted these amazing Spanish coins. "But when? It must have been over a century ago. Where did Reverend Gravitch find these coins?"

"You will have to take up your inquiries with him," Mr. Herrick said, "for I did not ask further into it. We shall be joining him for Sunday's service."

"I simply must find more," I confessed. I closed my fingers around the coins, gripping them tightly so as to never be pried away. Possessing even this one tiny morsel of a larger treasure whetted my appetite in a ferocious way. "I thank you for these. Yet, I am afraid even such an abundant gift cannot help both my company and the widows. I refuse to return to Kennebunkport without adequate compensation for my family's sins."

"Sins?" Mr. Herrick echoed. "Is it a sin to lose both your father and his ship in a storm? I fear Miss Tate, that you have unduly assumed Nature's wrath is your fault."

"You are right, sir. It is not," I agreed. "But was there any other target? As you say, I am the last of my line. I alone am the Tate expected to carry on what my ancestors have done."

He sighed. "Well, we shall do our best to ensure the Tate name shall not be slandered any further - either by the actions of its unworthy overseer or the lack of financial compensation brought home by its sole successor."

His words moved me. I looked up from the map table and regarded him with awe. He saw past my exterior and peered inside me as if he were a clockmaker rewinding my inner machinery. It felt unsettling, to say the least, how greatly he seemed to know me after spending less than twenty-four hours in my presence.

How could he know me so well, when others had utterly failed in their assessments? Only Mr. Godwin extended his attentions with more than the usual degree, yet even he maintained a respectable distance from my more intimate feelings. Like my spirit resided within a locked room he dared not explore.

But Mr. Herrick - Jonah - he blustered right into that inner chamber, key or no key, and took up residence there as if he'd always done so. He examined me with a microscope of exacting and accurate truth, proclaiming in his blunt way a very ungentleman-like but very real picture of my character.

He *knew* me, and no-one ever had before.

What in the world was I to make of this? I hadn't any idea. So, I was the first to quit my gaze from his and, blushing hotly, resume my study of the map table.

"It would be helpful to know what research you have already conducted," I mumbled. "Books you have read, and so forth."

He moved the Herrick Island map aside and lifted up a diagrammed chart. It was a large squiggling outline of Maine's southern coastal area spanning the New Hampshire border down by Kittery all the way up to midcoast Brunswick.

"Not much found in any local accounts, I'm afraid. It seems your ancestor is more legend than factual figure. Yet, I am certain if we study these tidal charts, a probable location for treasure will be found."

"We'll see."

He gave me a sideways squint, a smirk lifting his lips into a half-smile. Yes, Mr. Herrick, I will not believe until results are made manifest into something real. Fancies can never be a substitute for facts. He cleared his throat.

"The one account I was able to find about the pirate indicated he didn't venture any further up along the coast of Maine beyond his normal habitat."

He indicated the Isles of Shoals on the chart, a small cluster of islands directly off the coast of Portsmouth, New Hampshire. Those were the treacherous Isles which proved to be the final and deadliest nautical obstacle my father ever faced. It was intolerably hard not to think of him here, when the vaporous air misted and pulsed like ghosts. My memories of him were more alive on this island than at home. Like his spirit chose these barren rocks, tormenting me until his earthly work was at last completed. My sighing breath mixed with the ever-present fog.

"Miss Tate? Miss Tate."

I shook my head, clearing thoughts of Father like dust.

"Are you well?" Mr. Herrick was asking. "You have become pale."

"How can you tell?" I asked with a smile. "Even your own countenance takes on a golden hue in this room."

He hiked up his sleeve and displayed his hand, fingers as long and thin as a magician's.

"My, what a sight. Getting back to the pirate, I began with the assumption that he would have been approaching Herrick Island from the south. Should your ship choose to land here, where would you bury treasure?"

I studied the Herrick Island map, observing its various coves and irregular promontories jutting into the surrounding waters. Those huge rocks encircling the island were akin to a stone fence inhibiting any intruding visitors. There were only two places to land a ship safely: the dock where I landed or the shallow cove directly behind Fogbound Manor. I indicated both on the map.

"I assume this area behind the manor to be a shoreline of some length?"

"It is. Alas, I already deduced that to be the only place a pirate could land, so I searched there profusely."

He made this statement in a rather careless tone, which led me to guess he hadn't been as thorough as I could be.

"Then, allow me to assist you in a more exacting search," I offered. "I assume you have the digging tools and accoutrements for such an undertaking?"

He laughed. "Listen to my guest! Not only is she eager to begin, but ready to strike open the soil with a shovel! I shall never again doubt the passivity of women. I have at last found a creature to match my own passionate actions in both capability and urgency."

"None have ever called me passive, Mr. Herrick. Indeed, once I have set my mind upon an objective, I find the most secure footholds on my way towards obtaining it."

"No doubt." He pressed his lips together. "Let me see your hand, Miss Tate."

I hesitated. "I'd rather not, sir."

"Oh, do trust me. We are to be companions on this adventure, each as eager as the other towards this shared objective."

My eagerness was purely driven by financial motives, but I chose not to remind him of this. Tentatively, I held up my hand. He grasped my fingers, delicately yet firmly, and I was surprised by the warmth beneath his sallow skin. Though his appearance suggested the contrary, he was quite alive. With a quick flourish he raised my hand to his lips and kissed me. It was a move so forward and uncouth I immediately snatched my fingers from his grasp.

"Mr. Herrick, that was - "

"Not a gentlemanly thing to do?" He cocked his head, grinning as if he'd caught a prize fish. "You want so greatly to find this money, while I seek my own version of treasure. Here's hoping we're not both left wanting."

What should I care that he was seeking something as well? I simply could not grasp his varied behaviors and ways. Working alongside steady and rational Mr. Godwin for so many years had ill-prepared me for this man's topsy-turvy ridiculousness.

"I thank you for your time in the map room today, sir, but I must beg my absence from it the remainder of the afternoon."

"What, has your quota for fanciful notions been used up already?" He folded his arms, leaning against the table. "A lady can handle only one per day, I suppose."

"I can handle whatever notions you dream up," I said evenly, "but I cannot abide your behavior. As long as I am here on this island, conduct yourself in a less uncouth way. Good day."

I left his side and marched over to the door. Mr. Herrick stayed where he was, balanced upon the table, surrounded by charts and maps.

"Aren't you forgetting your sack of gold coins?" he called.

"I am here another three weeks, Mr. Herrick. When I depart, I will take every piece of gold that is rightfully mine."

With that, I let myself out and yanked the door closed behind me.

sixteen

His kiss on my hand was like an ember that set off a blaze through my skin. You may know my inner character Mr. Herrick, but you have not proven yourself worthy enough to stay in my presence.

Trembling with anger, I strode down the hall. Oh, this manor's perpetual gloom peeved me. I wished I could swat the pesky fog away and be done with it. I craved clarity - yes, clarity above all. Exactly what time it was, exactly where the treasure was, exactly how much money I'd find, exactly when I could board the mail boat and be out of here.

I reached the top of the main staircase, grabbed a fistful of my skirts, and started down. And when I arrived home - then what? Give the money to the widows and pledge my life to Mr. Godwin? I grimaced, almost tripping on the steps. Compared to this insane venture, getting married for neither love nor money seemed perfectly rational. That was what Father expected, what Grandmother encouraged, what Mr. Godwin proposed.

Where was my own voice within this cacophony of opinions?

I returned to the entrance hall and instinctively looked to the corner for a grandfather clock. Harriet, do you not recall? No clocks. Only the wind whooshing outside as if desperately trying to get in.

Once in the parlor, where I was thankfully alone, I noticed a writing desk beneath one of the tall diamond-paned windows. Ah! My letter would not be delivered until the next mail boat, but at least I could pen something to relieve my stormy mind.

The desk was quite ancient, made of scrolled mahogany with a faint, masculine scent of leather and tobacco. As I slid onto the cushioned chair, I realized this was where Mr. Herrick wrote his own letters to me. Indeed, I found the same crinkly golden parchment within the desk, and the long feathery pen he must have used. The ink had a fruity scent, like blackberries. Though I could have scratched out a novel given my agitated state, I forced myself to calm and began my letter.

3rd March, 1855

Dear Grandmother,

    I arrived safely upon Herrick Island and have now taken up residence at Fogbound Manor. Mr. Herrick is a person of exuberant outbursts and childish fancies, caught up in a futile treasure hunt that I fear is more a product of his overactive imagination than a real quest.

    Due to the urgency of the company's financial situation, my time is greatly shortened, and I am determined to be on the next boat off this island. Unfortunately, that will not be until this Friday.

    Do inform Mr. Godwin and Cousin Francis of my impending return.

At this, I paused. My letter sounded like the lofty ideals of a desperate writer. I set the pen down and leaned forward in the chair, placing my elbows on the desk and cupping my chin in my hands. A solution to my problems at the shipping company had presented itself already.

Was it so foolish to reject Mr. Godwin? Right now, it seemed even more foolish to journey one hundred miles, cross the sea, and be with Mr.

Herrick. Had I realized the master was even more ridiculous than I thought, Mr. Godwin was the obvious choice. I didn't love him. But perhaps marital happiness was too great an ideal to sacrifice my present situation. My legacy was to sustain my family's business.

"No matter what," I murmured aloud.

I'd never met a man I could love, so why was Mr. Godwin any different than all the others?

He was a good choice. I must tell him, as soon as I could. The mail boat returned on Friday. I would depart Herrick Island, go home, and beseech Mr. Godwin to reconsider his proposal and accept me. I was ready to face whatever future that might be. It was more sensible than seeking treasure.

Well, I'd made up my mind to leave on Friday, so there was no need to send word to Grandmother. I stood up from the desk and took the letter to the hearth fire, where it provided kindling for the crackling flames. As its form disintegrated into ash, I felt better. Be yourself, Harriet. Do not get caught up in silly adventures that chafe against your personality. Goodness, Mr. Godwin even had ten thousand dollars, which would add nicely to the little sack of gold coins.

A rumble of hunger stirred in my belly, and I made my way back to the staircase to return to my room and dress for dinner. Upon entering my bedchamber, I spied a small folded note upon the breakfast table. Mr. Herrick's shaky handwriting revealed a contrite request to join me for supper. I tossed it back on the table and sighed as loudly as Herrick Island wind. Oh, if I could only refuse.

It took me far longer than I thought it would to choose a suitable dress for my first dinner with Mr. Herrick. I pushed past my dresses, finally selecting one of a blue and cream silk with bell sleeves and three rows of tiered ruffles on the wide skirt. Its soft floral scent made me feel more than a little nostalgic for my bedchamber back at home.

Once I'd tucked my silent watch into my pocket, I left my bedchamber and walked down the fourth-floor hall. Every candle sconce was alighted, each casting a circle of warm feeble light on the faded wallpaper. I was hungry, tired, and felt a strange sense of restlessness, so when Mr.

Herrick met me at the bottom of the main staircase, I gave him a perfunctory nod and greeting.

"Good evening to you as well," he returned. "You are quite becoming, Miss Tate."

His own appearance was quite striking. He'd dressed in a black dinner suit with a cream waistcoat and matching cravat. The pale silk beside his sickly face gave him such a ghostly pallor he resembled a vampyre. His black hair was combed and tied back with a ribbon. The smile on his lips was mischievous and puckish, but he looked even thinner and balanced heavily upon his cane.

"You see," he said, offering his hand to me, "I can pass for a gentleman."

He expected me to take his hand after what he had done in the map room?

"I can escort myself," I said curtly.

I didn't like his wink and focused straight ahead as we entered the dining room together for the second time. It had been transformed from the elegant luncheon into an elaborately fine setting, complete with seashell and beach stone displays, an exquisite damask tablecloth the color of the wine, and a lovely floral dinner service.

"I had thought of inviting you to dine privately with me upstairs in my quarters," he said with a devilish smile, "but that might have seemed too forward."

"I should say so," I remarked. "Especially after your bold conduct. My desire to remain in your company would have thenceforth been nonexistent, and I would refuse to accompany your treasure search."

"No doubt. Oh, and Miss Tate - I should correct you and proclaim it *our* treasure search." Once seated across from me, he raised his wineglass. "To expectations," he toasted. "May we find joy when they are met, and retain our good humor when they are not."

I could find much kinship with his toast, and clinked my wineglass with his. My small gesture and smile brought an amused smirk to his lips.

"You are quite like a little bird," he commented. "Once in its familiar nest, it settles, becomes content, and even allows itself the pleasure of re-laxation."

"I can hardly call Fogbound Manor a nest."

He shrugged, swirling the wine about his glass. He downed it with a hearty swallow and gestured for more. My peace of mind was beginning to return, for I had a new plan. The more I thought about it, the more attractive an option it became. Mr. Godwin had even said I could keep my name upon the company. Should I bear him a son, it would ensure a new overseer and new captain.

"You seem distracted this evening," Mr. Herrick remarked. "Day-dreaming about what you'll do when you locate your fortune?"

"I do not dream, I plan."

"I do not plan, I dream," he retorted, mimicking me like a parrot.

"Quite accurate," I said. "I could have deduced such a statement two minutes after meeting you."

"You are put out with me. Do you expect me to apologize for kissing your hand this afternoon?"

"I expect no such civility from you, for you display nothing in your character to indicate you operate by a higher nature."

He laughed. "That's my Harriet. Your opinion is never wrong. It is like a fixed star I could navigate a fleet by."

I pursed my lips. Back to mocking me yet again. Mrs. Quinn entered at the head of a line of dinner servants. For the second time that day, I was the recipient of a humble, but ultimately satisfying meal. This one was of corned beef and boiled vegetables with herbs in a cream sauce. For the moment, I forgot about Mr. Herrick and his forward ways and enjoyed the meal.

"Quite delicious," Mr. Herrick said as he finished his course. "More wine, please. I do find my appetite to be even more lush than before my illness."

"What is your diagnosis?"

"Chronic heartbreak," he answered with a sober expression. At my frown, he giggled. "We'll get to that in a moment, my dear. Oh, I have received several diagnoses, each more ludicrous than the last. The Wenthams, whom you shall meet tomorrow after church, are of the opinion I have some type of bone-eating disease. I rather like that."

"You like being ill?"

"What a silly notion, and more than a little morbid considering my impending mortality. I'd as soon die from too much love." He indicated my left hand. "I see no wedding ring upon your finger, nor have I heard about any absent suitors. Tell me, pretty lady, has no-one back at home stolen your heart?"

I frowned, more than a little miffed. "I think it unlikely, Mr. Herrick, that a man would steal anything of mine without my knowledge."

He leaned forward over his empty plate and laughed. I found it uncomfortable to be the subject of such hearty amusement and put my wineglass down.

"You are quite the amusing companion! Perhaps I might perish of excess humor, for look at how merry you have made me." His laughter finally died down. "So, there is none to lay claim to your heart, I take it? Furthermore, I'd wager a dozen pirate treasures you have never lent a man your full affections."

I had no wish to affirm or deny this, despite my new commitment to become Mrs. Godwin. But could he receive my full affections? The more I thought about it, the more unlikely the outcome. Mr. Herrick was waiting for my reply, so I had to say something.

"My full affections shall not be lent to anyone, and that is how it shall ever be."

"I see," he said. "Well, as your love life is as sealed as a casket, then I guess the next subject should be mine."

"Please, Mr. Herrick, that topic is frankly none of my business or concern."

"It might not be your business, for that is obviously the treasure, but it might become of your concern."

I couldn't see why, and truthfully didn't care where Mr. Herrick's affections lay. He could be pining for a fisherman's daughter or the Queen of Sheba for all it mattered.

"I confess I am a man whose heart has been broken. I can see now why this topic doesn't pertain to you, Miss Tate, for you have never loved another as I have. Never have you surrendered that wonderful mind of yours in favor of your heart's desire. Nor would you allow yourself to forget the mental in favor of the emotional. I can see that quite clearly."

He spoke in such a blunt and uncomfortable manner I wanted nothing more than to cease it. I would never get used to being addressed in such a way.

"The object of my love abandoned me in favor of another. These isolated walls have proved more of a prison lately than a home of shared happiness. Fogbound Manor has a master, but no mistress. I may be standing on a shortened path to the grave, but I assure you, Miss Tate, that my feelings would not be any less strong from my illness. Indeed, being ill has made me even more susceptible to the temptations of the heart."

What to make of that declaration? I didn't care if he fancied one of his own scullery maids, if only he would let me be. Five more days, Harriet. In five days, that mail boat would return and I would be upon it.

"Nothing to say?" he uttered. "I may have found the one topic in which the logical Harriet Tate cannot calculate."

"Before I came to Herrick Island, my hand was asked for. I declined at the time, but a careful reconsideration has shown me the error of that decision. So, I shall be accepting the gentleman upon my return."

"Well!" Mr. Herrick sat back in his chair. His waxy pallor looked almost healthy thanks to his hearty meal. "I take it this is more of a business transaction than a lovebird pairing."

"Of course," I answered, surprised he'd even asked. "I see no reason to speculate upon the possibility of finances when I can be assured of such. He has offered me a sizable fortune, and I can count upon it."

"Off you go, then," he said with a smirk. "Off Herrick Island and back to Kennebunkport, where the next item on your list will be to produce a male heir for the company."

He'd insulted me, which by now I should have expected. Well, he'd not received the full extent of my anger yet. I had no problem giving it to him now, especially since he deserved it after his inelegant behavior in the map room.

"Your future may be shortened, as you put it," I returned, "but mine is not. What, pray tell, is your legacy, Mr. Herrick? To what higher purpose does your life serve? Do not denounce my choice, sir. You can either help me or let me be!"

I stood up and slammed my napkin down next to my empty plate. Mr. Herrick stared at me, his expression a mixture of awe and admiration. I didn't want him to admire me. I wanted him to help me obtain this money.

"I appreciate your hospitality, but I shall be departing on the next mail boat."

"Wait, please, Miss Tate," Mr. Herrick said, half-rising to his feet. "I - I took you for a woman of humor -"

"Humor?" I snapped. "I am about to file bankruptcy on my company and lose everything. That is no joking matter."

"I see that now," he said, in as serious a tone as he could muster. "Forgive me, my dear. You are as forthright as you are intelligent. Pardon a dying man for his follies, and let us make amends."

I slowly walked around the table to him. His weight balanced on the arm of the chair, for he could barely stand without help. He could collapse at any second. I wanted to feel something besides anger, like a sense of pity for him and his condition. Yet, I could not. He blocked what I wanted, and I utterly despised how much time we were wasting.

Time ...

I slipped my hand into my dress pocket and drew out my little watch. Cold and asleep, bereft of its ticking for far too long. My request to him was calm, calmer than I'd ever spoken.

"Tell me what time it is, Mr. Herrick, so that I may wind my watch."

He licked his dry lips. "I do not know the time, I'm afraid. However, there is a clock at the chapel. I am attending tomorrow's service there, if you care to join me. I promise you will know the time."

"Then I shall accompany you," I said. "Though as for this evening, I bid you good night."

He nodded. "Enjoy a restful sleep, Miss Tate. You have earned it."

I curtsied to him and left the dining room. Finally free of Mr. Herrick and his ridiculous conversations. If he coerced me into listening to more of his prattle, I just might scream loud enough to shake the ghosts.

The lack of his company soothed me more than his presence ever could.

seventeen

To say I slept fitfully that night would be an understatement. I lay prone beneath my bedclothes, a pressing headache tightening the back of my neck. My vision grew accustomed to the room's darkness, and I gazed at the twisting supine wallpaper pattern for many hours. Wind moaned against the windowpanes like a man dying. Twice I roused myself and tried to peer beyond the glass, to no avail. Fogbound Manor was, indeed, bound in fog.

I'd thought I felt trapped at my own house, but it was nothing compared to how I felt here. A restless caged thing, stirring up wildness I didn't know I possessed. Never had I felt so driftless, grasping for the certainty of a fixed star to guide me. Two months ago, my future was as mapped as if it had been laid out by the heavens. Now, I struggled with challenges that I'd never had to consider before.

Not to mention my supreme annoyance with Mr. Herrick. His blustery talk churned questions about who I really was. I kept reminding myself of my earlier promise to leave Herrick Island and accept Mr. Godwin's hand ... yet, the more I considered it, the more frustrated I became. If Mr. Herrick knew me completely and implicitly, then Mr. Godwin could not.

"How can I marry him?" I murmured aloud from my cold, uncomfortable seat near the window. I'd found the bed too coarse and sat wrapped in blankets on the chair, trying to find refuge against its headrest. My fitful rest didn't last long enough to revive me, and I was up with a candle far before the breakfast tray was delivered. I ate what I could, dressed in warm layers of extra corded and quilted petticoats beneath my woollen gray day dress, tucked my little watch in my pocket, and vacated the room.

No sooner had I set foot in the entrance hall, when Mr. Herrick appeared to join me. He thumped his cane heavily against the flagstone floor, echoing off the high cavernous walls. He was dressed to go out in a thick wool coat, muffler, and tipped hat.

"The carriage should be coming 'round shortly," he explained, and produced a note from within his jacket. "The Wenthams have accepted our invitation and will be joining us for dinner after the service. I also expect the driver should attend, as you were able to coerce him yesterday to do so."

Mr. Stokes held out my cloak and bonnet, and I donned them willingly. Mr. Herrick swept the front door open, and Sunday morning's vaporous oceanic chill crept into the manor.

"After you, my dear," he said. "Look at me, posing as a gentleman for his honored guest."

"I do appreciate it," I said, and meant it. His displays of civility were like wearing an itchy mask, which he couldn't wait to slip off and get back to being his more youthful self.

I passed by him and paused at the top of the huge stone staircase whilst he closed the door behind us. We descended the front steps to the carriageway. I turned about to gape at the sheer impressive size of Fogbound Manor. Mournful and castle-like, damp ocean air perpetually wetted its exterior to a dark slick gray. As if the manor arose from the sea's bottom and couldn't receive enough sunlight to dry it completely. Fog veiled its upper floors and misted about its turrets.

The carriage-way was quite crowded with a large party of servants and groundskeepers, including a sour-faced Mr. Penley. He was perched up top his black vehicle, reins limply in hand. His expression for his master was none too friendly at all, but when he noticed me, it was different somehow. I nodded to him in return. Mr. Herrick could tell we had exchanged glances, frowned at Mr. Penley, and forcibly ushered me into the carriage. It was all I could do not to fall into it, and, once seated, regarded him with disdain.

"What can you mean, Mr. Herrick, by such behavior?"

He huffed in after me and planted himself on the opposite seat. Then he whacked the ceiling with his cane.

"Drive on!" he shouted, as if it wasn't apparent. The carriage rocked to life, and we set off at once across the gravel. "Miss Tate, I am afraid I should apologize for my servant's conduct."

"Whatever for?" I asked. "Your conduct yesterday in the map room was far ruder than anything he has done."

"Are you to bring up that incident every hour that you remain here?" he muttered.

I shook my head, thoughts jumbled. I gave such a frustrated sigh my carriage window fogged.

"You make no sense, sir. No sense at all to someone like myself."

"Then accept it," he snapped. "You want me to be so consistent and practical and every other trait I never had nor will ever. You asked for respect for our different natures. Well, kindly display it towards me."

I could have chomped my own tongue off. Mr. Herrick drove me so mad I wanted to box his ears. But my anger mixed with a high degree of mortification. He was right.

"You put me in my place, sir," I said quietly.

He played with the curtain window, staring blankly out on the dull landscape. When he spoke again, his tone had softened.

"You are not the first, you know. To desire my character to be what it is not. Have you never spent time convincing someone to accept your real personality and not the one they've conjured for you?"

"No, I have not."

"Then you are fortunate." He leaned forward. "Ah, we are nearly there."

I rubbed the mist from my carriage window. We approached the little chapel from the west, the rising sun in front of us casting weakened rays upon the blocky, seaweed-strewn stones. It looked like a structure some mythic ocean-dwelling creature had made, crafted of solid ancient rocks tipped and mortared together. Like the moon to the earth, it was a perfect complementary design to Fogbound Manor. A squat belltower stretched up into the fog, misted by ocean spray, its surface glistening from the ever-present moisture. The bell tipped lazily, like it was rolling out of bed, and the sleepy gong vibrated the carriage. A minister appeared in the chapel doorway, clothed all in black save for the white collar at his throat.

Mr. Penley pulled the carriage up to the chapel and stopped. We'd driven so slowly across the narrow expanse of Herrick Island that those on foot had easily followed us. So, there was quite the crowd to join Reverend Gravitch for his morning sermon. Jonah took up his cane, and we both descended from the carriage. Mr. Penley held the door open for us, said nothing to his master, and quietly shut the carriage door behind me.

"Thank you," I said.

He nodded. But then Jonah offered his arm to me. I turned from Mr. Penley's curiously pained stare to take his master's arm. Through the wool I could feel his bones, and he walked unsteadily beside me as we crossed over to the chapel.

The Reverend clasped his fingertips together, regarding us with a curious stare. A white-haired gentleman with impeccable posture and a smooth countenance, he seemed younger than his years and full of vigor.

"Jonah," he acknowledged in a deep, rich voice perfect for orating. "I greet you with kinship, but I fear I must ask Lucas to drive you back home. You are in no state of health for this. I think often of your poor brother Elijah and should not like to see you follow him into such an early grave."

Jonah's lips thinned into a sour expression. "My health is not the island's concern, Reverend. I bring more good news than you do, at least. Allow me to introduce Miss Harriet Tate!"

This exclamation, like announcing a stage actor, caused me to blush and hide my embarrassment with a practiced curtsy.

"Reverend Gravitch," I said. "A pleasure to meet you. Mr. Herrick showed me the gold coins you gave him."

"The pleasure is mine, Miss Tate," the reverend said. "As for the coins, I received those as a gift from my brother."

"Oh. May I speak to him presently?"

The reverend tapped his fingers together. "He would be delighted to converse with you. Yet, he is in Rockland. I believe he is due to arrive on the mail boat this week, however."

How unfortunate and ill-timed. So, this brother was not on Herrick Island. It seemed I would have to resort to unearthing every sandy cove in search of treasure.

"Looking forward to seeing him," Jonah said off-handedly. "By the way, you are the only fellow upon the island in possession of a working clock. Miss Tate desires to wind her watch."

The reverend smiled. "By all means, you are free to use it. It is just inside the chapel. The elder Mr. Herrick was a clock-maker, but it seems his son has neglected to wind them. I do sympathize, Miss Tate, for one cannot see the sun clearly here to ascertain the correct time."

I bit my lip, my eyes on Jonah. He never mentioned his father was a clock-maker.

"Thank you, sir," I said to the reverend. "Come, Mr. Herrick, let us seat ourselves for the sermon."

"Glad to have Captain Tate's daughter visit us," the reverend said. "Always a pleasure to receive such illustrious guests. Jonah, do take heed of your health before it's too late."

"Oh, it's too late for me," Jonah said decidedly, and thrust his arm in mine to escort me into the chapel.

We passed from grayed foggy sunlight into a dimness similar to the manor. Jonah put his fingers over mine, and I deliberately removed them as we made our way up the central aisle. The chapel was snug and dry, with a high arched ceiling exactly alike to Fogbound Manor's parlor. Chunky stone walls featured gorgeous stained glass Gothic-style windows, letting in bits of colored light to shine upon the gray stone. Lit beeswax candles gave the chapel a smoky, honeyed scent. Dark mahogany pews were lined in red velvet cushions, and the other island's citizens were taking their seats.

"Mr. Herrick," I whispered fiercely. "I can walk unaided, unlike yourself."

"Even the Greeks had a crippled god, Miss Tate. Poor health is a sign of divine benevolence."

What could I say to such an untrue statement? Jonah led me right to the front pew and bade me to sit, which I did so. Though the pew was comfortable and a potbelly stove provided adequate heat, I did not feel at ease. The last time I'd been in a church had been for my father's funeral, and for some odd reason I could not shake my father's presence from this place. He hovered about, his wraith-like spirit weighing upon me, holding me down. While Jonah stepped across the aisle to say good morning to a handsome young couple, I was left to my own restless thoughts for the moment.

Suddenly, a sound reverberated through the chapel that I would have recognized anywhere, and it immediately made me smile. A clock chiming! I retrieved my watch from my pocket. Excitedly, I counted eight tones, and my hands shook as I wound my watch.

Tick. Tick.

The little hands had sprung to life again. It was eight o'clock in the morning on Sunday, the 4th of March, 1855. I had at last obtained my moorings again. No longer adrift at sea with neither clock nor sun to guide me.

Tick. Tick.

When Jonah beckoned for me to join him, I happily obliged. I tucked my watch back in my pocket and made my way across the aisle to pews on the other side. Upon my arrival, a handsome couple both rose to their feet in greeting. The young wife gave me a wide smile in kindness, and I smiled back. She was quite lovely, with curled brunette hair the color of burnished mahogany, and kindly dark eyes. When I turned to the husband, I received quite the shock and could not think of anything to say. It was the message rider!

"Miss Harriet Tate," Mr. Herrick was saying with his typical exuberance. "May I introduce you to Mr. and Mrs. Wentham. Nicholas here is the executor of my estate."

It was, indeed, the very same man whom I'd assumed to be merely a servant. It seemed he had a higher profession. Bereft of his thick riding jacket and hat, he appeared remarkably passive-looking. His complexion was fair and his gaze quite languid, as if he'd awakened from a nap. Of course, there was no doubt in my mind he remembered me.

"Mr. Wentham, is it?" I politely shook his hand when he offered. "Thank you for performing as Mr. Herrick's messenger."

"It did call me away from my work here," he said stiffly. "Upon my return, I told Jonah I'd never again set foot in Kennebunkport."

"That is quite the observation of a place you visited but twice," I said. "Why ever not?"

"Why, its citizens, of course," he said with a smirk. "How ill they treated one of their own."

Jonah looked at me pityingly, but I shook my head.

"Well, it was much deserved. I cannot blame Mrs. Percy for her behavior that morning. As you can see, I changed my mind and journeyed here to Herrick Island."

"So glad she has," Jonah said. "I don't doubt, Nicholas, that you will ensure I have my funeral in this chapel."

Mrs. Wentham laughed nervously. "Why, Jonah, that's so morbid. In fact, I think I see a little more color in your countenance."

Jonah shrugged. "Perhaps it is the prospect of seeing you again, Lucinda."

Mrs. Wentham smiled, but her eyes met mine. "Perhaps."

The door in the back of the chapel closed, and the Reverend began making his way up the aisle. Everybody in the pews behind us rose to their feet.

"Let us be seated," Jonah whispered.

He held out his arm to me once more, but I did not take it and returned to my pew, wondering what Mrs. Wentham had meant and why she had pointedly regarded me. The Reverend began his sermon by reciting the Lord's prayer. His voice was suitably pleasant and warm.

My thoughts returned again to Father. Why was his absence so palpable here? When I received news of the shipwreck, a sense of acceptance settled upon me. My mind became quickly reconciled to the fact he was never coming home. Why then, all this resurgence of emotion? His death awakened more feelings in me than his life ever did.

The Reverend looked up at us, one hand placed on the Bible and the other over his heart. "Lay not up for yourselves treasures upon earth, where moth and rust doth corrupt, and where thieves break through and steal. But lay up for yourselves treasures in heaven, where neither moth nor rust doth corrupt, and where thieves do not break through nor steal.

"For where your treasure is, there will your heart be also."

When the sermon ended, my thoughts and emotions were in such muddled confusion I didn't notice Jonah had placed his greenish fingers over mine. Startled, I shifted my hand away. He was out of place. I abruptly stood up.

"Harriet ... ?" he said softly.

How dare he call me by my first name. But what use was there to tell him not to? I had other matters to contemplate, for the Wenthams were to have dinner with us today. After the sermon they came over to join us.

"Nicholas. Lucinda," Jonah greeted. "Let us journey at once to Fogbound Manor."

Mrs. Wentham slipped her hands around her husband's arm. "I admit I was surprised when you also invited Lucas, but we shall all accept."

Her husband nodded. "Yes, dear."

I couldn't tell whether he was joking or not. We followed them towards the back of the chapel. The Reverend met us at the door.

"I am dearly glad my brother is arriving on the next mail boat, Jonah. You should be seen."

"I'm sure the good man will have his usual mortal prognosis," Jonah said. He gestured to the little churchyard beside the chapel. "The spot beside Elijah is prepared?"

"Indeed," the reverend answered. "The Herrick family has the most prominent location."

"And the Bible passages I asked for? Ready to recite those?"

"Yes, of course."

"We cannot be referring to your funeral, Mr. Herrick," I said to him. Then I turned to the reverend. "I do look forward to meeting your brother and speaking to him about the treasure."

"He has quite the information," the reverend said. "I'm sure he'd be glad to tell you all about it."

"Indeed." I smiled, and said to Jonah: "Thank you, sir. Let us return to Fogbound Manor."

We left the chapel and stepped out into the carriageway. Mr. and Mrs. Wentham were already seated in the carriage, with Mr. Penley standing outside chatting quietly to them. At the sight of his master, he climbed up and seated himself. I leaned in close to Jonah.

"I would ask that we not speak any more about funerals."

"Why ever not?" he asked loudly. "You'll probably be attending mine before you leave the island. If I am alive in a month, it will be a miracle."

We reached the carriage, and he held the door open for me. I stepped up inside and sat across from the Wenthams. Jonah followed and, right after shutting the door, planted his backside firmly on the seat beside me. He crossed his skinny arms, poking me in the ribs with his arrow-like elbows, and pouted. Like a child. The carriage pulled foward, and we were off back to the manor. Fed up with his moods, I stuck my hand in my pocket and drew out my watch.

"Oh, how lovely." Mrs. Wentham leaned forward, curious to see my most prized little possession. "It makes such a tiny ticking sound."

Mr. Wentham drew out his own watch and showed me. "What was it upon the coins you showed me, Miss Tate? *Tempus Rerum Imperator*. Time is sovereign over all things."

"I thought you did not know Latin, sir," I said quietly.

"A messenger may not, but a lawyer does." He gave a little sniff.

His face and personage were the same, but he acted so differently than at my house scarcely two weeks hence. He seemed put out, somehow, with my presence here. Jonah must have paid him handsomely for his duties in dispatching his mail, so who knew his reason for appearing less than cordial.

"I confess, sir," I said after a moment, "that I was also able to deduce the inscription on those coins."

"I beg pardon?" Mr. Wentham snapped his watch shut. "I did compliment you upon your intelligence, Miss Tate. Of course, that was before you did not take my advice against coming here."

"We are glad that you have come," his wife suddenly said. "In fact, you provide a more immediate audience for Jonah's pirate talk." She leaned forward and said in a loud whisper: "Between you and me, Nicholas is tired of hearing it."

"I wouldn't doubt it," I said.

The master hadn't said a word, and I glanced at him sideways. Mr. Wentham sniffed again. The uncomfortable conversation lapsed, and we pulled into Fogbound Manor's carriageway. Perhaps it was only the difference between those living on the mainland and those on the island. I'd had the luxury of a larger society. Could I even imagine only three neighbors my whole life? How exposing, like the contents of my private self were an open field for anyone to traipse through. Perhaps Jonah was changeable merely to keep his own real self hidden.

The carriage stopped, and Lucas Penley jumped down from his perch. He paused outside the window, peering in at Mrs. Wentham with a look of intense scrutiny. She swept out of the carriage, her husband followed suit, and soon all four of us had disembarked. Jonah swiped his cane about and ordered us all into the manor at once due to the weather. I was about to remark the weather was as fine as it could ever be on Herrick Island, but he was already striding towards the front steps.

Mrs. Wentham took my arm in a sisterly way. "Jonah is a man with a great and unpredictable character. I don't know how you've managed."

"Me neither," I muttered.

She glanced at her strolling husband. They both chuckled in unison at what I had said.

"Yes, Miss Tate," Mr. Wentham said, "Count me as quite pleased that you have come to Fogbound Manor."

He ascended the wide staircase to open the front door for us. It was not until his wife and then myself had passed through when I realized a fifth figure slowly walked behind me. Mr. Penley paused at the doorway, eyeing Mr. Wentham.

"I'm to dinner, too," he grumbled.

"So it seems." Mr. Wentham heaved a great sigh, but kept the door open for him. "Enter then, Lucas."

After we were all present in the entrance hall, I tried to seek out the carriage driver to make eye contact with him. To let him know that he was not the only soul who felt like they didn't belong here. Somehow, I felt connected with him. I sensed we shared that as a common ground.

Lucas, I wanted to say. Return with me to your carriage, and let us away from here. But Fogbound Manor's darkness concealed him. I could only hear Jonah's voice, muffled and coarse, urging us all into the dining room. I lingered as long as I could, sought him out, and swept at once over to him.

"Lucas," I said softly.

Oh, he heard me. He half-turned, our eyes met, and he had enough time before Mr. Wentham noticed to smile at me. It softened his features and the scowl melted. Like one candle flame in winter, I felt the glow of his well-concealed kindness.

It was the only human warmth I'd ever found on Herrick Island.

eighteen

❋

My first dinner with Jonah last night had not gone well, so I wasn't eager to spend another with him. More table guests provided a pleasing liveliness and differing topics of conversation. Whenever I felt ill at ease, I reached beneath the table into my dress pocket and closed my fingers around my watch. I could feel its ticking through my skin.

Mrs. Wentham sparkled with a feminine life all her own. She bustled about with charm and social graces which delighted all male members of the party. Jonah basked in the pleasure of her little touches and regarded her with more loving looks than her own husband. Her flirtatious nature reminded me of school-girls I'd grown up, whose only occupation in life was to simply be their own girlish selves. Her husband didn't succumb to her charms, but rather interjected his own dry and direct opinions about the dinner into the conversation whenever he saw fit to draw attention to himself.

Lucas was as ill at ease as could be, staring at Mrs. Wentham so directly I was surprised she didn't call attention to his behavior. He fidgeted with his napkin, slouched in his seat, and hardly uttered more than two

words the entire dinner. Jonah infuriated him, and Mrs. Wentham fasci-
nated him. I hoped it wasn't due to fanciful imaginings that I thought he
smiled at me once or twice.

I'd not contributed much to the general conversation, when the topic
abruptly shifted to the treasure. Jonah's morbidity about dying disappeared, replaced by his regular enthusiasm. He waved his wineglass about,
nonchalantly spilling drops on the tablecloth as emphasis.

"Harriet will help me explore the beach behind the manor. She has
decided to further analyze ground I have already covered. I told her I'd
already searched, but she is the most persistent little thing."

The way he talked! I'd never stop feeling annoyed by it. I set my napkin down and was about to say something about it, when he chattered on.

"It's such an asset to her character, though. Harriet has the finest
mind of any person, man or woman, I've come across. Behind that placid
exterior is the mental aptitude to not only locate the pirate's gold, but use
its wealth to the utmost both for her own benefit and others."

What? I was so confused by this convoluted combination of praise
and mockery I couldn't think. I was also unprepared for my dinner companions' reactions. Mrs. Wentham raised her glass to me, snickering a little.

"To Miss Tate, then," Mrs. Wentham said. "For it seems it as good as
found thanks to her efforts."

"If it exists, then Miss Tate shall find it," Mr. Wentham added.

My cheeks colored. Lucas hunched his shoulders and glared down at
his plate.

"Mr. Penley." He did not look up, yet I pressed on. "Will you kindly
take me out on a carriage ride tomorrow?"

"Harriet, my goodness," Jonah cut in. "You would delay your treasure
hunt?"

"I shall be here until Friday, Mr. Herrick. That's plenty of time for us
to search the shoreline. Did we not make excellent progress in the map
room yesterday?"

He frowned and leaned back. "Well, Lucas. Take her out. You leave
at eight o'clock tomorrow morning."

"Now that I have rewound my watch," I said with a smug smile, "I shall be on time."

"Enjoy her company while you can," Jonah added, "for she is leaving us and will be married shortly to a suitor waiting with lovesick anticipation in Kennebunkport."

Lucas turned stone-faced and didn't utter a word. His angry silence blackened my feelings against Jonah. He may have treated me as an intellectual equal at first, but his inappropriate conduct and blunt statements patronized me. His rude words had also pushed Lucas to the breaking point. He set down his water goblet and screeched his chair backwards.

"Thank you for dinner," he muttered. "Good night."

"Lucas," Mrs. Wentham said. "My dear, will you not stay?"

"I have to feed the horses."

"Quite a dutiful servant," Jonah remarked, "but you have not yet heard what I wish to say. There's a reason Nicholas and I were discussing my will earlier, for it pertains to you in a most pertinent manner."

"Then tell me," Lucas growled. "Be out with it."

Jonah wadded up his napkin and plunked it on his plate. Then he pushed back his chair and shakily got to his feet. I half-rose to assist him, but he waved me off. He infuriated me as much as Lucas, but I couldn't stand by and not help him when he was so ill. Jonah grabbed his cane, which had been leaning against his chair, and made a huge sweeping gesture.

"Do you like my house?" he asked loudly.

Confused, Lucas folded his arms.

"Well, do you?" he repeated.

"Mr. Herrick –" I began.

"Harriet," Jonah interrupted, "I am glad you are here as witness. You both as well, Nicholas and Lucinda. During these final weeks of my life, I have struggled with one pressing question. Can anybody guess what that is?" He glared at me. "I know you can, for it's also a question that you struggle with."

"I'm afraid I do not understand."

"Think!" he exclaimed. "Why should I praise your intelligence so highly amongst my peers, when you do not grasp my meaning? I am the last Herrick."

"You keep reminding me that you are." I balled my hands into fists beneath the table, but I finally realized what he meant. "As I am the last Tate. Who is the heir to Fogbound Manor?"

"There!" He waved his cane so wildly I thought he might split his spine. "How can I not find such fated kinship with her? Harriet Tate clearly understands. She cannot inherit her home nor oversee her company. But this, my friends, is the question forced upon me. Who will be my heir? That is why, Lucas Penley, you are here."

Riveted to my chair, I had never seen such a display my whole life. I couldn't move if I tried. Jonah Herrick, what in the world are you doing? He wavered and at last his skinny frame collapsed back into the chair. Then he planted his sharp elbows on the table and leaned forward towards Lucas, his pale cheeks sunken in the candlelight.

"What an idea, isn't it? That a Penley will get my home. As soon as my corpse is cold, you can move right in."

"Jonah," Mrs. Wentham murmured.

"Fine justice for you, Lucas." Jonah gestured for more wine. "The Herricks will be gone at last. I must commend your patience, boy. I know I don't possess it."

I could not believe what I was hearing - that Fogbound Manor was bequeathed to a carriage driver! It made even less sense than Cousin Francis inheriting, but at least he was my father's nephew. The new heir grew even angrier.

"You always played cruel pranks," Lucas muttered. "But this is beyond even you."

"Oh, no, you mistake me." Jonah gulped his wine. "Nicholas is here to draft my will, and everyone present shall add their signature. Discount my joking manner, for I am serious, Lucas. I am bequeathing you Fogbound Manor."

Lucas glanced over at Mrs. Wentham. "Why not give it to Lucinda? She's older."

Jonah sat back in his seat. "Lucinda had her chance to take part in my life. She said no, which makes her unworthy of the Herrick legacy. Once I am gone, you may give your sister whatever you wish. But I wouldn't let her have one seaweed-soaked rock if I were you."

So that was why Lucas and Lucinda looked at each other that way. They were siblings. Lucinda was so shocked and so pale she couldn't speak. Her husband laid a soothing hand on hers. While he grounded her visible distress, Lucas at last got to his feet.

"I ain't lookin' at your will, Jonah. Give me what you want, or don't give me anything at all. Doesn't matter to me."

"Oh, but it does matter," Jonah said softly. "As Harriet well knows."

I ignored Jonah and looked up at Lucas. "Good night, Lucas. I shall see you in the morning."

I received no such goodwill in return. He bent down, gave his sister's hand a reassuring kiss, and strode from the dining room. The front door's slam was like the closing of a casket lid. I did not envy Lucas's position at all. I had my own familial obligations to struggle with.

Mr. Wentham yawned. "Even without Lucas, we can still draft up the will, Jonah. There is time to renegotiate the terms of the inheritance, since I don't think you will succumb to your illness today."

"The good Lord will take me when He wants to," Jonah said. "I have the best of both worlds, Nicholas. I can stay on this earth with Harriet to search for treasure, or I can be reunited with my brother Elijah on the heavenly plane. It matters not to me."

"Will you be all right, my dear?" Mr. Wentham gently asked his wife.

At her tearful nod, he stood from the table and gestured to the parlor. Then he calmly and placidly walked from the room. Jonah also stood, but before he left, he made sure to address Mrs. Wentham and restate his decision.

"Ask Harriet about what it means to leave a legacy. I have a choice, Lucinda."

"Yes," she said softly, "you do. But having the power of choice doesn't mean you get to disregard everyone's feelings."

He shrugged, straightening. "You disregarded mine."

Without a final farewell to her or myself, he left the dining room.

nineteen

While certainly not knowing what to say after Jonah's rude departure, I inwardly smiled at his boldness. I'd known him less than three full days, and not one hour had been dull or predictable. One had to admire the sheer energy required to not care a whit what others thought. It was alien to me.

"May - may I call you Harriet?"

"You may," I answered, unsure as to why Mrs. Wentham addressed me. If she hoped to seek solace from a fellow female companion, I had none to offer her.

"It's Lucinda, as well. No one prefers formality on Herrick Island."

That I could wholeheartedly agree with. "Mr. Herrick has dictated a strange manner of behavior to be practiced by all here. It is not what I am used to, I admit."

She daubed her eyes, her sadness and shock quietly disappearing like soft tidewaters. She gazed towards the door from whence the master had vacated, and I suddenly remembered what he'd said to me last night. He'd had his heart broken. Now I was sharing a table with the person who'd done this very dishonor. Jonah was right, that I had no similar situation to compare.

"I would like to speak with my brother." She expertly folded her napkin and placed it on her cleared plate. "Will you not join me, Harriet?"

Was she joking? After such an animated dinner, I wished for nothing more than a relaxing evening. My hesitation brought another prompt from her.

"You did ask him to journey with you tomorrow, did you not?"

"I did, but that does not mean –"

"Perhaps it does," she interrupted. Her tone was quiet yet forceful. "I saw the way you looked upon him. Did you think me to be a rival in his affections?"

"Mrs. Wentham, might I remind you that I am soon to be engaged."

"But you are not yet. I feel you should reassure Lucas that his chances are not yet wholly diminished."

What a way to surmise such bold accusations. She was as forthright as Jonah. No wonder he had fallen so quickly for her demeanor. But she reminded me of the shape-shifting nature of several girls I'd known in school. Girlish and sweet amongst some company, as merciless as a snake amongst others. I'd find no comfortable friendship with her, not that I was seeking any. I at last got to my feet, more determined to reassure Lucas of my non-attachments than at his sister's beckoning.

Mrs. Wentham joined me, and we walked alongside one another on our way out of the dining room. She said not a word until the moment I reached for my cloak.

"There is a passage through the manor over to the stables." She paused beneath an oil lantern and lifted it off its hook. "Allow me to show you. I was privy to using it myself as a child."

I listened for her muffled footsteps as I followed her through the dank and gloomy first-floor halls. We passed in and out of varying shades of grayish light, some patches paler than others, though no sunshine penetrated Herrick Island's mist. Outside, the sea's tides whooshed insistently. Jonah's tremendous outbursts, so thunderous and proclaiming, crashed about my thoughts. He confounded me, he praised me, he confused me, he incited pity within me. He was a dozen men bottled into one, and the pressure cracked like glass walls. It agitated us both.

"How much further?" I called.

Mrs. Wentham's oil lantern bobbed towards me through the gloom until her face emerged, as if she resided within the mist.

"Take five steps forward, but careful not to smack your nose."

She stepped aside for me to take the lead. I marched past her with my hand slightly outstretched. My fingertips brushed against wood as moist as skin, and I stopped. Beyond, the musky dank smell of wet hay wafted through the walls.

"Give it a push, Harriet."

"Miss Tate," I said automatically. Her expression in the dark was invisible, but I could feel her stiffen beside me. So much for informality.

I groped for the cold wet doorknob and turned it. The door gave easier than I thought, and, once opened, revealed the full smell of the stables. I stepped through the doorway towards a lighter pale glow, and soon discovered it came from a large metal lantern. This lantern was placed on a rickety stool in the center of a wide hall of horse stalls, at least four on each side. As I tentatively walked about the stables, the stone floor made my footsteps click loudly. The sound alerted someone else to my presence, and from one of the stables Lucas emerged.

The exertion of stall-mucking had caused a sweaty sheen to glisten along his jawline. He tossed a dirty towel back into the darkness behind him. He'd unbuttoned the top of his henley shirt and rolled up the sleeve-cuffs as well. Suspenders dangled by his knees, and heavy canvas trousers were shoved into thick mud-caked boots. A horse nickered from a stall close by.

Mrs. Wentham sidled up beside me and set her oil lantern on the floor, brightening the stables. Lucas didn't look too pleased to her.

"A fine job of it you did there," he muttered. "He's not supposed to leave it to me."

"Nicholas is doing his best on that account." She produced a handkerchief, startlingly white and pristine, and approached her brother. "Let me wipe you down a bit. Clean up the new master!"

Her shrill laugh made me wince. What had she come here for? To patronize and tease Lucas? She patted her own cheeks before tucking the delicate square of silk away.

"You must see that this is all a giant folly. Another of Jonah's cruel tricks. I wouldn't wish to play that game with you, my dear. Not since you are to inherit."

"There is another option," I offered. "Lacking an heir, the estate will pass to whichever new bidder offers the largest asking price. It will be akin to purchasing any other type of property."

"Precisely," came Lucas's terse answer. "As it should be."

"Mr. Herrick can name anyone he wants as his successor," I said quietly. "If my own father had wished to break with tradition, then my name would be upon the company's deed. A legacy can be changed, by the one who bequeaths it."

"Jonah is offering something extraordinary," Lucinda urged. "You would do this for me. I assure you I shall not force you to stay here on the island. Not if you don't wish to. But to pass up this opportunity would be madness."

Lucas nodded. "Lucinda, I don't want Fogbound Manor. And he won't give it to you. Buy it after his death."

Yet, her staunch spirit could not accept such an answer. She wanted the manor, and I understood what that was like. To be a woman standing right next to her dream without any possibility of taking it or receiving it. She could walk its halls, climb its stairs, and pass through its doorways. But she would never own it.

"Lucas, I have brought Miss Tate here with me tonight. You and I both see how greatly Jonah has come to endear himself to her. Though, she does not know the full extent of the master's character, and how vin-dictively cruel he can be on a mere whim. She does not know how he and his drunkard of a brother bound and tortured Lucas for hours on end. My brother was not their servant, but their slave to satisfy any evil fancy they could conjure. Those ... those damn boys."

Lucas stepped away from us until his back nudged against a stall door. He reached up and gripped the iron bars like a man falling. The pain when he had looked at Jonah. A wounded animal. And now Jonah wanted to give his own victim the entire manor? What, was this to be a guilty apology in the form of stone and fog, to make up for his hellish sins?

I took a step towards Lucas. "It is the very fact that Mr. Herrick has never told me of his past actions that causes me to believe this. Lucas, I see it in your eyes how he has treated you. Unforgivable."

Lucas at last relaxed, his shoulder muscles ceasing tautness. He lowered his arms gently to his sides and turned his body towards me. His scowl was gone, replaced by a more open look to his face.

"After Jonah dies, I'm leaving."

I could find nothing to argue against this declaration. Even if he did receive the manor, he could turn over ownership of it to his sister at any time. Then she could have the home she wanted, and he'd be free of the Herricks at last.

"In time, you will become mistress of this place," I said to Mrs. Wentham. "Your brother can sell it to you for a dollar, if he chooses. In my own father's will, I was expressly forbidden from becoming company overseer."

"That is why Nicholas is with him now," she explained. "For Jonah will be as cruel as your father and write a clause that bans me from ever returning to Herrick Island, let alone receiving the manor."

"Indeed." I thought for a second, but could find no other alternative. "I can foresee only one option, although it requires that you trust me, Mrs. Wentham."

"Only insofar as you remain trustworthy, Miss Tate."

I grimly chuckled. "I am too poor to be swindled, have no property or family goods to bargain with, and can only claim a meager fortune of a dozen gold coins. So, Mrs. Wentham, I may be a lady of high standing and excellent family name, but I offer nothing of value to you."

She looked at me curiously. "Then, what do you propose?"

"That I become the heir to Fogbound Manor."

Lucas's scowl at once reappeared, while his sister gave a mirthless laugh.

"Even if you convince Jonah to bequeath you the manor, what prevents you from carrying out his final wishes?" she asked. "You could banish the name of Penley forever and reinstate yourself as a wealthy lady."

"You wouldn't," Lucas said to me. "Lucinda, she's even more eager than myself to leave Herrick Island."

"Your reactions are expected," I said stiffly. "Doubt and aversion to the idea. Yet, like I said earlier, it is the best option. It removes Lucas as the heir. With Mr. Wentham's knowledge of the law, he can successfully negotiate the terms to transfer ownership. All I would require is a sum of two thousand dollars to bring home."

"As a dowry for your intended?" Lucinda asked.

"Yes." My affections for Mr. Godwin were growing dimmer by the moment, but it was what I'd chosen for my company and my family. "I see that as the best course."

Lucas leaned over and picked up an iron pitchfork. "Best for you."

"It is not only best for me," I disagreed, "and it requires your trust."

"Wait, Lucas." His sister approached me. "I see quite the benefit to this bargaining arrangement. Let me discuss it with Nicholas before I completely confer."

"So be it." Before I excused myself, I felt I had to tell her. I had to prevent another from what I suffered. "But, Mrs. Wentham, as one who might forfeit my home and company to bankruptcy, I assure you that if you do not recognize this opportunity, then you will lose everything. You will always be close to what you want, but never truly obtain it. That is a suffering I don't wish on anyone."

"Well," she said with an annoying shrug, "that is why I married a lawyer. He has educated me on how I can obtain this property, and it is all in how Jonah's will is worded. His will can be manipulated and determine a new legacy."

She blew a kiss to her brother, then slipped out the back of the stables. I could hear her boots clicking across the stones. Lucas clanged the pitchfork against the floor.

"Jonah won't agree to your decision, Miss Tate."

"Probably not," I agreed. "But it does help your position. I want ..."

I want to leave with you, I almost said. I want to forget about Jonah and fog and treasure and my dead father's sins, and leave Herrick Island forever. I smiled, though this time for him, it was a genuine smile.

"I want you to call me Harriet."

He did smile back, a little. I didn't know why I desired to apologize for what his master had put him through, but it seemed an unjust punishment for no crime ever committed. Forced to pay for something that was never his fault.

God in heaven, I knew how that felt.

twenty

✳

Whilst rounding the landing on my way downstairs, I pulled out my little lady's watch and checked the time. Three minutes until eight o'clock. I snapped the case shut and continued down to the entrance hall, my hand on the mahogany banister. I had no desire to see any of the manor's other occupants this morning. Though I was curious to speak to Mr. Wentham about what alterations he had made with Jonah to the will. The master would be shocked, to say the least, at my proposed change.

I met no-one in the entrance hall, not even a servant, and dressed warmly to go out in my cloak, scarf, bonnet, and mittens. The early March weather was still a far cry from spring, and a wintry chill slipped between the blocky stone walls and past my flannel petticoats. Once attired, I went outside and shut the door behind me. A thin layer of ice made the front steps treacherous, and I carefully tiptoed down to the carriageway. Lucas had not yet arrived.

I shielded my eyes from the dim morning sun and gazed up the full breadth of Fogbound Manor. Gulls swooped lazily about its turreted towers, and only one window glowed warmly. Its enormous charcoal-colored exterior held a host of new emotions for me embedded within the damp stone. Did I truly want to become its heir, even if for only a few short weeks? How much was the estate even worth? It couldn't be a paltry sum, since Lucinda Wentham desired it so greatly. If I was exclusively looking out for my own interests, I'd sell it for as high a price as I could and take those thousands of dollars in profit back to Kennebunkport.

The thought made me smile. Well, if Mrs. Wentham did not prove to be an adequate successor, I might proceed without her. Just like my father, indeed, to find the female option so lacking. But in this case, it would be due to the merits of character, not traditional principle.

Crunching along behind me came the sound of wheels on gravel. Lucas had brought a small black two-seated carriage with an exposed place for the driver up front. A pair of white horses drove it up alongside me, and he stopped them with only a tiny jerk on the reins. An expert driver.

"It turns easier than the larger one," he explained. "Better for a short ride."

"How convenient," I said.

As he stepped down to help me inside, I recalled with mixed feelings that this was exactly the type of carriage Mr. Godwin owned. A fact that never need be mentioned to Lucas. I accepted his hand and hoisted myself up inside the carriage, then took a seat off to one side behind him, so we could converse. He sat creakily down in the driver's seat, picked up the reins, and we started off down the carriageway leading towards the road we'd taken when I first arrived last Friday.

We'd only progressed a few hundred yards when Lucas guided the horses to turn left. We departed the main road and drove along a faint path that resembled a wagon-trail through the forest. Sparsely situated trees allowed plenty of room to pass beneath their tall mottled pine trunks. Lumpy gray and brown rocks emerged from the forest floor, dusted with dull pine needles and dead leaves. I could smell the woodsy scents of fir, spruce, and the musky earth beneath. Far above us, interlaced pine branches provided further shade from the weak March sunlight, and the forest's cozy dimness wrapped about me.

After an hour of quiet travel, we reached a large clearing. Chunky low rock walls sloped up on either side, and in the center was a packed earthen floor. Gray light blanketed the clearing with a hazy mist. Lucas halted the carriage.

"An old cabin was here," he said.

He got out of the carriage, and gestured for me to join him. The ground was still frosty from winter, and only the slightest breeze from the ocean wafted into this secluded place. Lucas lifted up the carriage seat I'd just vacated, and brought out a large muslin sack, its contents clanking.

"Over here."

I followed him to the edge of the clearing, where we came upon a campsite set up next to the remains of a charred brick chimney. Two large boulders were positioned in front of the chimney, and I seated myself on one of them while Lucas busied himself with starting a fire. He used old boards from a stack by the chimney as kindling, he'd brought matches, and soon a cozy blaze crackled within the outdoor fireplace. I removed my mittens and warmed my fingers, breathing in the wonderfully smoky scent. It relaxed and revived me, and I settled in quite comfortably.

With the fire heartily burning, Lucas set up a cast iron spit roaster, and soon was dutifully turning a chicken, potatoes, and onions for our luncheon.

"Thank you," I said quietly. "For preparing all of this."

He crouched before the roaster and said nothing. At least he was not scowling. I knew he was not happy about my decision last night, but I couldn't think of any other way to set him free. His master had only days to live, and after that, he'd be leaving the island permanently.

"They used to bring me here," he said abruptly. "Jonah and Elijah. Their father was the cruelest man I ever knew. Elijah's face was always bruised. Jonah limped from all the whippings. Then they're dragging me out here, tying me up to these bricks, and beating me. I think my dried blood is on half these bricks."

I shivered. How pale and ethereal my own father's unkindness compared to these paternal actions.

"I ... I am sorry."

He grunted. "You did nothing."

I looked down at my hands, firelight dancing over my skin. "I know, Lucas. Yet, I do feel I understand –"

"Oh, you do?" he interrupted.

His question echoed in the silent clearing. I suddenly felt quite chastened. What business had I to involve myself in what his sister wanted or the lawyer or even his damn master?

"Quite right," I said tersely. "I do not understand. Thank you, Lucas, for reminding me."

He threw me a glance over his shoulder, slightly confused. Yet, I felt anything but confusion. My quest had resumed its laser-like clarity in my thoughts. Harriet Tate, what caused you to be so side-tracked? Pray that you not so easily forget your place again. Lucas focused his attention back on the roasting and slowly turned the spit. I sat in stony silence until he spoke again. His voice was quieter, softer.

"Convince Jonah to become the heir, if that is what you truly want. But Harriet, do not give the manor to my sister."

It was like a warning to me. I pursed my lips, thinking intently as to how to resolve this matter. The fire crackled amongst the bricks.

"Then Mr. Herrick leaves no heir. Whomever becomes Fogbound Manor's new owner will be free to make their own choices."

Cruel deeds aside, the Herrick family could not suffer the same fate as my own Tate name. Jonah would lose his home, his family money, and all claims to the entire island.

Lucas smiled grimly. "Serves him right, is what I say."

"You'd also rather your sister not inherit what she has so greatly desired?"

He shruffed, absentmindedly turning the spit roaster.

"It's fair," he finally said.

"I hardly think so," I disagreed. "Was it fair that my father kept me from inheriting? Why legacies cannot be based on merit rather than such superficial traditions is beyond my comprehension."

Lucas abruptly stood up, stomped over to the muslin sack, and pulled out a pair of plates with serving utensils. He skewered the chicken and vegetables off the spit roaster, arranged them haphazardly on a plate, and shoved it at me. I'd hardly time to utter thanks before he dished up his own meal, planted his backside on the other boulder, and began noisily eating. I quietly turned from him, picked up the hot chicken in my fingers, and ate like a messy child. Oh, but it was so delicious! I hardly cared. For once in my life, I dined on something with no thought as to manners or formalities.

Having had his fill, Lucas sat on the ground, tucked his back against the boulder, and stretched his arms behind his head. His boots were warmed by the firelight.

"Do you really think there is pirate treasure on this island?" I asked.

"Of course not."

"I am to join Mr. Herrick at the shoreline tomorrow to search for it. But I am becoming convinced I'll find little more than driftwood."

"It's difficult for ships to land here, due to the shape of the island," he said. "I can only remember one arriving, and that was years ago."

"What do you recall about it?"

"There was an injured man onboard. Doctor Gravitch saw to him. It kept the Herrick boys occupied and away from me. I came out here and camped for a few days before they noticed I was gone. Never saw any of the sailors."

"Doctor Gravitch?" I asked. "A relative of the reverend?"

"His brother."

"Ah." The man whom I should ask about the coins. "He is due to arrive on Friday."

"Well, Jonah is dying. No matter if some doctor gets here or not. Nothing can save him now." Lucas picked up a stick and poked at the embers. He glanced up at the sky. "We should head back, before dark."

I got to my feet and helped him pack the kitchen items away in the muslin sack. I pushed sand on the fire to douse it, and we at last returned to the carriage. After he'd tucked the muslin sack away beneath the seat, he bid for me to climb up. I hesitated.

"Lucas?"

"Yes."

"Why do you not want your sister to inherit Fogbound Manor?"

"Just don't let her have it," he retorted. "Trust me."

I sighed in frustration. "If you do not tell me, then I cannot make an informed decision. No matter how much Fogbound Manor is worth, I do not wish to inherit it. I have my own home to save."

He steadied the bridle of his horse to soothe her. She submitted to his touch, her long eyelashes fluttering. I stepped closer to Lucas, and gently ran my fingers along the mare's side. She was warm and round, smelling sweetly like hay. Lucas softly rubbed her nose.

"Lucinda is not like you," he said. "You want to do better with what you have been given. She merely wants the title and the prestige. How others would see her, without knowing how falsely she behaves."

"Then prevent her from inheriting," I urged. "Once you own the manor, you can sell it. It must be worth a tidy profit, at least."

"Profit," he growled. "It's blood money, Harriet. Call me poor and low, if you like. I scraped by long enough. But I'd rather scrape than be made rich off the property of such –"

His anger, ferocious in its intensity and longevity, cut his own words off. He stopped, breathing hard. I could not look at him, but I felt his wrath. He seethed with such a burning hatred, it lit his veins on fire. He exhaled a loud sigh.

"You sell it and collect the profits. It's the best dowry you're ever gonna get from Herrick Island."

"Who says I wish a dowry?" I snapped.

"Aren't you running back home to get married?"

"Only to help my company." I folded my arms, anger stiffening my spine. "Call me wealthy and snobbish, if you like. But if I do not have that money by the first of April, I lose it all."

"And this fellow offers that." He shook his head. "Money don't mean a damn thing, Harriet. Rich people got nothin' to offer but their foot on your back. When you arrived here, I thought you were different. But this marrying to get money - it's as dumb as anything Jonah ever did."

I should have been furious for him saying such a thing. I should have wanted to strike him across his stubbled jaw. But I didn't. He was hurting, like I was, about the past. He couldn't forget it or let it go, and it was wrapped in layers upon layers of deep bitterness and regret. When he looked at Jonah, it would come to the surface and he'd hurt all over again. I was beginning to feel the same way about this place. It summoned painful memories like a conjurer, never allowing us to forget.

How could we, when the foggy air writhed with haunting ghosts?

I breathed in the scent of the pines, never tearing my gaze form Lucas. Then I stepped forward and laid my hand on his. He didn't move, but his fingers twitched beneath my touch.

"When I leave, come with me," I whispered. "And never think on this place again."

He turned his wrist and interlaced his fingers with mine, drawing me slowly towards him. He reached up gently, as if I was one of his shy mares, and caressed my cheek with his fingertip. He left a trail of warmth down my face, like he was scarring me.

"I'll accept the inheritance," he said softly. "Yet, you must do something for me."

"If I can." Suddenly nervous, I couldn't help saying it. "I want to help you."

"Then stay with me. Here. You never need marry if you don't wish to. Forget about being a Tate. Let it go, Harriet."

To forget ... I knew why he asked such a thing of me, but I could never accept. It would be like dying, leaving a shade of my essence too pale to catch the light.

He knew my answer must be no, and he pulled away ever so slightly. Yet I couldn't forsake his warmth. I pressed up against him and laid my head on his soft woolen chest. He gently circled his arms about my shoulders and held me whilst I submerged in his kindness, relaxing within his scent. My eyes filled with tears. He'd laid a path open for me, welcoming and caring. A future more dear than the past ever could be.

But I'd rather perish than let myself forget who I really was.

twenty-one

Lucas spoke no more about Fogbound Manor or the inheritance, and I retired at once to my bedchamber upon returning. He'd only wanted the place if I agreed to stay here with him, as a companion of sorts. I privately admitted his companionship might bring greater comfort and perhaps even love over time, but with the mail boat's pending arrival in a few days, I had to regain my true focus. I was running out of time.

"Find the money and return to Kennebunkport," I said aloud.

My breath fogged on the mullioned glass windowpanes, and the dark sea beyond my window whooshed in reply. Lucas will inherit, I will have my treasure, and we shall both depart Herrick Island forever, never to think of its suffocating spirit again.

Sullen after my day with his servant, Jonah wouldn't address me at breakfast the next morning, so it was I who prompted the idea of heading at once to the seashore. When his reply was a pouting silence, I repeated my request.

"Then, you will bring the shovel, I hope?" I asked. "Mr. Herrick, if I am to locate –"

"Yes, yes," he said irritably. "The Wenthams can seek it with you. I must remember how ill I am and decline to accompany the party."

"Lucas will not be joining us, either." Mrs. Wentham stirred her tea cup and licked the spoon. "He and Harriet had an understanding yesterday, so he wouldn't dream of intruding on her quest at all."

"Understanding!" Jonah barked. "The way I understand it, ladies of proper society do not take private carriage rides with low servants."

"Since when did you care about propriety or society?" I questioned. "Or, for that matter, your own illness?"

"Since when did you care about anything regarding my opinion or welfare?" Jonah retorted. "It's about the money. That's the one thing you Tates value above all else."

"There's little point in denying it," I said dryly. "Oddly, that is the same reason Lucas gave for denouncing my character. While you sulk about that, I shall in the meantime resume my quest. It's the reason I am here, after all. Good day."

I gave a departing nod to the Wenthams and made my way out of the dining room. Jonah didn't follow me, and I headed upstairs to the second floor. The map room was locked, so I let myself in with the key and soon located the shovel, along with a second one fashioned of heavier metal.

I'd no sooner returned to the entrance hall when I saw the master, his hand on the front doorknob. He wasn't dressed to go out. I stoically walked over to the hall tree, set the shovels against the wall, and began to put on my cloak and mittens.

"Is that true?" he demanded.

"What are you speaking of?" I asked wearily.

"That Lucas denounced your character."

I pulled my cloak hood over my hair. "Yes, it is true. Criticize me for the financial security I desire so greatly, but I am no liar."

"Neither is he," Jonah said. "Undoubtedly he couldn't wait to tell you of my exemplary actions as a boy."

"He spoke of it." I picked up the two shovels. "Are you to join me, sir, or not?"

He smirked. "It looks like you have decided to bring your own shovel, my dear. Are you up for a little grave-digging afterwards? I might not survive this jaunt."

"Grave-digging, I hear?" asked the placid voice of Mr. Wentham. He appeared in the dining room doorway, accompanied by his wife who sniffed at Jonah like a dog. "Not until you sign a name to your will, Jonah Herrick."

Jonah reached forward and snatched one of the shovels from me, then leaned heavily on his cane and thumped over to the hall tree.

"Stokes!" he cried. "Where is that old fool? I wish to go out."

"What of naming Lucas as your heir?" I asked, confused. "Was that not what you proclaimed at dinner?"

"Are you ready to find your money, Miss Tate, or not?" He dressed haphazardly in a coat and hat. "Let us to the beach!"

He made quite the show of yanking open the door and clopping out to the front steps. I shook my head. If I wasn't careful, Jonah would change his mind as abruptly as he changed moods and name one of the Wenthams as his heir. I was starting to believe Lucas that his sister wasn't worthy of the title. And Mr. Wentham's behavior on this island was so wholly different than in Kennebunkport he put me ill at ease. No, it was becoming clear that if I was to satisfy both Lucas's and my own future desires, I'd have to be the one named as heir in the will.

But would Jonah accept such a thing? I couldn't wager on it.

Nor, for that matter, could I wager on finding little more than broken shells on this beach hunt. I gripped the cold shovel handle and followed Jonah outside to the carriageway. Stabbing his cane into the gravel, he marched away from Fogbound Manor towards the stables. A cold wind had sprung up, slicing through the fog and instantly freezing the inside of my nose. I snuggled further into my cloak and hurried to catch up with the master.

"Mr. Herrick," I gasped. "Are you not to wait for the Wenthams to join us?"

He thrust the cane forward like a spear. "Onwards to the treasure, dear Harriet. The mail boat arrives Friday morning and I can't let you depart empty-handed."

His words might have been charitable, but his voice was drenched in bitterness. In a few minutes we came within sight of the stables. The familiar scent of horse leather made my breath catch. I shan't dare tell the master what his servant confessed to me. Grave-digging, indeed. With a pronouncement like that, I might as well stop his weak heart with my own hands.

Just beyond the stables, Jonah headed straight to a footpath next to Fogbound Manor that curved between two enormous rocks.

"After you, madam."

"I can hardly be expected to know where the treasure is if I have not ventured there before," I pointed out.

"Miss Tate, you are observant as ever. I was merely trying to appear a gentleman to such a kind lady as yourself."

I don't know why I blushed then, but I did – warmth flaming my cheeks despite the clammy, windy cold. I abruptly picked up my skirts and stepped through the rock crevice. I stood at the top of a narrow hill overlooking the beach. It was about as wide as the looming manor behind it, and bore the full brunt of the mansion's gloomy shadow. Typically for a Maine beach, there was no sand but rather a flattened carpet of small smooth rocks and shells gently sloping down to the lapping waves. Beyond the shoreline, cresting Atlantic waters spread as far out to the horizon as could be imagined. We were upon the last, tiny outpost before the comforting human touch of civilization vanished and Nature's wildness intervened.

The sea was all that lay outside Man's influence. Borderless, mapless, timeless. It refused to succumb to laws or rules. If it wanted life, it took it. Such an unearthly practice for a substance unique to Earth. No other planet possessed an ocean. Perhaps I'd rather have been moon-born, for her dusty presence was far more soothing.

The wind took pity on us and died down a little, so that by the time we picked our way down to the pebbled shore, my numb cheeks had a chance to warm themselves.

"What a sight!" Jonah exclaimed. "Has it been since the pirate himself that a Tate has set foot on these shores?"

"I am inclined to think so."

"Look upon my own resting spot."

He indicated a tumbled group of huge rocks abutting the beach. One was the size and general shape of a chair. Jonah excitedly stepped past me and demonstrated this purpose for me. A section facing the sea featured a natural seat and backrest. He propped his foot on a piece of driftwood, stuck his shovel into the rocks, and leaned as if he lounged in an easy chair.

"Jonah," I said aloud, then clapped a hand over my lips.

He looked at me. "Yes, Miss Tate?"

"Forgive me," I said. "That was not what I meant to say."

"You mean you did not mean to say my name?" he asked. "I see little harm in calling a person by their name. Don't you think?"

"I shall call you by your surname only," I quickly replied.

"Indeed," he said, "and I was right when I bet that you would come to call me Jonah. For that is not what is proper, correct?"

Proper, my foot. He knew what was proper and what was not - yet still insisted on carrying on such frustrating mockery.

"Is this what island living is like?" I demanded. "So little society that you drop social customs in favor of common vernacular, no matter how crude?"

For a second, he appeared taken aback by my tone. Not that I regretted speaking to him in that way.

"Island living," he repeated slowly. He stared out over the pebbly beach to the choppy waves beyond. "Living on an island is like living upon a star. I am surrounded by an ocean stretching as far out beyond the horizon as the blackness beyond the star. Yet I am connected to others through the light."

I hadn't heard him speak this way before. A tenderness in his voice, soft and sad.

"My family has always been island people. We cannot be like those on the mainland, even someone like you who spent your entire life beside the sea. You do not know the isolation that comes from such little society. I can count the number of people I have become deeply acquainted with on one hand. Yet why should I need more society? Wouldn't it unnecessarily draw attention from my quest?"

"I was referring to the way ladies and gentlemen address one another."

"Oh, that again." He rolled his eyes, then leaned back and laughed. "From the tone of your letters, I had little idea how humorous you are. Yet I must say that every day since you arrived has given me another reason to find amusement from your ingrained beliefs."

"Not beliefs, but common sense," I corrected. "Without at least some companionship, you are liable to follow your fancies further and further into an idealistic state, forgetting that practicality and sense will aid you more."

"Well, then wouldn't you say you fit that role perfectly?" He grinned again. "How I do love that look upon your face."

"What look?" I asked sourly.

"An expression of frustrated acquiescence. You know I am right, yet it still annoys you."

"I wish to begin the search," I said, changing the subject. "Where is the location you have tried?"

"Ah, of course."

In one easy move, Jonah slid his thin body from the rock. He stepped across the pebbled sandy floor over to a group of jutting boulders as large as my mansion back home in Kennebunkport. They were colored a damp charcoal gray, constantly wetted by the sea spray.

"Come!" He turned back and beckoned for me. "You shall see."

Clutching my shovel and my skirts, I followed the shoreline over to the boulders. Little foamy wavelets slipped up the beach, nearly touched my shoes, and then slipped back down again. I breathed deeply of the salty air, listening to the circling gulls caw to one another.

Jonah waited for me, one hand on a huge boulder looming twenty feet above us. Its massive bulk buried in the brown sand, a thin rocky ledge sticking out towards the sea.

"Have your shovel?" he asked, holding up his own.

I nodded. "Of course."

"Hmm," he grunted. "What I am about to show you is what I believe to be the most likely location where the treasure was buried. It is a secluded spot, quite dark, so I hope you are ready to enter it."

"Yes, let us at once."

"All right, dearest lady. Follow me."

He stuck his cane in the sand as ballast against his weight and pivoted around on it, so with one large step he'd disappeared behind the rocky ledge. It was like he'd vanished into the sea. Amused, I tiptoed over to the ledge and peered around its side.

It was a cave! The boulder disguised a large mouth-like opening within and plenty of room to enter. With the shovel in one hand and my skirts in the other, I took a little jump over the waters and landed right inside.

"Hello! Hello!" Jonah called. His voice echoed off the wet rock walls. He laughed, and his laughter bounced all around me. "This is where I'd bury treasure."

"Indeed." My own voice also echoed back to me. "A perfect location, inside such a naturally formed cave."

"Ah, she approves!" Jonah came up to me and reached for my shovel. "If you will permit me, my dear."

"Of course not," I said. "You have not the strength to carry it, let alone dig."

He dropped his hand, breathing harder. The way he looked at me was like that morning in front of the map room. The sea waves sloshed at our feet, and I could feel a little of Jonah's warmth radiating from his body. He ran a hand through his dark, wet hair.

"You're right," he said softly. "I lack the strength. But you do not. Did your father know about you? How strong and intelligent you are?"

"He was never home long enough to know me."

Jonah's eyes were sad. "How can that be, Harriet? When I have been privileged enough to call you my guest for four days, and four lifetimes would never be enough to know you?"

"Jonah," I whispered. This time I let myself say his name. "Will you do something for me?"

His eyes widened. He hadn't been expecting my question.

"It depends on what you desire," he said guardedly. "Some requests, you see, are easier to fulfill than others."

"It is a simple enough task, if you should accept it." I took a deep breath. "Name me as the heir to Fogbound Manor."

He looked down, then gently reached forward and took my hand. His fingers were warm and smooth. He brought my hand to his lips, like he had in the map room, and gave me a kiss so tender and adoring my heart quivered. Twice now he had openly displayed affections towards me, and twice he'd caught me off guard with the surging intensity of his emotions. Still holding my hand, he moved closer to me.

"No, Harriet," he said. "I will not name you as heir."

"Your reason?"

"I should ask you the same question, which I can readily answer." He gripped my fingers, like we were melded together. "Lucas doesn't want it, and I wouldn't dream of giving it to either of the Wenthams. You are not as well-acquainted with Lucinda as I am. Perhaps you see yourself in her, a woman denied an inheritance she so desperately desires. So, before my bones turn cold in my grave, you'll immediately either bequeath it to her or sell it to her."

I struggled to free myself, but my struggle was weak. "Jonah, your family has displayed such cruelty to the Penleys, it is a wonder you don't deserve what they do with your legacy."

"And yet your own father was cruel," he pointed out. "Any fool spending ten minutes in your presence sees how worthy you are of his inheritance. I don't need to have known him to come to such a conclusion."

I had not the will to argue with him further. With his eyes upon me and our shovels buried in the sand at our feet, I suddenly realized the truth. A truth I'd known since his first letter, yet could not wholly face until this moment. I couldn't even look him in the eye as I spoke.

"There is no treasure in this cave is there, Jonah?"

"As smart as ever. But perhaps you are the type of woman who had to come all the way here and stand on this wet patch of barren sand to realize you are so much more than a box of gold coins."

He finally released his hold on me. I broke from him and stumbled to the mouth of the cave. Wind whooshed about me, waves pulsed at my feet, and I allowed myself to feel the full extent of the ocean's pulsing. Wash over me, cleanse me, heal me, baptize me anew. How I desired to be free of this island, of this need for the money. I only longed for freedom.

"Miss Tate? Miss Tate!"

Lucinda Wentham was calling from the beach. I stared out over the expanse of the ocean and wiped my tears. What was there to weep for? A dream that would never become real? Money that remained a fantasy? Lucas's own words were bitter in my mind. *Money don't mean a damn thing.*

No treasure, no inheritance. I'd leave as empty-handed as a ghost, no wealth to call my own. I didn't even want to think about how to tell Grandmother or Mr. Godwin. Cousin Francis would run my company into the ground, I'd lose my home, and my name would be lost. More lost than I could ever fathom.

"Miss Tate?" Lucinda called again.

I looked back at Jonah. "Was there ever even a pirate by the name of Tate?"

"Oh, you have many ancestors," he said slowly. "Captains, all of them. But who is to say one of them was a pirate?"

"Then why am I here?" I wiped my cheek. "Why tempt me to come find something that doesn't exist?"

He smiled. "You are so much more than your family, Harriet. I promise you'll realize you did come here and find something real."

"Not real enough," I whispered. "I can't save my family on promises."

I picked up my skirts and left his side. Did I hate him for his false temptations or hate myself for taking a chance to believe in him? No more than I despised him for indulging in delusional glories. My last hope for finding the treasure perished within me, and as I emerged from the cave, I felt I could begin to understand why he'd built this whole life in his mind.

He was dying. And until the day I left his island, Jonah and I were on this star in the vast blackness of space together.

twenty-two

After meeting me at the top of the beach slope, Lucinda accompanied me back to the manor. When she pressed for information about my impending inheritance, I felt numb and gave her a terse answer. She clucked her tongue at my failure. I stopped in the carriageway, miffed by her insistence upon disregarding my personal feelings in favor of her own.

"What can be done, Mrs. Wentham? I asked him to name me, and he would not. Further, my search of the beach proved absolutely fruitless. I conclude that there is no reason for me to remain here on Herrick Island acquainted with either your brother or Jonah. They certainly have their own unfinished business to attend to."

"So, that is what you have decided." She gestured up towards the manor. "It's supposed to be mine, Harriet. Before Elijah Herrick died, he said he would marry me and then I would have become mistress of this house!"

I stared at her in disgust. She'd have chosen to marry a man proven to be vindictively cruel towards her own brother? What, she expected that Elijah as a husband would have treated her differently? I couldn't fathom going to such an extreme length, even to obtain the manor.

"I suggest you take the matter up with Jonah," I said. "You will find him at the shoreline. I do not wonder that you made a grave mistake in rejecting his marriage proposal. Then you would be in the position right now of inheriting."

"Well, I did not love him." She folded her arms and laughed grimly. "He wasn't dying when he asked me. I assumed I'd have to spend the rest of my life playing wife to such a man. Believe me, I'd say anything right now to change his mind."

"Nothing will."

Her error was more than one of timing. After seeing the place where the Herrick brothers exercised their anger on Lucas with bricks and boards … Lucinda had been willing to overlook such wrath, but I never could. She had to face her prospects, and it was time for me to wake from this foggy dream and face my own.

I wouldn't even give her the courtesy of a proper farewell and stomped up the front steps to the manor. I could see my bleak future as if it had already happened. The voyage to Kennebunkport, quietly sobbing in the back of the carriage. The icy trudge up to my house. Grandmother in the parlor, expectant and waiting. Mr. Godwin at the company, still holding out some discernible scrap of hope I'd accept him. Cousin Francis at my old desk, as smug and stupid as any blundering captain whose own ship sank beneath him.

It only needed the gentlest of nudges, to cause the whole thing to crumble. I couldn't be any less ready to leave, and I couldn't more ready to go. I was trapped between worlds, a haunting phantom in a purgatory of her own making.

"Why, Miss Tate. Do come in."

I slipped my hand into my pocket for my lady's watch, and clutched it as I followed the voice through the entrance hall. I'd no sooner stepped inside the parlor when I saw Mr. Wentham standing by the fireplace. My first instinct was to vacate the room immediately, and I stopped only a few feet past the door.

"Good evening, Mr. Wentham."

He gestured to the large parlor windows, which had a clear view of the outside carriageway.

"You have put my wife ill at ease, Miss Tate. I do not think she is pleased with your choice to inherit."

"I beg pardon?" I said crossly. "Jonah has not yet named a successor. I thought he was to bequeath it to Lucas."

Mr. Wentham bit his lip, eyes hardening at my scornful tone. I resolved right then to do whatever it took to remove the Wenthams from the island after Jonah's death. Even if I had to perform such a task in Kennebunkport.

"If Jonah leaves no heir," he said, "I have been appointed executor of the estate. I could easily write in any name I choose."

"I presume that name would be yours, sir," I said dryly.

"That is precisely what I'd like to discuss. Have a seat, Miss Tate. Care for a drink?"

"No, sir."

He moved away from the fireplace and walked over to a little cabinet, where he removed the bottle of cognac Jonah had first showed me Saturday morning. As he poured it into a glass, he kept an eye on me like he wanted to pin me to the floor. At last, I took his suggestion and slowly seated myself.

"I am the best option to inherit." He capped the bottle, replaced it, and walked over towards me. "However, Jonah informed me last night that he shall name you, Miss Tate. He knows he has not long to live, so this shall be put into effect immediately. He wants everyone assembled as witnesses tomorrow."

After my conversation with Jonah at the beach, I highly doubted that he would have told me one truth and Mr. Wentham another. One of them was lying, and I could not positively be sure which. Of Mr. Wentham's character, I could only claim not to know him as well as I wanted. Well, I had called Jonah's bluff on his numerical aptitude, and I could do the same with Mr. Wentham.

"Then I shall be ready to accept what Jonah bestows on me."

"You will, will you?" Mr. Wentham parked himself on the parlor sofa, glass in one hand, and leaned forward as if expecting a criminal confession. "I admit that your arrival here on Herrick Island was unexpected. Who would have thought that the daughter of Maine's finest sea captain would believe in the mad, reclusive Jonah Herrick's ramblings about pirates and treasure? Upon first meeting you, I'd assumed you to be too high-born and bred to consider such nonsense."

"It is nonsense," I agreed. "That has always been my opinion and shall remain so. I was also proved right on that account, since I left the shoreline this afternoon empty-handed. There never was and never will be any treasure on Herrick Island."

"Oh, but there is." He shifted his glass to one hand, and with the other hand leaned back and tapped the stone walls. "How much do you think Fogbound Manor is worth?"

"I have considered its value before," I admitted, "and speculate it must be a great amount. After I have inherited, I can easily sell it and obtain a tidy profit. It should be more than enough to save both my company and home from bankruptcy."

Mr. Wentham took a sip of his drink, swirling it about in his mouth. His face was quite placid, eyes blankly staring at me, mouth drawn in a straight line.

"A tidy profit, indeed. You are correct that it is a great amount. The manor is valued at five hundred thousand dollars. Half a million, as they say."

"Quite the sum."

I kept my own face as expressionless as his, but my knees began to quake. Half a ... half a million! My goodness, no wonder Lucinda Wentham did all she could to inherit, and why her brother despised every penny of it. I couldn't even wrap my own mathematical mind around such an amount. Yet, Jonah said he'd never leave it to the Wenthams.

"Of course, such a fortune attracts fortune-hunters," he continued. "Thus, when Jonah and I amended his will last night, I made sure to include an important amendment. Whomever inherits the manor must provide within forty-eight hours ten percent of the property value. If this amount is not produced, then the manor is immediately placed under the executor's rule as his own personal asset. Miss Tate, I must protect Fogbound Manor from falling into the wrong hands."

Oh, so he assumed me to be a greedy fortune-hunter? This amendment benefitted only one person, and it wasn't me.

"So, as I understand it," I said, "two days after Jonah's death I am to purchase my own inherited property with fifty thousand dollars. Who am I paying?"

"Myself, of course. It covers estate and legal fees."

"I'm sure it does," I quipped. "I also presume that you have in your possession just such an amount in case Jonah changes his mind and bequeaths the manor to your wife?"

Mr. Wentham smiled, lazily sipping his drink. "Both Mrs. Wentham and I are in total agreement about who should inherit. I will not even charge her any interest for the loan."

"How benevolent."

I stared across at him. For the first time, I felt an odd and unexpected sympathy for my father. He'd had to choose a successor. He knew he was leaving his company and home to his ridiculous nephew. Yet, what choice did he have? I wasn't a son.

"It is just as well," Mr. Wentham continued, "that I might have tossed Jonah's first letter into the sea. Even if he did pass the manor to you, we both know you couldn't afford it."

"Not in my current circumstances," I said. "But I highly doubt Jonah shall bequeath the manor to me. The mail boat arrives on Friday, and I shall be on it. I depart without the inheritance, but I do leave with my dignity intact."

"I believe you'll find poverty to be quite undignified." He swallowed the rest of his drink. "I must say I look forward to your impending departure. As you can imagine, I need no further impediments or obstacles preventing me from obtaining what I want."

Oh, he must covet Fogbound Manor even more than his wife did. I suddenly realized why Jonah had said that he wouldn't give the manor to me. He was protecting me from a legal entanglement, for he knew I couldn't pay fifty thousand dollars to Mr. Wentham within two days. For that matter, neither could Lucas.

"There might not be any opposition from me," I said, "but I would not be so confident, sir. The fact Jonah has not named a successor is quite telling. He still has the power to choose."

Mr. Wentham looked down at his empty glass. "Oh, I don't foresee that happening, Miss Tate. His illness is so advanced. I suspect he won't live more than a week."

"Then you have not much time, have you?"

He didn't answer me, but the look on his face was of such satisfaction, my stomach felt tight. Who knows how long he'd been planning for this. Mr. and Mrs. Herrick were gone, Elijah was dead, and Jonah would never recover. In less than a month, Nicholas and Lucinda Wentham would be the new master and mistress of Fogbound Manor. Neither Jonah or Lucas desired such an outcome.

Mr. Wentham got to his feet and set the glass on the mantel. He turned it about, the cut crystal catching the firelight with each rotation. Addressing me once more, he chuckled a bit.

"It's too bad Jonah's pirate nonsense has proven to be nothing but a dream. If there was, indeed, a treasure, you could easily afford to inherit Fogbound Manor. You'd be wealthier than even Captain Tate ever dreamed of being."

Tick. Tick. Tick.

I slipped my hand into my pocket and drew out my watch. I slowly rewound it, keeping track of the time.

"Mr. Wentham, I don't dream. I plan. And I plan on going home soon. Good night, sir."

He bowed to me as an insipid gesture of feigned politeness and slowly made his way from the parlor. I watched the firelight dance across the surface of my watch, lighting up each Roman numeral. Time is sovereign over all things. How useless to try and stop the clock. It was as useless as trying to save my company or save Jonah.

My breath caught. He knew he would lose everything after his death, and he didn't want me to face even more loss. He couldn't tell me. He could only protect me.

"Thank you, Jonah," I whispered.

Let me sit here within these finite moments, before I am gone and you are gone as well.

What little time we have.

twenty-three

I was up early the next morning, and somehow the skies seemed lighter. I watched the clouds gently shift about, as if nudged by some great force. I couldn't see any sunlight, per se, but the atmosphere featured a less smudgy gray hue. As if the ghosts perpetually living about here dispersed. My conversation with Mr. Wentham in the parlor last night gave me more than a few thoughts to mull over, and I was lost in thought whilst enjoying my breakfast when Mrs. Quinn knocked upon my door.

"Good morning," I greeted cordially.

"Meow." The orange cat Jonah had affectionately nicknamed Mr. Quinn slipped in front of his namesake and silently hopped up onto my bed.

"Ill creature. Should have drowned it," the housekeeper muttered. She thrust an envelope at me, crinkled and dirtied by her hand. "To the parlor at once, Miss Tate."

"I will."

I took the envelope and waited until she left before lifting the flap. It was another of Jonah's notes, scrawled as per his usual writing, and contained an invitation to take part in the reading of the will. I glanced over at the orange cat, snoozing and purring with both round eyes open and fixed upon me.

"Did you know your home is worth half a million dollars?" I asked.

He blinked first one eye and then the other. An early spring breeze fluttered past the windows in the sitting-area. Half a million. I had to inherit it. Without sacks of gold coins to take home, my next best option was to become Fogbound Manor's new owner. Five hundred thousand dollars. I could easily postpone filing bankruptcy if I was also involved in the sale of the manor. Could there be any greater prize to triumphantly bring home? Oh, the look on my cousin's face when I told him! How Grandmother would weep with joy that her son's name would never be forgotten. My own independence from both man and materialism secured as if by royal decree.

Yet, what of Mr. Wentham's infernal legal fees? Mr. Godwin didn't have enough, and I was in no position to borrow the amount from anyone I knew. The shipwreck financially crippled poor Kennebunkport. I also thought too greatly of Father here and longed to forget about him.

The more I considered it, the more fruitless an outcome it seemed. Harriet Tate to own Fogbound Manor? How ludicrous. There was no way possible I could magically conjure fifty thousand dollars. Besides, it was already Wednesday morning. I had less than thirty-six hours before I left the island. Mountainous problems faced me back at home, and such a bleak future made me feel more and more overwhelmed.

Doing the right thing felt wrong, and doing the wrong thing also felt wrong.

After leaving my room, I easily found my way through Fogbound Manor's twisting gloomy halls. Every scrap of faded wallpaper and every sputtering candle suddenly had a value in my mind. Half a million. It was like these floorboards and peeling plaster walls were suddenly fashioned of pirate coins.

I finally turned the corner at the main staircase landing and stepped down to the entrance hall. Muffled voices came from two men standing just inside the front doors. Wan candlelight revealed a face I hadn't expected to see – that of Reverend Gravitch. He patted Mr. Stokes on the shoulder, inquiring politely after the old butler's health.

"Good morning, Miss Tate," he said in his rich voice. "It seems we both shall bear witness to Jonah's reading today."

He gently took my hand and kissed it with practiced grace and gentility.

"Thank you, sir. He does desire his final wishes be carried out in a proper manner." I offered my arm, and he took it. We slowly walked from the entrance hall into the parlor. "It is clearly important that his estate passes to the rightful heir."

"As well it should," the reverend agreed. "He's trying to avoid what happened after his own parents passed away. Those legal proceedings were quite the entanglement. Mr. Wentham was kind enough to straighten the whole mess out. But Jonah was not due to inherit anything. It would have all passed to Elijah."

A realization dawned on me, that I hadn't considered. "Jonah never planned on becoming the last of the Herricks, did he?"

"Of course not. His brother was in excellent health up until the day he was found."

"Found, sir?"

"Oh, yes." The reverend patted my hand. "Poor Elijah Herrick drowned at the shoreline where he'd played as a boy so many years."

"My goodness."

Elijah had died on the same beach where Jonah had taken me to search for treasure. So many ghosts here.

The parlor soon filled with the other guests of Fogbound Manor, including the Wenthams, of course, as well as Lucas. He lingered just inside the room's doorway, scuffing a boot across the stone floor, hands jammed in his pockets. I wondered if he was packed and ready to leave the island.

Jonah at last entered the parlor. The combination of naturally low lighting and his own illness made him startlingly frail. He wobbled precariously as he clutched his cane. Mr. and Mrs. Wentham were enjoying how close to death's door he appeared, and both even commented on it from what I could hear across the room. Jonah announced that he was glad we had come, and we were to go into the library for the official reading of the will. The reverend took my arm again and kindly escorted me down the hall. We slowly followed the others until we'd come to yet another of the manor's enormous rooms.

Perfectly round and high-ceilinged, the library had been set up for the reading. A mahogany podium sat on a thick table, and leather chairs were positioned in front of it. The room was completely lined in windowed bookcases, each featuring a lock and dangling key. Like the rest of the manor it was dimly lit, so I couldn't read the book titles at all. Only a few sputtering sconces and a single candle by the podium provided any relief from the gloom. As I took my seat beneath one of the sconces, I could hear the sea's insistent sloshing just beyond the wall. We must be within one of the turrets in the back of the manor.

The reverend sat next to me, with Lucinda on his other side. Lucas moved one of the chairs as far from the podium as possible and planted himself in it. I could see him from out of the corner of my eye. His scowl was even deeper, and he hadn't yet removed his coat. After helping his wife to sit, Mr. Wentham stood right next to the podium.

Jonah leaned his cane against the table and balanced his slim weight upon the podium, gripping it so as not to fall over. His skinny fingers were shockingly pale against the dark wood. Wreathed by black hair, his whitened face resembled a ghost peering out from the bookcases. Mr. Wentham leaned over and smoothed the crinkled edges of the will. He looked as smug as a predator. How could he not feel satisfied, when he'd written his own future into a legal document?

Jonah chuckled. "Your assistance is much appreciated, Nicholas. It is a good thing Reverend Gravitch has come, should I be forced to utter my last rites."

Why did it seem as if we were already at his funeral? All assembled, listening not to a will reading, but to his eulogy.

"Well," Jonah continued, "let me say before I begin, that this is normally done after I am deceased. However, Miss Tate has voiced her decision to depart on Friday, so this shall be carried out before that time. Her part to play in the proceedings will be revealed in a moment."

Lucinda glanced at me, then just as quickly looked to her husband.

His expression did not alter, nor did I expect it to. Even if I was to inherit, it would be a mere forty-eight hour celebration before my impoverished situation forced me to hand Mr. Wentham the manor's keys. Any part I played in these proceedings would all come to naught, anyway.

"It is my will to now read the will." Jonah laughed at his own joke. "My Last Will and Testament. Of course, it is also the last will of the Herricks. Some of you may believe that, unlike Captain Tate, I did not name a successor. However, you are mistaken. The heir is named in this document."

Before he began, I took stock of those in the room. Besides Mr. Wentham, who amongst us could afford that fifty thousand dollar fee? No one, as far as I knew.

"With all witnesses present, I now read to you my final wishes." As Jonah leaned over, his arms trembled. Oh, he was so gravely ill. "I, Jonah Herrick, of Fogbound Manor, Herrick Island, Maine, of sound and disposing mind, memory, and understanding, do give and bequeath my entire estate, the whole of the geography of Herrick Island, and all property within its boundaries to Miss Harriet Tate of Kennebunkport, Maine."

"One moment!" Mr. Wentham immediately gripped Jonah's shoulder, nearly causing him to collapse to the floor, and pointed an accusing finger at me. "Miss Tate has made her opinion about this matter adequately clear, Jonah. She neither wants nor needs Fogbound Manor."

I sat riveted to my chair, unable to comprehend what Jonah was doing. Could his sickness have finally eclipsed his sanity? There was no way on God's green earth I could afford to become Fogbound Manor's heir. How cruel to dangle such a prize before me, when it would never be mine.

"Jonah?"

My plea was unheard, for Lucinda Wentham caught his attention first. She'd clamored to her feet and in two seconds was up at the table by his side. She snatched the will off the podium, scanning it like a hawk. Lucas slouched even further in his seat, rolling his eyes at the ridiculous carnival display of behavior. I leaned towards him. He had to know I was as surprised as everyone else.

"Lucas, this is not of my doing."

He propped his chin on his hands, glancing sideways at me. "Not of mine, either. Good luck with your manor."

"It won't be mine for long, not if Mr. Wentham is correct about its assessed value."

"Of course I am correct," Mr. Wentham snapped.

He finally let go of Jonah, only to console his wife. Lucinda was not taking this news well at all, and had abruptly begun to weep. What an actress, I thought. That half a million dollar fortune slipped away from her. With Jonah's impending death and how the Herrick brothers victimized Lucas - none of it meant anything to her. I couldn't be more grateful I'd taken Lucas's advice and not bequeathed the manor to her. Weary of the bickering and ready to end it, I jumped to my feet.

"Jonah!" Good thing I now had his attention. "Will you kindly enlighten us all as to the reason why you have named me?"

Reverend Gravitch broke his own silence as well. "Yes, Jonah. I would dearly like to know."

The master was the only one in the room who hadn't uttered a thing. He took up his cane and pushed past Mr. Wentham, then shakily made his way towards me. Click, step. Click, step. Pity filled my heart. Yes, pity, for how doggedly he clung to life.

"Tut, tut, Miss Tate," Jonah said. "I can't have you looking at me like that. Hold your compassion for the moment, if you would."

I pressed my lips together. Why now, after so many days spent infuriated with him, did I feel such tenderness? Jonah half-turned and gestured towards Mr. Wentham with his cane.

"No doubt Mr. Wentham has informed you there is also a brand-new amendment, just recently added to my will?"

"He did," I said.

Jonah smiled. "Then I have done nothing to vex you. Assuming you are not able to provide the ten percent in legal fees within forty-eight hours after my death, then the property automatically passes to Mr. Wentham."

"I do not foresee I can provide such an amount," I said tersely. "It is beyond my means."

Lucinda daubed her eyes with a handkerchief, her mood improving considerably. "Then, if my husband is to receive the property after all, why not simply name him as the heir?"

"Why indeed?" Jonah muttered. "Mrs. Wentham, it has been made plain to me that neither you nor your husband see my manor for what it is. I trust that Harriet does, and so she would be more than able to carry out my final wishes."

"What are you talking about?" Mr. Wentham said irritably. I couldn't imagine why he was so peeved when he was due to inherit such a massive fortune.

As an answer, Jonah took up his cane once more and shuffled his way over to Lucas. The younger of the Penley siblings barely regarded him, preferring instead to stare straight ahead, his chin jutted and fingers gripping the arm of the chair. Jonah paused before him, leaning down so I had to strain to catch what he said.

"I don't suspect it will be even forty-eight hours after my funeral that you will be gone from this place forever. I can only imagine how you must feel towards me, for what I have done to you."

Lucas scoffed. "Just try. I encourage you."

"I encourage you to blame me, Lucas. It was my doing. Elijah is gone, so I cannot speak for his conduct. But my own was deplorable. It took my worsening illness and Harriet's reprimanding for me to at last see the error of my ways. I have no right to ask for your forgiveness, and once you'd rejected the inheritance, I knew you never would."

Lucas tightened his grip on the chair, his chin wavering. How many times had he been dragged to that chimney in the woods? How many times had the Herrick brothers beat him with chains and bricks, his screams echoing through the dense forest ... I could picture that awful place as if we'd all been transported there. I couldn't tell if Jonah's apology was sincere, and Lucas couldn't fully trust him, either. Jonah took a deep breath.

"My father was a man of unspeakable cruelty. He does not deserve to be remembered, and I am ready to let his lineage perish. The name of Herrick shall be erased from this island. I deeply desire this, Harriet, and

I know you will do it for me."

Jonah Herrick to be no more? Fogbound Manor and Herrick Island would be renamed, and it would all vanish into the haze of time.

"I will," I said. "Let everyone here know that it shall be done."

"Well, Jonah," Mr. Wentham said. "Do you not think I could rename Fogbound Manor? Or my wife? We are perfectly capable of calling it Wentham Manor and renaming it Wentham Island. I can sign my name to the deed tonight."

"Ah! I am glad you have mentioned the deed, good sir." Jonah limped back to the podium and retrieved a second document beneath the will. "Miss Tate, if you would kindly come forward and accept your inheritance."

Trembling, I approached Jonah and Mr. Wentham at the podium. This is how events should have transpired at my own home. What an odd set of circumstances for it to happen here, at Fogbound Manor of all places! A formal-looking piece of parchment sat before us, with an inkwell and feather pen beside it. Mr. Wentham gripped his wife's hands. Her tears had turned to grim anger, and she glowered at me. Jonah began reading the deed of sale.

"This real estate deed for the property of Herrick Island, including Fogbound Manor and all buildings under its jurisdiction, is executed on the 7th of March, 1855, by the Grantor, Mr. Jonah Herrick, to the Grantee, Miss Harriet Tate. In witness thereof, the said Grantor has signed in the presence of Miss Harriet Tate, as Grantee." He paused. "Mr. Lucas Penley, will you please come up and add your name to the deed as witness?"

Jonah dipped the pen and scratched his name on the Grantor line. He handed it to me with a wink. I gladly took it and, with them all standing by me, signed my name to the deed. Within two minutes, I'd become heiress and owner to an entire island and huge manor worth five hundred thousand dollars. I had only days to enjoy what had become legally mine, before I must turn it all over to Mr. Wentham. Lucas also added his name to the deed.

"Congratulations, Harriet."

He bid us all a good day and excused himself to return to the stables. Reverend Gravitch also got to his feet.

"Well, this has caused quite the excitement this morning, Jonah. I do hope it hasn't been too injurious to your health."

"Of course not." Jonah smiled at me. "Now that I am no longer the owner of Fogbound Manor, I shall sleep well knowing a Tate has my best interest in mind."

Blush crept up to my cheeks. Lucinda narrowed her eyes at me. Did she still think I'd turn right around and give her the manor? Even if her husband added a dozen damning amendments, I would do anything possible to keep that from occurring.

"Oh, and Reverend Gravitch," Jonah continued, "might you be so kind as to escort the Wenthams back to their lodgings? I'm attending Sunday's service, so will see you at that time."

"My pleasure. A good day to you, Miss Tate. I hope you have an easy journey on your return home." The reverend shook Jonah's hand. "You made an excellent choice, Jonah."

"Thank you, Reverend Gravitch."

"Come along, Mr. and Mrs. Wentham." The reverend gestured to his two guests, then walked from the library.

But the Wenthams were not quite ready to depart. Lucinda had not endeared herself to me at all, and her husband was merely a smarter version of my money-hungry cousin. What power could he hope to wield over me or Jonah or any other standing in his way? I no more feared him than a shrew. Jonah had also anticipated his anger.

"A good afternoon to you, Nicholas." His words were pleasant, but his tone was threatening. "Did you not understand you are no longer welcome here? After I am resting with the angels, I shall not be around to remove you from this house."

"But she will be." Mr. Wentham pointed to me. "A shame on you and your family, Jonah Herrick. Allowing yourself to be misled by your heart's affections towards manipulation by this undeserving woman."

Bristling at his tone, I took a step closer towards Jonah. If I was to make a mortal enemy of Mr. Wentham, so be it. I'd rather burn my bridges than endure with flimsy foundations built of deceit and loathing.

"You are quite bold in your accusations, sir," I said coldly. "Perhaps you do not yet realize that I will do everything in my power to evict you from my island."

"My, my," Jonah said. "If only I'd live long enough to see that downfall. I envy you, Harriet."

Mr. Wentham laughed out loud. "Jonah, you will be dead soon, and Miss Tate can't afford the fees to the property you have bequeathed her. Have you forgotten she is now poor? Fogbound Manor will be mine in a matter of days. May that comfort you in your eternal rest."

"Oh, Jonah! You disgust me," Lucinda added spitefully. "I will not mourn you or your name after you are gone!"

She grabbed fistfuls of her skirts, stamped her foot, and marched to the doorway. Her husband was all too pleased to follow suit. Like a pair of self-righteous royals, they linked arm and arm and headed out of the library. What a pompous show. Jonah chuckled.

"You didn't think this old desolate rock could contain such entertaining characters, did you Harriet?"

"Quite entertaining." I paused. "But Mr. Wentham is right. I cannot afford a ten percent legal fee. The inheritance will not be mine to enjoy for long."

"Ah, Harriet. Always worried about the future, when the time to enjoy your life is now."

He reached into his waistcoat and took out his little pocket-watch. He hadn't wound it, and both its hands pointed towards the twelve.

"There is one more thing I'd like you to do. After my father died, I removed every clock and watch in this manor. Once I am gone, you may bring these timepieces back into your new home. Take this, as well."

I held out my hands, and he placed the little watch in my cupped palms. His fingers were warm and his touch felt soothing.

"I have left you everything," he said simply. "You no longer have to return to Kennebunkport to marry. This manor is your wealth, now. I am the one who can give you what your father could not - a legacy in your own name."

"My father ..." I echoed. I closed my fingers around the watch, obscuring the little clock face from view. "Every day that I have been here has been spent thinking about him. He's haunting me, and I wish nothing more than to be let alone."

"You see?" he whispered softly. "How being the last of your family has burdened you? Let me ease it."

"I can never be unburdened. Not like you."

"What in God's name makes us so damn different?"

"Jonah, you were a son!"

He looked startled at my abrupt tone, and for the briefest moment I regretted what I'd said, but my utterance had been like the unleashing of the tide that, once begun, could not be stopped.

"A son," I repeated, my voice breaking. "Father was angry with me. He was angry I would not marry and my prospects were dwindling. He was angry I had spent so much time at the shipping office. He saw no merit in my hard work or my efforts. He saw me only as the sons he'd buried."

That was the legacy I could never fulfill. I could not be the next Captain Tate, and he hated me for it.

"You see, Jonah? Whatever sins you committed, at least you were a gentleman. What claim did I have in my Father's life - to his fortunes or his affections? Oh, I learned to be the son he wanted, but it would never be good enough."

I left Jonah's side, my face in hands. My future was set upon me when I first drew breath, and there wasn't anything I could do about it. I could not escape my legacy, no matter what inheritance was given to me.

"You know, Harriet," Jonah said softly, "it was honorable of your father to take care of you in such a manner. Though you may disagree with his methods, he wasn't weak like my father."

"Honorable," I repeated, slowly. To say I disagreed with him was a vast understatement. I couldn't believe he had used such a word to describe my father. "Jonah, he left. He always left. To call that honorable is horrifically inaccurate."

"But he was successful. Surely you see honor in that."

"I see responsibility," I contradicted, "but not honor. It is not honorable to leave your family behind for years at a time so you can control your tiny, insignificant world upon your ship."

"You never had the pleasure of meeting my father," Jonah said. "You would have gladly traded his cruel presence for his honorable absence."

"What trade is there in that?" I demanded. "Is it so difficult for a man to be both present and responsible towards his family? I stayed with my mother, and she died when he was away at sea. I stayed with my grandmother, even through her frequent illnesses. I stayed, and he always left. If there is honor in that, I wish to never meet an honorable man again."

Jonah was silent for several moments. I felt strange and unsettled, my words hanging in the air between us like matte fog. What was the point? It wasn't going to change anything. It wasn't going to repair the feelings between Father and myself. It wasn't going to reverse the storm that smashed the *Phoenix*. Mr. Wentham would still get the manor, and I was still going to return home to file bankruptcy. It wasn't going to change anything.

Jonah took a deep breath and exhaled, his chest sinking beneath his waistcoat. He looked so weak today, his thin arms pale bones inside his jacket, his body wasting away. We should not argue, we should not quarrel. How inefficient to spend his final days engaged in conflict.

"Well, Harriet," he said, "you can rest assured I'll stay. I am bound to this island, and I shall never set foot off it again. You are leaving. Call that what you will."

He took up his cane and walked past me, thumping out of the library and down the hall. I did want to leave. I didn't know how I felt about him and the manor and my father and everything here.

I only knew I had to say good-bye to it all.

twenty-four

✳

Even the ghosts in the fog let me be after a day of such emotional turmoil, and I found my spirits much renewed the following morning. The weather also cooperated, for it was quite light out and spring-scented breezes wafted past the manor. I went to the windows and pushed them open. Dawning of a new era, indeed.

It was my final full day on Herrick Island, and I had awakened as mistress of this manor. For years, I'd desired to become owner of my home and company. Who would have predicted Jonah Herrick would be the one to offer me such a future?

A legacy in my own name.

I slowly walked about my bedchamber, remembering all the nights I'd fretted. I touched the upholstery on the chairs, the soft wool blanket, the old furniture. Each item of decoration seemed transformed before my eyes. I'd told Jonah I could hardly call Fogbound Manor a nest, but that was before it was mine.

Now, I felt so differently about it that I could scarce believe it. Passing by the mirror, I couldn't help but observe my features. Yes, I looked the same. But how much had changed!

I couldn't bear to hand it all over to Mr. Wentham. It stiffened my spine and set my jaw merely to think of it. There must be some way to retain my holdings. I had to see Jonah about it at once.

I hurriedly dressed and slipped downstairs to the second floor. When I spied that warming golden glow beneath the map room door, I paused in the hallway, feeling nervous. What caused my footsteps to halt and my heart to beat faster? Certainly not the prospect of being with Jonah again. I cleared my throat, reached up, and knocked on the door.

"Enter," sounded the command from within, hurried and distracted.

The moment I opened the door, Fogbound Manor's former master began issuing orders.

"Set the tea tray down and depart quickly, madam, for I am not to be disturbed the remainder of the morning. Do let your lower help know of this."

I closed the door behind me. He assumed me to be Mrs. Quinn and did not raise his gaze from the map table to ascertain whether I was or not. My presence wasn't expected at all. I marched right up to the wide circular table and leaned upon it, balancing my weight on my palms and peering as intently at the map as Jonah.

"What are you looking at?" I asked.

Jonah jumped. "Good God, woman!" he cried. "What, you wish to usher me even earlier into my grave? My word!"

"I take it my arrival is unexpected."

He took out a handkerchief and dramatically wiped his brow. "That, my dear, is about the truest thing you have ever uttered. What wonderful creatures women are. Keeping us gentlemen on our toes with their changeable minds."

I smiled. "What makes my mind so changeable?"

"Have the past seventy-two hours entirely departed from your memories? I disappointed you with the lack of treasure found on the island, then I unwittingly bequeathed to you a manor you don't want, and then I brought up painful recollections of your father. I could name at least twenty other sins of character I've committed, if you'd like me to go on."

"No, no." What fun delight I took in listening to him relay his faults to me. "I can recollect more on my own, I assure you."

He tucked his handkerchief away in his pocket. "You seem, madam, in better spirits than yesterday. I take it your inheritance pleases you?"

"Only so long as I can claim it, Jonah. That is why I have sought your company again today. I must find some way to retain ownership."

"Ah, I see." He leaned against the map table, folding his arms over his skinny chest. "So, it is not the actual monetary value of this manor that appeases you, but the mere fact that you can own it. I suspected you would feel that way. It's gratifying to know I was correct!"

"How astute," I remarked. "Now you can rest assured that Tates are not as financially motivated as you thought we were."

"It seems that is rather a Wentham trait." He snickered. "As well as a Scully one, I presume?"

"Yes, indeed. Cousin Francis will enjoy my triumphant return as the mistress of Fogbound Manor. He'll immediately give himself a raise in salary."

"You can deny him every penny, if you wish. I made sure to include a clause in the will that any monies contained in the sale of the manor belong exclusively to its owner."

"Its owner." I smiled ruefully. "Tell me, Jonah, how you are so confident that I can retain ownership, when I can't pay Mr. Wentham's legal fees?"

He shrugged. "You're the smartest woman I have ever met. I am sure you can come up with a solution."

"Intelligence does not always equal financial success." I noticed the little sack of golden coins still sat upon the map table. "I can take back this small fortune to Kennebunkport."

"That is to be used to help the widows," Jonah reminded me. "Or, so you said."

"Indeed, I did."

We fell into silence. He cocked his head at me, observing my reaction to all of this. How could I feel so fortunate and yet so unlucky at the same time? To own this manor without having the chance to keep it?

"You are returning tomorrow, then?"

I wished he hadn't asked.

"I am, Jonah. Yet, I must ask you something." I took a step closer to him. "Do you want me to sell your home?"

"It is not mine any longer. That question is for you to answer."

I folded my arms across my chest. "If I sell it, then I will have more than enough money to save my shipping company and my house. But I will never have the ability to own property again. I will also lose ..."

My voice trailed off. I couldn't imagine not having him here any longer, as a part of this island. Could I forsake all that had happened?

I took a deep breath. "I will also lose this home. A home you have given me. It is a difficult choice to make."

He moved towards me and put his thin fingers on mine. "I think you have already made your choice, Harriet. And it is the right one. Your name is on your shipping company. Your family legacy will live on."

I bit my lip, my throat full. Fogbound Manor's isolating and oceanic beauty played such a dreamlike lullabye, dulling my senses. I wished I could stay within this map room all my days, with Jonah beside me, seeking treasure. But what kind of reality would that be? I'd find nothing but barren sand, Jonah would still leave me, and the dream would end. He faced it with more courage than I felt. Yes, I had already made my choice. It was only a matter of summoning the strength to face the consequences. Tears filled my eyes.

"Mr. Wentham will take the manor, Jonah. I wish I could keep it."

"Do you, now?" he whispered. "Even if you did have the money, would you still choose to stay? Or would you sell it to save your company?"

"I don't know, Jonah."

He intertwined his fingers with mine and brought my hand to his lips. As he kissed my skin, I stilled my body and allowed myself to feel the gentleness and tenderness of his touch. Oh, there was indeed more warmth here than I'd first discovered. Like so many things of greatness, it was secretly hidden. I'd at last found it, and I turned my face towards its rays. He drew me closer to him, sliding his warm hands up my arms until he'd clasped my shoulders. He bent his face, catching my sorrowful gaze.

"Come with me. I want to show you something."

He reached for his cane, pushed open the door, and, still holding my hand, led me slowly down the hall until we'd reached the main staircase. He bid me to come down, and I followed in daze, my tears silently dropping like rain down my cheeks. We turned the corner at the landing and walked down to the entrance hall. Pausing at the front doors, he gently reached up and wiped my tears with his palm, then handed me my cloak. I didn't question and dressed to go out without saying a word. I couldn't take my eyes off of him for a moment. I drank in the sight of him, as one who would leave tomorrow and never see him again. My feelings for him engulfed me, and I was helpless in the face of their tidal power. I closed my eyes and let it sweep me along. Where we were going, I did not know. I only wanted to follow him.

Jonah opened the door, and we slipped outside onto the front stoop. As he shut the door behind us, I breathed deeply. Fogbound Manor bathed in its perpetual mist. A light spring scent danced on the fog, like an airier cloud. Jonah and I descended the steps down to the carriageway. He again took my hand, which I willingly offered to him, and we walked through the earth-scented fog past the stables and over to the rock crevice. He was leading me back to the little beach cove.

We stepped through the rock crevice and walked down to the water together. The light colored the rocks a pale, pearly gray, and the wind was gentle, almost playful. I inhaled the salty, refreshing air, listening to the waves slosh against the shore. The Atlantic appeared as the same foreboding, undulating mass, its color a little less gray and more blue to reflect the sky.

Jonah stuck his cane into the sand, making little holes as we slowly strolled along the shoreline. We walked parallel to the waves, moving from the rock cave towards the opposite end of the beach. I enjoyed our shared silence, each bundled up in wool against the cold, our shoulders pressed together, hands clasped.

When we reached the far left-hand side of the beach, Jonah showed me a small path winding up through the rocks. He planted his cane between little pebbles and hoisted himself up. As I followed him, I gripped handfuls of dried sturdy dune grass to steady myself. He stopped about ten feet above the ocean's surface and walked out on a large loaf-shaped rock that jutted out towards the waters. Its wide flat surface could have easily fit a parked carriage. This perch afforded a perfect balcony over the sea, as if we were theatregoers observing a play. The wind blew out the length of Jonah's scarf, the fringe dancing. He peered over the edge of the rock, staring down into the swirling waters below.

"Look down there. I wanted to show you a new place to search for treasure."

He half-turned to look at me. Pale spring light illuminated his skin, as white as the sea foam.

"I was only joking," he said with a smirk. "To lighten the mood, as it were."

He addressed me as if I was the same woman who had arrived at Fogbound Manor so many nights ago. Were my feelings not plain, as if I projected my own soul through my eyes and skin? It couldn't be more obvious, and I smiled at his boyish ignorance.

"Yes, let us get started. Have you brought the shovels?"

His brow wrinkled in confusion. "You mock me, it appears. I should be used to such treatment, for I am all too adept at being the mocker."

"No, Jonah," I said, and my husky tone made him stare at me. "I do not mock you. I bear you no more strife."

My mind eased, and my words vanished from my thoughts. Morning fog had burned away, and I could see all of him in the clear, slanted light. I stepped even closer, a breeze slipping between us.

"Thank you for bequeathing me the manor. I have made my decision."

"Oh? Then, let's hear it."

"I shall sell my company and my home. I can make enough profit to afford the legal fee, so look for me to return to pay Mr. Wentham. I do not have a lot of time, but I will do what I can to save the manor."

He bit his lip, looking down at the quartz veins in the rock beneath his feet. "And this is how you want to treat what your family has built? You will regret it, Harriet."

"I will regret leaving Fogbound Manor more."

"You say this only to cheer me on our last day together." He finally met my eyes, his hair blowing about his face. "Your presence has made my final days on this earth more dear to me than all the years before it. But I cannot let you give up what means so much to you."

I had to say it. It was my last time to tell him.

"You mean that much to me, Jonah. This is what I want."

I stepped up to him, closing the windy gap between us. His arm slid about my waist in a strong, tender grip, pulling me towards him until we were waistcoat to bodice in an enfolded embrace. He pressed against me with such fervor I lost my breath. His chest was so thin, his body light and warm. I was surprised he was more robust in physical form than he appeared, and it felt strengthening. I gradually found my breath again, and it curled in my body in such a soft way I couldn't help surrendering. As the waters covered the sand, so he covered me.

"Yes," he whispered tenderly in my ear. "None other knows you like I do. What ordinary man would?"

Crushed against him, I could not feel any less whole. I nestled against his thick wool coat, completely safe and sound.

"Jonah," I whispered.

He swept his arm up, his fingertips brushing against the bare skin of my neck. He kissed my skin where he could, his breath gliding along my body. Then he kissed me, and I disappeared inside his love. He was marking me as his, pressing me with his own insignia like a poker brand. Heat seized me, made me want to receive his full passion in return, so we could match energies and blaze life into this cold, isolated island.

At last, I pulled back from him. My arms still locked about his warmth, my eyes closed so as to enjoy every touch from him. He rested his chin on my shoulder and held me. I inhaled and breathed out, a long full breath that filled me with a sense of contentment I thought I could never feel. I ... I was happy here, with him.

"Harriet?" he said softly. "Look at me."

I lifted my face and slowly opened my eyes. His were dark, trimmed with such thick lashes. He traced his finger down my cheek.

"I am in a perpetual waiting," he confessed. "You'd gladly wait for me to recover and I can see in your eyes that you long for it. But Harriet, we are living in the waiting. Life in the waiting before death can be a better kind of living than any other." His fingers slipped beneath my chin. "Can it not?"

I didn't know how to answer, or even if the hard, agonizing lump in my throat would let me speak. I had to leave, so what else could I do but live in the now? His coming death pained me. But I still struggled to create, in the waiting, a happiness we could both gain pleasure from.

"Then," I whispered, "let me wait here with you."

My arm was around his neck and I sank into his sickly, warm embrace. His kiss swept me from my own senses and created a barrier against our common enemy of time.

Let me shun the clock. Let me love him, and live in the waiting.

* * *

As Jonah and I made our way back up the beach together, the fading light revealed an approaching cloudbank dark and heavy on the horizon - another of Herrick's Island storms about to visit us. My right hand was clasped in Jonah's, and he crested the top of the beach with me. One would think my love to be a healthy man, though he had to borrowed my strength for he claimed none of his own. Walking beside Jonah felt like a rightful home. He had often shown me exaggerated affection, but now, assured of mine in return, he could showcase it in its most blossomed form. When he asked me to dine with him, I acquiesced with a kiss upon his hand.

"I admit to being a man not easily surprised," he said with a laugh. "Yet I do believe none other than the lovely Harriet Tate has the power to shock me."

"You will be more surprised when you hear of my new name for Fogbound Manor." By now, we had returned to the carriageway, and I stopped just at the foot of the front steps. I broke from him and looked up at the huge mansion rising above us. "Welcome to the Tate Manor."

He leaned heavily on his cane and coughed. "Harriet, I do believe it's a good name. You'll enjoy it."

"Are you all right?" I asked.

He held his hand to his dry lips and coughed again. "I think it best that we get inside, my dear."

I immediately shouldered his weight with my body and helped him up the stairs into the manor. Mr. Stokes was just inside the door and took hold of Jonah's arm to steady him.

"I'll ... join ... you for dinner tonight, Harriet," Jonah wheezed.

I shook my head. "That will not be happening. Mr. Stokes, please take him to bed, and tell the cook to make up a beef tea tonic."

The butler nodded. "Yes, miss."

Jonah coughed again, then smiled. "Isn't she a right good mistress of this old place? Giving orders as if she's always done so."

"Hopefully, it eases your mind," I said quietly. "Rest yourself now, Jonah."

He kissed my hand one last time, his lips cold. Then his faithful servant helped him up the main staircase. Once they'd both turned the landing and were out of sight, my chin quavered and I began to weep again.

"Everything will be all right," I whispered to myself. "You'll sell your home and be back here before ..."

No, I couldn't. I'd return far too late to see him again. It would take more than a week, and I'd receive a note from Mr. Wentham gloating about his new property. I'd be forced to hand over my inheritance and sever all ties with the manor – and Jonah – forever.

I could bear facing such a bleak future if I wasn't so in love.

twenty-five

✴

Dark clouds approached the island, their charcoal gray underbellies heavy with rain about to fall. A storm was coming.

Mrs. Quinn herself delivered my breakfast tray, and she also had a singular request from her invalid master. Bed-ridden and ill, he wanted to wish me a good journey, but I was not to see him before I left.

"Why ever not?" I demanded. "You will tell me where his chambers are, Mrs. Quinn."

She wiped her hands on her dirty apron. "Whose orders am I a-following now, missy?"

"Mine, madam. I am the owner of Fogbound Manor."

She stared at me, one hard-eyed gaze. But I was easily six inches taller than her and used my full height to my advantage.

"My carpet-bag is packed for today's journey, so please have it taken down to the entrance hall. Then I ask that you take me to Mr. Herrick's room at once."

At last, she broke eye contact and stepped from the doorway. I understood that she wanted me to follow her, so I grabbed a shawl and hurried down the dark passages. Mrs. Quinn's little chamberstick made barely a dent in the foggy gloom as we made our way through Fogbound

Manor's upper hallways. What made him think after our time together yesterday that I could possibly depart without a farewell?

Mrs. Quinn abruptly stopped right in the middle of a hallway and pointed her crooked finger.

"Keep goin'. Last room at the end."

"Thank you," I quipped and brushed past her.

Once Mrs. Quinn's candlelight had disappeared, I was in near darkness. Pattering rain on the roof caused me to frown, for it meant my trip to the dock would be less than pleasant. I continued down the hall, passing intermittent doors and blackened chimney lamps on rickety ancient hall tables. At last, I came to the end and passed underneath a large archway into the master bedchamber.

The room's size was massive, rivaling the enormous parlor downstairs, yet its furnishings were so simple and plain that it resembled a monastery. A stark black iron bed with a scattering of white bed linens, several chests of drawers, some chairs, and a couple of plain round tea tables were all the furnishings. Was this truly Jonah's room? It was so unlike him in exacting detail and sparseness. He was wrapped in blankets in a high-backed chair by a weak hearth fire. A poker lay across his lap, and the orange cat curled on his legs.

"Do you never simply obey orders?" Jonah asked. "I specifically told Mrs. Quinn to have you leave at once."

"Jonah." I took a step closer, trying not to openly weep. His cheeks were so sunken, his hair thinned. "You send me away, after what we shared on the beach?"

"I can't have you see me like this." He tucked his chin towards his thin chest and coughed. "I gave you what I could, Harriet."

"And if I stay?"

He slowly shook his head, coughing again. "If you do not have the money to pay Mr. Wentham after my death, then everything you worked for will be lost. I trust you, my dear. Now, you must go."

I picked up the cat and set him on the floor, then gathered my dress and sank to my knees. I took Jonah's hands within my own and kissed them like he had kissed mine. I curled my fingers around his thin wrists.

We stayed locked together for as long as I could. I listened to his labored breathing and pressed my face against his sunken cheeks. My feelings broke and washed over the shoreline within me, and I gladly let it happen.

He slipped his fingers beneath my chin and lifted my face. "When you first arrived, I felt condemned to desire a lady as cold and mechanical as a clock. I thought that if I were to open the door to your body, I'd find metal parts therein. But as I grew to know you, I realized it was not coldness but grief and regret. Once I knew that all you wanted in life was to be recognized for how intelligent you are, then it was easy to turn you from a clock back into a woman."

I wiped the tears on my cheeks, smiling sadly. "I wish I could say that others in my life have been so understanding. But it's enough simply to know that you are."

"I know you, my dear. To be a woman of your intellectual capacity is as rare a thing as can be imagined. Like a treasure, it is not an ordinary gift meant for the ordinary person." His voice dropped. "Your mind enhances your other womanly qualities to their utmost, like shading adds depth to a painting. I'd not care for you so deeply if you were not so brilliant."

My mind, of which he had so highly spoken of, suddenly became as blank as a gray sky. I had been perched on a crowded precipice, waiting for another to recognize me for who I was. Not what anyone else wished me to be, not conforming to any preconceived definition of how I should be or aspired to be. No, this man, as singular and maddening and amazing as he was -

This man saw me for me ... and loved me for it.

"Beseech me to remain here with you, as your companion."

"Dearest Harriet. What you gave me here at Fogbound Manor was the greatest single adventure of my life. It was not common. It was not ordinary. It was not meant for souls that are so greatly unlike yours and mine that even if they could comprehend what we have they wouldn't deserve to feel it." He bent closer, his forehead pressed against mine. "I only want to help you realize how extraordinary you really are."

He kissed my forehead, and I forced myself to rise to my feet. We gripped hands for as long as I dared, then I lay his thin fingers on his lap. He rested his face against the curve of the chair and beheld me.

"Farewell, Jonah."

Remember me this way. May our shared love be a beacon through the fog of absence that we both must face. I will carry your memory with me, as a candle to light dark passages.

Like skin, the mundane had been shed, and I emerged from his chambers feeling whole and complete. I draped my shawl about my shoulders and picked my way down the passage back to the map room on the second floor. There was one more item I must take with me.

The map room was dark, not a single lamp lit. Gray light filtered through the room like smoked fog. Hazy, diffuse, shadows intermingled and blended. The map table was cleared of all items except for the map of Herrick Island and the sack of gold coins.

I went to the map table and drew the sack towards me. I untied its strings and lifted up a cold coin. I told you, Jonah, that I wouldn't forget the money bequeathed to me. It is the only monetary legacy I have received, but it means more than a pirate's ship of gold.

The hours are soon here when Jonah would be gone. No longer his voice in my ear, his footstep upon the threshold. It's as if his absence was already with me, courting me like a lover.

When I pressed the coin to my lips, my breath warmed the polished gold. My lips he kissed, my soul he joined. I occupied our love fully, like a garment stitched and tailored only for us. He could not help but adore me the rest of his days, but know this –

I will love him the rest of mine.

With the gold coins cradled in my arms, I slowly went downstairs to the entrance hall, then began dressing in my cloak and bonnet. Mr. Stokes picked up my carpet-bag.

"A good luck to you, Miss Tate," he said. "So's you know, I'll be watchin' over Master Herrick."

"Thank you, Mr. Stokes." My breath blended with the gloomy fog in the hall. "Let Reverend Gravitch know that he might not make it to the service this Sunday."

"Yes, miss."

"Look for me to return on the next mail boat. I shall be back in a week's time."

"Good-bye, miss."

I turned to Mr. Stokes and took my carpet-bag, the sack of coins nestled under my other arm. He turned and shuffled off into the darkness of the manor. I wished I could stay. For days, I'd been anxiously awaiting Friday morning to leave. Now that it was here, I'd rather stand in the face of the ticking clock and push its hands back.

Give me more time. Just a little more time.

Lucas drove the carriage up to the front of the manor, then climbed down in the rain. His boots thudded in the carriageway. The front door abruptly swung open, and Lucas bustled in from the rain. It dripped off his coat and wetted the stones at his feet. His arrival was like the death knell for my presence at Fogbound Manor. I'd never see Jonah again. He'd die without me, and I'd return to this manor only to live as a victim of his haunted love the rest of my life.

Lucas took the carpet-bag from my fingers. "Coming?"

"I am."

I walked past him through the front doorway and stepped out of the manor, my throat so full, my heart so sorrowful. Good God, leaving felt like the most unnatural thing I could do. Jonah's love was enough to convince me I had to stay, but I wouldn't keep the manor.

I walked across the carriageway, striding through the rainy mist, and pulled open the carriage door myself. While Lucas stood behind me, I stepped up inside. He put my bag inside with me, then slammed the door. I was cocooned in the soft velvet seats, a small cool window to rest my hot forehead against. In a few short hours, I'd be upon that boat and off we'd sail.

Away from Jonah.

Lucas hiked himself up to the driver's seat. I held my forehead in my hands, and the fog obscured my tears from view. If only I had found that infernal treasure. Then I'd be able to give it to Mr. Wentham and return. All I had after seven days upon Herrick Island was ...

"His love," I whispered aloud.

Lucas slapped the reins, and the carriage jerked to life. I couldn't help but gaze upon Fogbound Manor one last time. I saw no master in the window, but I knew he was there. He'd be there long after his spirit departed his body. Watching from the glowing paned windows, occupying his favorite chair by the parlor fire, haunting the foggy beach.

Wheels clinked over the gravel, and we drove away. The fog now became my dear enemy, for it obscured the manor from view. The carriage climbed upon the rocky path, winding in and out of dark crags. Soft drizzle slipped down the windowpane like tears. I reached up and traced the pattern as it bent and twisted like a rivulet.

The carriage began to move a little faster. Above me, the sky was a darkening gray as ominous as the jagged rocks about me. I don't know why, but I began to grow fearful. I scooted to the end of the carriage seat to look out the other window, but a wet stony surface was all there was to be seen, as if I was riding in Neptune's carriage underwater. I tried to peer upwards, but the rain had whipped into a maelstrom and drops shot from the heavens like a firing squad.

Was it my imagination, or had Lucas sped up the horses yet again? We seemed to be moving even faster, the island spinning about us, churning us and forcing us to flee from its wrath.

Unexpectedly, the carriage began to lean precariously towards the left. My stomach dropped into a place of fear deep in my belly. I sat up straight, bracing my knees against the opposite seat and squeezing my body into the back of the carriage. A branch or a rock - I knew not which - smashed the carriage window where I had been sitting only moments before, and shards flew about the interior like glass birds. I cried out and held up my right arm to shield myself from injury.

When suddenly, the carriage tipped.

I barely had time to register what was going on before everything around me - the seats, the floor, the ceiling, the broken windows - tilted and spun. Up and over, up and over. My left arm smashed into the ceiling, and I shrieked in pain from the force of the impact. I tumbled like dice, slamming into the seats over and over. My body flung against the carriage wall, tinkling glass in my ear, a scream like a banshee howling above the rain. I flailed about with my right hand. Anything to grab, anything to hold onto! Yet my efforts were in vain, and all I could do was watch my battered body collide with the seats again.

No sooner had I gripped the torn fabric when the carriage abruptly stopped. The jolt tossed me onto the floor, where my face hit a hard, wet surface so jarringly I slumped on my swollen cheek.

Cold and shivering, I slipped into darkness.

twenty-six

✳

Drip drip. Drip drip.

A soft trickle leaked down onto my shoulder, wetting the wool of my dress. I groaned softly. Even this slight pressure caused a waving heave of pain to swell through me. I opened my eyes, and it took me a moment to gauge my surroundings. I was staring at intricate ridges sewn into the velvet fabric of the seat edge in front of me. I lay on my right side, placed neatly on the floor between the two carriage seats, like a corpse in a sideways coffin. I gingerly turned my neck, so my face was more or less tilted upwards. There was a long torn rent in the carriage roof, as if a giant snapped open the whole conveyance like a Christmas cracker. Rain slipped through this opening and pattered my skin.

Judging from the pain and the limp way it lay across my torso, my left arm was most likely broken. I still felt my fingertips and tapped my thigh slightly, but no other movement could occur without punches of nauseating pain. I was nearly sick from the intensity, so I closed my eyes and pressed my forehead into the edge of the carriage seat until it passed.

How could I rise, without the use of my arm? I must find some way to get up, for despite massive soreness and bruising, my other limbs were still in order. I might even find a way to return to Fogbound Manor.

God in heaven, Lucas! A bolt of sorrow more fierce than shoulder pain brought hot tears to my eyes. He must have been thrown from the carriage upon the rocks.

"Lucas!"

My hoarse whisper barely reached my own ears. The screaming in the rain must have been him.

There was another sound more powerful than my lungs could create - that of the mighty Atlantic. It crashed ceaselessly against the rocks outside the crumpled carriage. I could smell its pungent brine from here. A seagull cawed nearby, flapping its wings. We must have tumbled from the path down that steep embankment I could well remember from my first carriage ride last week.

A fresh wave of pain ravaged my bruised body, and I buried my face in the crook of my right arm. I don't know how long I lay there on the carriage floor. The dripping water from above, the soft rain falling through the rent in the roof, the seagulls with their oddly soothing cries, and the ever-present ocean lulled me into a weakened stupor.

When I at last awakened, I believed I still dozed and Lucas couldn't be real. The entire carriage tipped sideways from his weight, and there was a squealing, scraping noise as he yanked open the askew door. He crawled in on the velvet seat above me, dripping fresh droplets on my skirts, his face splotchy and reddened with cold. But his hands were warm, and when he placed gentle fingers on my broken arm, I couldn't help but cry out - and knew he was alive.

"Lucas," I murmured.

He reached up and loosened his cravat, then untwisted it from his neck and pressed it against the side of my face. Its soft cotton felt soothing against my skin. I felt all scraped up, raw, and bruised.

"It's all right." He glanced down at my arm. "Can you move it at all?"

I slowly shook my head, causing an aching nerve to speed down my chest.

"Only my fingers, a little. I believe it to be broken."

He pursed his lips, balancing his weight on the seats above me.

"No other pain elsewhere," I said. "I grant you permission to move me as best you see fit."

"I see." His brow crinkled a little as he winced.

I shifted my neck to see him better. A purplish stain, like a watercolor print, crept from his hairline down his cheek.

"How did you survive the fall?"

"Once I felt the carriage tip over, I got off as quickly as I could and held on. Knocked my head against the rock." He paused, his eyes as full of pain as I'd ever seen. "I watched you fall, Harriet. I couldn't imagine that you lived."

"I - I heard a scream," I whispered. "I thought ... "

He shook his head. "My horses."

"How terrible. I know how much you cared for them."

His expression was tender. Then, in one swift movement, he shifted his body weight so his foot was planted on the small section of the floor behind my bent knees. He knelt down until the entire length of his chest softly pressed upon my body. I'd never been so close to him before, and could breathe in his warm oceany scent. With one hand gripping a fistful of the carriage seat for balance, he slipped his other hand under me. His shoulder was a powerful pillow for me to rest against as he strained his back to lift me. I pushed myself up with my right arm to help him, and as soon as I got to a half-sitting position, was able to twist my knees and balance myself. My left arm dangled at an awkward angle. I squeezed my own hand against my chest, biting my lips against the pain.

"Now, I can help you up," he said.

He braced both feet on the part of the floor I had recently vacated, which provided more leverage for him to lift me up onto the carriage seat. I struggled with my legs and finally twisted my body into a sitting position. Gasping from the exertion, I leaned back against the seat and closed my eyes. A fearful groaning, scraping sound came from the tipped carriage. Lucas hauled himself up next to me and sat down heavily, his damp forehead against my shoulder, his breathing labored.

"Dear God," he murmured. "I fear I'll never get off this damned island."

"I am simply glad you're all right," I said. "I'll rest a bit, but then I must get to the dock, Lucas. It's imperative that I catch the mail boat."

He glanced down at my arm. "Let's just get you out of this carriage first."

"As soon as I can. We need to hurry."

"I know, Harriet," he snapped. He bit his lip. "Sorry. I have an idea your arm is broken."

I winced against the pain. "If it isn't, it certainly hurts as if it is."

He leaned down and picked up his fallen cravat. He untwisted it out to a long length of cotton and bade me to lift my broken arm. I used my right hand to gently grasp and lift, a movement that couldn't have caused more agony. I held the excruciating position while he wrapped the cotton about my shoulder and arm, creating a sling. I could at last relax my shoulder, reducing a great deal of suffering. Once the nausea had subsided, I inspected his primitive, though effective medical treatment. The cotton was wrapped and tied as neatly as could be.

"Thank you."

He wiped his brow and sat back upon the seat. "Fished on my uncle's boat at times awhile back. Handy skill, tying knots."

"It's well done."

I started to get up from the carriage seat, but all of a sudden the whole thing began to tip. Lucas stuck out his arm and prevented my weight from pitching forward.

"Lean back," he ordered.

I shifted my torso and pressed myself against the carriage seat. The pain in my arm combined with how nauseous I felt made me close to tears. Jonah, I am trying. I want to do what is right by you. I am trying to get out of here.

But the effort was too great, and I sat beside Lucas on the carriage seat for a long while. His breathing slowed, my arm felt much better, and we were able to take what comfort we could. Outside, the ocean's swirling tides and seagull caws reminded me so greatly of being back on the beach with Jonah yesterday I pretended I was there.

"Is there any chance the carriage will tip further, into the sea?" I asked quietly.

"Yes."

"How far are we from the dock?"

"Within a mile or two." He glanced at me. "But you are not well enough to make a three-day journey back to Kennebunkport."

"Lucas, I can't stay." I turned my face away from him, staring beyond the wet broken glass out through what remained of the scrunched carriage window. "Help me get out of here."

"I can, but then I'm taking you back to the manor."

"No."

"Harriet, you know the captain doesn't dock at Herrick Island for long. We are probably too late to catch the mail boat."

It was not my own mistake, but the clock that failed me. I slipped my shaking right hand inside my dress pocket.

Tick. Tick.

My watch had not stopped, but I wanted to throw it into the sea. I hated sitting here, in so much pain and with my own legacy slipping away from me. Maybe I'll just wait until one of Herrick Island's breezes sweeps me off the rocks and into the sea. Jonah would soon be with me, and we'd reunite in our oceanic heaven together.

Lucas pointed at the huge rent in the carriage roof. The gray sky had lightened a bit, and the raindrops were ceasing. The storm, so quickly a deluge, was passing.

"It'll be getting on dark soon. Are you well enough to stand?"

"I do not think so," I whispered, hating to admit my physical weakness.

He leaned forward, scrutinizing my broken arm.

"The doctor," he finally said. "He was due to arrive today, anyhow."

Through my pain, surprise seemed to awaken me. What were the chances the doctor was to arrive the same day as this accident? It was my best option for recovery, and I urged Lucas to leave while there was still some semblance of daylight.

"I should go back to the manor and tell Jonah to change his mind," he muttered. "There ain't no treasure, but I'd make a tidy profit, as you said. Sell its contents and pry its worthless rocks from the beach."

A cold shiver set my teeth to chattering, but it was not from the March weather.

"Well, I plan on evicting your sister permanently from my island. Perhaps I should do the same for you."

He leaned forward tensely, a hand on his pale bruised forehead, peering at me sideways.

"Oh, Harriet Tate thinks she knows. Just because she gets to become wealthy all over again. How 'bout I go to your mansion, huh? Rip the clapboards off your family's house? I bet it's a nice sea captain's home, filled with expensive things to pawn."

I licked my lips, a sour taste. "Obviously, you're not willing to accept Jonah's apology."

"You ain't said you're sorry, either."

"What have I done?" I demanded. "You asked me not to bequeath your sister the manor, and I won't. I should be thanking you, for you showed me her true character. Do you believe I should be sorry for wanting to own Fogbound Manor?"

"It's not about Fogbound Manor." He leaned forward and traced his hand down my cheek, like he had in the forest. "I wanted you to be with me."

I reached up and took his hand, then slowly moved his fingers away from my face. He stiffened, watching me warily, but even his tension couldn't mask how gently he touched me.

"You can still stay at Fogbound Manor," I whispered. "But I cannot give you what you want."

"You're going to return and marry Jonah now, aren't you?"

I jammed his hand into his lap. "I will never marry. Thank you for giving me the opportunity to tell you that. Neither will I ever share ownership of my home with anyone."

He shrugged. "Then there's nothing for me here."

The rain finally ceased. It was time for Lucas to go. He hunched his coat over his shoulders.

"Don't know when I'll return." He lifted the seat of the opposite bench and retrieved an old musty blanket. "Here."

I nodded my thanks, grateful for it to relieve the chill. Then he left my side, his warmth vanishing into the misty sea-scented air. I thought he might leave without saying anything, but he turned back.

"You're a strange woman, Harriet Tate. Ever since you set foot here, I've been trying to figure you. You come here for money to save your house, but you're willing to become mistress of Fogbound Manor. You care so much about what your father wanted, then you're ready to sell it all. Is that what it's like being a Tate?"

I gritted my teeth. "I have met so many like you, Lucas. You know not of what you speak. Ordinary people just don't understand."

"You could be a Herrick talking like that. Thinking status equals happiness. Well, you'll be back with your Jonah soon enough. All you wealthy people deserve each other. Someone like me don't understand your false problems."

Frowning, he alighted out of the carriage in one swift move. He was gone, back out into the rain, which mingled with the fog in a damp coverlet. His boots scraped the rocks above, and I could hear him climbing up the slope to the road. My arm ached, and I wanted to weep for Jonah.

He understood. He didn't treat me so degradingly. He knew me more clearly than I could know myself, and had reveled in my true personality.

I slipped sideways onto the seat, curled up beneath the warm old blanket. I tried not to think of the future I must now face, without the manor and without Jonah. I tried to remember what it was like to sit with him in the parlor, enjoying his conversation, but my thoughts were like a misty haze of pain and exhaustion.

I'd lost everything I ever cared about.

twenty-seven

"Harriet?"

A man's voice called to me through the melting fog, like sunlight chasing dew. Stiffness drenched my entire body. My voice, thin and whispery, could barely speak his name before I heard his boots on the rocks.

"Harriet!"

Lucas was here again. His body weight shifted the carriage, and he placed a warm hand on my blanketed thigh. He was no longer tender, but rough, fearful. I coughed, causing ribs to swell and stretch. I winced.

"I'm awake, Lucas. I'm all right."

"Good." Any previous display of kindness had vanished from his demeanor. "The doctor is up on the road. Let's get you out."

"What of my carpet-bag? And the coins?"

He glanced beyond me to the rest of the carriage. "I don't see them."

Cold air chilled me as he pulled the blanket from my shoulders. I was curled up on the seat, shivering, and his arms clasping me felt like iron clamps. I groaned from more than pain. All of my money was gone. I was completely penniless. The carriage creaked beneath his weight.

"It's not important, anyhow," he said. "You're going to hurt. But you must help me. Push yourself up."

What did he care about the importance of those coins? My jellied legs could barely move enough to kick a feather, so I do not know how I found the strength to support myself as Lucas tipped me onto my back and gently eased me out through the broken carriage door. After a few minutes of maneuvering, he managed to free himself and was fully out of the carriage. He wedged his boot in a rock crevice for stability, hooked his arms around my waist in the most uncouth way a man could, and pulled. Rolling waves of nausea gripped my empty stomach. To keep from collapsing, I clamped onto the bent doorframe.

"Let go," he panted.

"I'll fall."

"I can't pull if you're holding the carriage. Let go."

I closed my eyes and let go of the carriage. From somewhere underneath the vehicle, a piece snapped like kindling. Like a dying animal, the carriage slipped beneath me down the rocky slope, freeing me at the same time it plunged towards the waves below. My feet thunked onto the rocks, Lucas held me to keep me from falling, and we both watched the doomed carriage collapse into the sea. The ocean was pleased with its newest victim, and helped it sink beneath the briny foam.

Lucas breathed heavily in my ear, his arms still wrapped around me. The pressure of his body made my bruised and battered skin ache. He warmed me only slightly, for I'd developed a violent chill. My teeth chattered in my head. I felt myself curling over, slipping down into the sea like the carriage. While I struggled to stay conscious, Lucas kept me anchored towards him.

"Mr. Penley!" A foreign voice, crisp and commanding. "Bring her up here at once. I need to see to her."

"We must ... go," I grunted. "Even the wealthy need help at times, you know."

"Let's get you on your feet, then."

He helped me sit up straight, balancing myself on the weight of my backside. The rock's pocked surface positioned me on a slant. If a passerby should see me, I resembled a beachgoer enjoying an afternoon by the seaside. Lucas crouched beside me and helped me roll my weight onto my knees. I used my right arm to hold my broken one tightly clamped to my chest. Lucas supported me as he got to a standing position, all the while easing me like a spooked horse.

"Can you stand?" he asked. "I need you to."

Dizzied, I clung to Lucas, one foot planted sideways behind me to keep from sliding down the rocky slope. I felt so much taller than my previous height, as if I'd suddenly grown another two feet. I closed my eyes and curled towards Lucas's body like an invalid.

Step by shaky step, Lucas helped me climb up the slope towards the road. I struggled with dry heaves from exertion, and my feet felt disconnected from my body. The air warmed as we climbed, and I quickly became too hot. Lucas helped me remove my cloak, but long before we reached the summit I knew I had a fever. I hardly remember the last few steps, and was in no mood to rejoice over seeing someone who could help me.

An unknown gentleman possessing the air of authority akin to a doctor rushed over to assist Lucas. He muttered something to my savior, who appeared more than a little scornful upon hearing such news, and that is all I recall before I pitched forward into the doctor's arms.

* * *

When I awoke the following morning, I was back in my old bedchamber at Fogbound Manor. The past twenty-four hours melted away like the god of time toyed with me. Again I could hear the soft pattering of rain against the mullioned windows, listen to the wind rustling against the manor's blocky structure, smell the smoky fire in the fireplace, and snuggle in my own bed under the sheets. Perhaps I should stop shoving against Fate and succumb to what was clearly my destiny – stay here with Jonah until his final hour.

The door creaked and a servant entered with a tray. She set it on the side table and was almost out of the room when she noticed I was awake.

"Good to have you back, miss," she said pleasantly. "I'll let the doctor know you've awakened."

"Have you seen Mr. Herrick at all?"

"No, miss." She shook her head. "I can fetch Mrs. Quinn to perform such a duty, if you wish."

"I do. I ask that she be sent for as soon as possible, to give me an update on Mr. Herrick's state of health."

"Yes, miss." She gave a little curtsy and left.

I stared up at the orange wallpaper on the slanted ceiling. The back of my neck was damp with sweat, and my fever had broken. While I waited, I tentatively tested my left arm. It was far too swollen and bruised to move a great deal. Lucas's first sling had been replaced with one just as neatly tied. The pain reduced to a dull ache focused on the lower part of my arm, about three inches above my wrist. That spot was far too painful to touch.

"A good morning to you, Miss Tate."

I didn't look up. "I am well enough, sir."

Doctor Gravitch set his black bag on the side table. His light eyes and wrinkled skin were quite different from his reverend brother's features, though both had the same deep-voiced air of confidence. He peered down at me like a boy looking at a bug through a magnifying glass. I didn't like being the specimen and squirmed under the scrutiny.

"I was summoned to look after Mr. Herrick, but it seems you are the more pertinent case. Let's take a look."

Instinctively, I drew the bedclothes up further, but he gave me that doctor's fierce stare, and I relented. After Mother's death, doctors poked and prodded at me for weeks looking for any signs of trauma or illness. I had rarely been in the presence of a medical professional since. Mostly quacks, anyhow, hawking their cure-alls from wagons and street-corners. Never in my life would I purchase those poisons.

"I will not take your medicine," I said, gritting my teeth while he examined my arm.

"Have I mentioned any to take?" His brow furrowed and he bent my upper arm until my shoulder zinged with pain. "As I thought. A little fracture. I've seen worse. You will be back to rights within six to eight weeks, I should think. No mobility."

He had the audacity to deliver this order while manipulating the very bone I broke.

"Have you also seen Jonah?" I forgot to call him Mr. Herrick, but the doctor didn't seem to notice.

"I have." He stood back from the bed, folding his arms. At least he was finally looking at me like a fellow human being and not a patient. "He waved off my inspection and bid me come here at once to see to you. He is eagerly awaiting my prognosis of your condition."

"Tell him I'm fine." I was not fine, but that was more due to emotional upheaval. I'd missed the mail boat entirely and there was no way to return to Kennebunkport. "I am more concerned about his state of health."

The doctor sighed. "Of that, I can offer no solace, Miss Tate. I implore you to see to him soon. My diagnosis is of the utmost seriousness. However, he insists upon attending tomorrow's Sunday service."

"Thank you, sir. For bringing me back here, and your expertise."

"You are welcome. Rest up now."

He retrieved his bag and left my chambers. I had to admit I dodged a mighty blow to my health by having such a competent and educated doctor see to me right after the accident. Though the god of time might play with me, the god of good fortune was a noticeable ally.

Perhaps there was still a way to save Fogbound Manor.

twenty-eight

✳

The following morning, after a full day of rest, I roused myself from bed and went to the window. Herrick Island's storm had long since moved off, and steady dripping wetted the glass panes. Snow was melting.

Tick. Tick.

I took out my little lady's watch and slowly rewound the dial. Such a tiny thing, fitting neatly in my palm. I closed my fingers over it, leaned forward, and set it on the window-sill. Jonah's health faded fast, and I had not much time.

My trip downstairs through Fogbound Manor's halls was painful. With every step, my arm ached and chafed against my body. My fingers felt numb, and my whole body was sore from my tumble in the carriage. Doomed horses screaming, crunching and breaking glass, the precarious tipping. A miracle I'd survived.

I met the doctor on the second floor, right at the top of the main staircase. He'd just come from Jonah's room.

"You seem much improved," he commented, "though I cannot say the same for the master. He will not be joining you for church."

"Can you not bid him to come, just for the morning? We'd be back well in time for luncheon."

"Of course not. He needs rest, not a trip outside."

My mind begged for it not to be true, that the sheer vital force of Jonah's energetic, changeable spirit be more fairy-like than mortal. Stay far from the door of death, my dear. Stay with me instead.

The doctor coughed. "Miss Tate, if you would please."

"Will you be attending?" I asked.

He shook his head. "I am on my way to the kitchen for more broth. Do tell my brother to return after the sermon."

He turned and briskly made his way down the second-floor hall. I took up a handful of my skirts, my fingers squeezing the light wool fabric. Perhaps I should go to Jonah. Did he not need me? But then I wouldn't be able to bring the reverend back to Fogbound Manor.

I donned my outer things and stepped outside the manor. The sight of the carriage caused me to stop abruptly. Lucas had brought the two-seat carriage we'd taken to the forest. Two brown mares with dark manes stood at attention. He glanced at me, his usual scowl like a dark furrow. I took a deep breath and tied my bonnet with one hand as I walked across the gravel.

Lucas wouldn't look at me as I boarded the carriage. He muttered something crude beneath his breath, then slammed the door shut. I leaned against the seat, feeling ill as the familiar bumping and swaying of the carriage recalled my accident all too vividly. I squeezed my eyes shut to keep from weeping and held my hands to my face.

Would Jonah be alive when I returned?

A few minutes later, we pulled up to the chapel. Who should be standing at the doorway, leering like vultures over a fresh kill? Onlythe Wenthams. Lucinda was grinning from ear to ear as if I arrived for a happy occasion. Mr. Wentham took his hat off in a fake polite way, then swept over and opened the carriage door with such a dramatic flourish one would think I was royal.

"Miss Tate." He held out a hand to help me. "How sorry I am to hear of your accident."

I refused his assistance and stomped down to the gravel. "I beg to differ, sir. I despise it when gentlemen say they are sorry when they are not. I am now completely deprived of any means of paying your fee for the manor. This, no doubt, pleases you greatly."

"My goodness, Miss Tate." Lucinda sniffed. "Only after I told you how much I wanted to become mistress did you coerce Jonah into giving it to you. Such a change of heart."

"Have you forgotten our conversation? Jonah didn't want to give me the manor." Pain clanged in my arm, and I clutched my shoulder. "May his departure from this earth be a comfort to you both. I suspect I will see you at the funeral."

I would have gladly pushed them into the mail boat myself, setting them off from Herrick Island's shores forever. To see them take control of the manor made me so angry I barely acknowledged the reverend and marched inside the chapel to take my seat on the front pew. The Wenthams sat on the other side of the aisle, snickering and whispering like thieves before a robbery. It didn't take long for the few churchgoers to appear. Reverend Gravitch closed the doors and made his way up the aisle. Before ascending the podium, he paused in front of me.

"Why, Miss Tate," he said softly. "I do not see Jonah here."

My lower lip shook. "He is indisposed, sir. The doctor requests that you come to see him after your sermon."

The reverend sighed. "I knew this day would come. I take comfort in seeing you recovered from your accident, and will accompany you back to the manor."

"We are coming as well," Mr. Wentham announced. The greedy wretch had overheard us. "I have my own last words to say to Mr. Herrick."

"I bet you do!" I snapped.

Lucinda glared at me. "Don't speak to my husband in such a tone, you vicious harpy."

The reverend frowned. "Mr. and Mrs. Wentham, in the presence of one so humble and selfless as our Savior, I bid you both be silent. Miss Tate, your heart is aching with loss and despair. I ask that you find goodness in all that has happened." He knelt down and reached out to take my hand. "God works in mysterious ways, but people also have the ability to work wonders. There is an art to finding treasure, isn't there?"

My eyes filled with tears, and I squeezed his fingers. "I don't know, sir."

"I think you do. What a storm took, gave you new life. There is no loss without something found."

I lost so much, and I still had more loss to face. I silently prayed for the courage to face it.

Reverend Gravitch got to his feet and went to the pulpit. His sermon was on the subject of time. I sat quietly in the snug, warm chapel, a spring breeze rustling leaves outside, and the swishing sound of the sea as Herrick Island's background music. When the clock began to strike its tones, I felt calm and centered. The sea knows no time, nor do the birds and the fishes. Clouds move according to their own clockless rhythm, and storms come and go by a timekeeper's table all their own. To everything there is a season, and a time to every purpose under heaven.

Let me wait here, without clocks or schedules or plans, and stay with Jonah until his final hour.

twenty-nine

✳

Reverend Gravitch and the Wenthams squeezed into the small carriage on the way back to Fogbound Manor, so I elected to go on foot. The ground felt softer, and did I spy a flash of green shoots amongst the constant brown and gray?

I rounded the short road, and the huge foggy shape of the manor came into view. The reverend and the Wenthams had already gone inside. Lucas perched on the carriage, limply holding the reins.

"You're all right," he said gruffly.

"I am."

I walked past him on my way to the front steps. What else could be said, that hadn't been uttered in the carriage? If things had been different between Jonah and me, then perhaps I would have accepted Lucas's offer when we were in the forest together. But Jonah knew me like no other. He saw past my brusqueness and authoritative manner. He didn't want me to give up being myself.

The parlor was all in a commotion, for the master himself was present. Amidst the clamor of voices, I quietly entered the room. Between the reverend, the doctor, and the squawking Wenthams, I glimpsed dark mussed hair. With a surprising burst of energy, Jonah fended off the doctor's attentions and rose at once to his feet.

"Harriet!" he cried.

Everyone in the room turned towards me. The Wenthams glowered, the doctor leaned over with a hand on Jonah to steady him, and the reverend assisted his brother. I jutted my chin, as the lady of good breeding that I was. Mr. Wentham's sneer made me smile. What a newspaper caricature he was. I'd have fun at his expense for as long as I could.

"Jonah," I greeted with a loving smile. "How good of you to come down, though you should be in bed."

"And you should be in Kennebunkport!" His enthusiasm morphed at once to compassion, as he beheld my arm in the little sling. "My dear Harriet, you have suffered such an injury. If only I could take all your pain upon myself."

"Then I am glad you can't," I said, "for it would be too much to bear right now."

"Tut, tut." He elbowed the doctor aside. "I'll not have you think any less of me for my illness. No pity for poor dying Jonah. Reverend, my cane if you would."

"You should not tax yourself too greatly, sir," Mr. Wentham purred. "This disease eats away at your bones as we speak. Why hasten it?"

"Why indeed?" Jonah retorted. He snatched his cane and pointed it at Mr. Wentham. "It is fortunate you have invited yourself to my home. So that I may be so bold as to order you to pack your things and vacate my island at once!"

Mr. Wentham grabbed his wife's hand and they both stomped over to Jonah, bearing down upon him like a Herrick Island storm. But their threatening presence was soon eclipsed by Jonah's poor health. His body could not sustain such an energetic spirit, and he collapsed into his chair. His cheeks were twin circles of bright pink color amidst his deathly pale face. The doctor reached from around his own neck and retrieved what looked like a long tubular device. He pressed the end of it against Jonah's chest, listened for a moment, then gestured for assistance.

"We must get him upstairs. His heart is having palpitations."

"At once," I said. "Doctor, put your arms about his neck and support his legs with your arms. Reverend, lift him on his other side. It's a long climb upstairs."

"Mr. Wentham." The doctor pointed to Jonah's feet. "Take him up with us. Gently, now."

The lawyer snorted. "Are you mad, sir? After what he said to me? I shall not do anything of the sort. Come, Lucinda, we are leaving."

"You both stay here," Reverend Gravitch commanded to the Wenthams. His biblical-sounding voice shocked them, and they froze. "Neither of you are welcome at the chapel. Shame on you, for your lack of compassion in this dying man's hour of need. Refuse to help him, and help will be refused to you."

Mr. Wentham's lip curled, and he smoothed down his waistcoat. "Very well, Reverend Gravitch. Deny us food and lodging. But know this – you are speaking to the future master of Fogbound Manor. And I will have no qualms in turning you out!"

"He will not," Jonah said weakly. "Pay him no mind, Reverend."

"Jonah, calm yourself." I looked pleadingly at the doctor. "Please hurry, sir. Do what you can to help him."

"We shall. Now, stand back."

Mr. Wentham and his wife moved off to the edge of the parlor, conversing fiercely with one another. I helped situate Jonah within the arms of both the doctor and the reverend, and then slowly followed them to the parlor doorway. As we passed by, Mr. Wentham abruptly opened the cabinet door and yanked out the bottle of cognac.

"A toast to your short life, Jonah. May your damned soul enjoy its unresting immortality."

"Stop!" Jonah halted the doctor, and then leaned forward, wobbling on his knees. I steadied him with my good shoulder, my hand clasped in his. "You are right, Nicholas. My soul will stay here, and it will never rest. For I am to be with my Harriet for all time."

"How romantic. She'll be in the poorhouse before long," Mr. Wentham jeered. "What an ideal place for your ghost to haunt."

"Will you please!" I snapped. "Out of their way."

Lucinda sniffed. "Well, if she isn't a captain's daughter! What, you think just because Daddy commanded a ship that you can command us?"

"Don't forget, my dear," her husband added, "that she was born a lady."

"Ha!" Lucinda barked. "It is far better to be a lady of money than a lady born. Come, my husband. Let us away from her low presence, and enjoy a walk on our grounds."

She held up her elbow, and her husband wrapped his hands about her arm like a snake gripping its prey. I'd not uttered a word during this threatening exchange, for I couldn't bear to give them the satisfaction of my wrath. It was too precious to waste on such filth. Just before they left, however, there was someone else who wished to speak his mind.

"You're not to come to my funeral," Jonah whispered hoarsely. "Either one of you. If they do, Reverend, see to it that they are removed at once."

The reverend nodded. "It will be done."

Both of them stared at Jonah, but he would entertain no refusal of this declaration. At last, with a couple more sniffs and their noses in the air as high as could be, they marched out of the parlor and slammed the front door behind them. I gripped my love's hand in solace. His feeble touch comforted me.

Doctor Gravitch cleared his throat. "Now, if you are quite ready, my brother, let us bring him upstairs. Jonah, it's time."

With a reluctance brought about by the deepest of my heart's devotions, I let go of Jonah. I could not have him suffer even one more shadow of pain if I could help it. I tugged on the doctor's jacket.

"Let me not stand idly by. Tell me what I can do."

His brow furrowed, then he gave a pert little nod. "Fetch my blood-letting bowl and needle from the kitchen. Bring them upstairs."

"Yes, sir."

I hurried from the parlor and headed down the back hall, not knowing how to get to the kitchen or where I was half the time. As I ran, my throat felt hard and I wept for Jonah. I'd known this day was coming, but I still couldn't face it. Give me more time!

My beloved manor took pity on the poor girl wandering its halls and revealed a whiff of beef broth coming from a nearby passage. I followed the scent until I'd come upon a low, plain door set right into the thick stony wall. I could smell bread baking and heard the familiar clang of a stewpot's lid. Thank God I'd found the kitchen.

I lifted the latch and shoved the door open with my good shoulder. The kitchen was huge, twice the size of the parlor. A massive hearth stretched along one entire wall, full of bubbling cooking pots and steaming teakettles. On a side table, I spied the doctor's bloodletting equipment – a curved bowl with a section cut out of it, and a case of sharp-looking tools. I grabbed a towel and filled the bowl with hot water, then made my way out of the kitchen.

Fog engulfed me within the halls, and I lost all sense of natural clarity of sight. Strange shapes appeared from the near-darkness, only to be revealed as common furnishings like hall tables and paintings. Yes, Jonah. Haunt me. Haunt me if I am to return to Kennebunkport. Haunt me wherever you can find me. A light of some sort, glowing and rimmed with an aura, appeared at the far end of the hall. Could it be? It was a lit wall sconce – and what door should it be illuminating, but Jonah's?

I entered his bedchamber, where more candles provided weak low lighting. It was as if I'd come upon a dream, fading and cloudy around the edges.

When I saw him in the bed, it was no dream but a vision of a darker sort. He lay pale and wasting, his head propped upon pillows, his corpse-like form the same color as the pale sheets. Seated beside him was the doctor. He pushed up the white linen sleeve of Jonah's shirt, exposing his thin greenish-hued left arm. Reverend Gravitch stood by the bed, a Bible in his arms, his expression grave.

"Good, Miss Tate." The doctor reached for his medical things. "Ah, and hot water. You have yourself an intelligent lady, Jonah."

"Of course I do." Jonah's voice was weak, as if laced with fog. "She'll look after this old place for me. No one could do it better."

The doctor took the bloodletting equipment from me, then began opening the case and taking out his tools. I slowly shifted Jonah's legs aside and sat on the bed by him. I could feel his warmth through the cotton sheets. He reached down and clasped my right hand. A dreadful silence descended. I couldn't even hear the ocean any longer. Jonah closed his eyes while the doctor tied a tourniquet around his arm and proceeded with the bloodletting. A crimson drip, startlingly bright in the dimness, leaked from his skin and gathered in a dark pool in the bowl.

"Your watch has stopped ticking," Jonah murmured.

"Yes, it is stopped." I took a deep breath. "I let it stop."

"Do you still have my own watch?"

"I do."

"Good." He sighed. "Promise me you'll wind it. After I'm gone."

I bowed my forehead down to his body, resting my face upon him, covering the lower half of his body with my warmth.

"I will."

I laid upon Jonah for as long as I could, pressing my fractured arm against my chest, suspending my body above his so as not to cause him any bruising. I could bear the pain, if he could bear his own. I felt more helpless in those moments than ever in my life. So small in the face of things I could not halt or change. I had been made strong through what had been taken from me. I did my duty and obeyed to the best of my ability, and if I had not, then I could endure the consequences. I had no right to ask.

But Jonah ...

Why take him from me? What lesson was I so dearly in need of receiving? For I knew of loss. God, I did know.

At length, with Jonah near to a swoon, the doctor placed wadded cotton on his wound and removed the bloodletting bowl.

"I'll take this down to the kitchen."

"Thank you, sir." I raised my head from Jonah's warmth. "You've eased his suffering greatly."

"I've done what I can, Miss Tate."

The doctor gathered his equipment and softly left the room, then closed the door behind him. Jonah tucked against the pillows and appeared asleep. I could detect the faintest rising and falling of his chest. Reverend Gravitch came around to the side of Jonah's bed and took his seat upon the stool his brother had used. He placed his Bible on his lap, his skin so healthy compared to the young master.

"Before you came up to the room tonight, Jonah made a special request for you."

"Oh?" I rested my hand on Jonah's leg. "What would that be, sir?"

"How his funeral should be." The reverend paused. "He said to tell me what you wanted, and he would approve of it."

I knew what I didn't want, and that was for it to be like my father's funeral. Empty words, little solace, every face a widow.

"When I attended my own father's funeral, it was one of such hollow comfort and coldness. But for Jonah, I wish him to be remembered with better feelings." I gave a sad smile. "I shall be there, to give the eulogy. It will be more than my duty. It will be my last gift to him."

The reverend's eyes glistened. He nodded. "Yes, Miss Tate. I approve of this completely."

I nodded, too emotional to speak of this any longer. Would that I could push it farther into the future, begging more time. I want more time. I never had enough time to know my father, but I had plenty of time to know Jonah. And it brought me the realization that no amount of time could ever be enough.

"I am sorry, my dear." He leaned forward and touched my good shoulder. "I know how greatly you wanted this manor. Enjoy your last moments within it."

"I will. This hearth is always a welcome place for you."

"Thank you. There is nothing Jonah need say to me that he has not already. May he rest easy in heaven with his brother."

He smiled sadly and slowly got to his feet. He paused by the bedside for a long moment, gazing fondly down at the resting man. Then he bid me a sorrowful farewell and left the room.

At last, Jonah and I were alone together.

thirty

✳

"Jonah?" I whispered.

He shifted sleepily on the bed, and I caught his scent. Again, I was beside him upon the rock overlooking the sea – fired by his love, enveloped in his embrace. Crack by tiny chip and crack, he broke down the walls and barriers within me, as a stonemason knows where to place his chisel to split rock. Parts of myself replaced by the us that we created, together. It was no longer Harriet without Jonah, but a new me. My love for him its own accompaniment to the rest of myself.

Yet that day, like so many others during my time here, vanished. In the darkness, his face was so pale and sickly it was almost angelic.

"I will grieve for you," I murmured aloud.

Yes, I would. I'd not spend one future hour without him. So many ghosts here, wandering in and out of these tiny, isolated lives. He'd become another, the friendliest and most loving.

"Harriet?"

"I'm here." I leaned down, my ear close to his lips. "Jonah."

He lifted his fingers and curled them beneath my chin. I softly turned my face, and we shared a kiss so tender it was like seawater slipping over stones. I didn't know love could exist like this. I didn't know anything. He drew his fingers up the length of my face and stroked my hair.

"Are you well?" he murmured. "I fear for you, my dear. It is the great sorrow of my final hour that I should leave you alone without me."

I shook my head slowly, and placed my hand on his. "I am not afraid of loneliness, nor shall I feel your absence. As long as I stay, you will be with me."

"Then stay."

Oh, I would. I'd obey this master as long as he lived. His spirit ebbed from him with each passing breath, but at least for this one moment, he could share his living warmth with me. It was the last thing he could give me, and his act of selflessness broke my reserve as if he'd melted it.

"How completely you have entered me, soul to soul. There is no greater depth than where you are within me, Jonah. I am not only your benefactor." My voice was trembling. The way he touched me was so achingly loving. "I am yours."

He trembled beneath me, his body like a shivering bird. "Do admit it, Harriet. I was right all along. You as the perfect one to complement my faults and virtues."

A tear trickled down my cheek. "We are the last of our kind, are we not? So very alike."

He laughed a little, his voice reedy and thin. "Not at all."

I touched his thin face, and he bent to kiss me once more. We were as different as the rocks and the sea, but on this tiny island, straddling the threshold between worlds, we could share our time together. I am paused beside you, Jonah, in these moments. I live in the now.

He was too weak to utter another word. He was slipping quietly from me, like fog parting above the sea. I could feel the last strength of adoration through his fingers, as our hands pressed against each other. I slowly lowered my cheek until it brushed against his open linen shirt, and the heat of my skin warmed his chest where I lay.

"I won't leave," I murmured. "I won't ever leave."

I could not see his smile, but I heard his final sigh and I felt his quiet contentment spread out around him. There I lay, until my own warmth was the only earthly bond between us. He had left me, for he was breathing no longer.

My Jonah at last had gone.

thirty-one

✳

"Miss Tate?" Reverend Gravitch said gently. "It's time."

"I thank you, Reverend."

I shook his warm hand, then stepped forward towards Jonah's little grave. It was set in the earth beside his brother. A simple curved granite stone, of the same color and appearance as the rock we'd stood upon at the shoreline. The salty ocean air played with my cloak, and my hair breezed about my face. The fog had pulled back a little, nesting within its own cloudlike airiness. I felt like Jonah was here, listening to me.

"When I gave my father's eulogy, I spoke of a man I hardly knew. He never stayed onshore for long, and the sea was his true home. He now rests at the bottom of the Isles of Shoals. But this man, Jonah Herrick of Fogbound Manor, Herrick Island ... This man, I did know."

I closed my eyes and breathed of the fog and the sea. It filled me, passing through my lips and dousing my lungs. Stay with me, my love. Stay here, as I shall stay.

"Jonah understood me, in a way no other never has. I did not have to dim my own light nor submerge any part of myself. I was not the Harriet Tate my own father desired, but the woman I really am. Jonah knew what it was like to leave a legacy. It means we are each a captain of our own ship.

We assume the helm, and we chart our course forward. There is no predestined path, there is no pre-set legacy. You are who you make of yourself."

Now, I was ready to let it go and captain my own future, creating hours so new I couldn't predict what would happen from one moment to the next.

"Thank you for saving me, Jonah." I knelt by his gravestone and laid my hand on its welcoming coolness. "Thank you for freeing me."

I didn't want a legacy any longer. I only wanted to stay here on Herrick Island, beside him forever.

The others dispersed back to Fogbound Manor, and I stayed for a long time beside my love's grave. I could recall so many things he'd said to me. The feel of his passionate kisses on my hand, his warm embrace alighting fire within me.

I walked away from the churchyard and followed the sandy path back towards Fogbound Manor. While approaching from the east, my boots crunching on the path, I soon came upon the rock crevice that led to the beach. He'd never be with me again, he'd never take me by the hand and lead me there. I'd have to do it for us.

I stepped between the rocks and stood at the top of the beach overlooking the pebbled shore and the Atlantic swishing and swirling on the sand. I breathed deeply of the ocean air. I caught a whiff of spring, new life on the wind. Yet as soon as it passed by my face, it vanished and the fog eclipsed it completely.

How gray and mournful this island was, for the earth wept at his loss. The tides had gone out, leaving me alone on the emptiness of a beach. But when the tides came back in to shore, they'd bring the dawn of a new bounty. I would reach down and gather armfuls of the sea's treasures, washed in foamy brine. I could feel the clock wheel turn. A time for everything under heaven.

I made my way down the rocky beach towards the waters. Each footstep carried me closer to that mesmerizing boundary between sea and land. Sand below and fog above, and the ever-present wind kissing me with breezy lips.

Water lapped around my boots, leaving squiggles of wet foam on the thin leather. My reflection rippled and skipped across the surface. A face young of year but wise of time. I gave a sad smile. Yes, my grandmother was right. How alike I was to my father. But since Jonah had loved me, I could look past the resemblance I hated, and find my own version of myself to see.

I am here, Jonah. I stand on our beach. I cannot reach you, I cannot join you. I keep hearing you say over and over that you promised I'd find something real. I did, did I not? The stones beneath my feet, your hand on mine, your love melting my skin. From wherever you are, do you look down upon me and believe we are never to be parted?

I slowly reached into my pocket, and drew out his little watch. A tiny timepiece stopped in its ticking. I carried him with me now, his love a breath of warmth intertwining through me like foam through sea waters.

"I adore you," I whispered into the wind. "I always will."

Will you wind my watch for me? He'd requested. Yes, my love. I will keep this promise and any other you'd have me make.

I cupped the watch in my hand, carefully pulled out the little dial, and began turning it. It made a tiny clicking sound. After winding the dial several times, I pushed it back in. There, now his watch was wound and able to keep time once more.

I waited for the hands to move, but they did not. Puzzled, I held the little clock up to my ear. I couldn't hear any movement of its inner gears. It couldn't be broken. I wound it again, and again heard nothing.

I clicked the top button of the watch to open its back. The curved circle of gold popped open. And what should I find therein ... but a tiny gold key. It was wrapped in a single crumpled scrap of paper and had prevented the little watch from working.

Trembling, I took out the key. It flashed a beam of golden light across my skin, and fog drew back as if surprised. Could it be? No, there wasn't possibly any way. It was too ridiculous to think of. He would have told me.

My fingers were shaking as I slowly unfolded the little scrap of paper. On its parchment surface was one phrase, scrawled in a shaky handwriting I'd recognize even if I'd been struck blind:

the map room

thirty-two

✳

Jonah wanted me to find something. I knew he did.

The little key warmed in my hand. I closed my fingers around it and held it to my lips. I kissed my skin where Jonah had kissed me. What did you leave me, my love? What am I to find?

I picked up my skirts, turned about, and headed up the beach slope. I crossed over the uneven stones, and the sounds of the tides grew fainter behind me. I pulled myself up the beach and headed through the rock crevice. My heart pounded through my whole chest, and I couldn't feel my legs. Jonah's love rushed through me, and I felt like the closer I got to Fogbound Manor, the closer he was to me. The fog was dim and eerie along the road, enveloping the manor in misty wisps. I could see his smile as if he waited at the window for me.

My boots crunched on the gravel carriageway, and I hurried up the front steps. I pulled open the double doors and slipped into the entrance hall. I half-expected Jonah to be there in the parlor waiting for me. *"Harriet!"* His shout echoing in my ears. Could it be only yesterday that I'd said good bye? I gripped the key, took up a handful of my skirts, and started up the main staircase. I turned the corner at the landing, and climbed the final steps to the second floor.

Foggy darkness descended as I slowly walked down the hall towards the map room door. Memories of Jonah draped over me. That first time we came here, with him looking at me the way he did. His face shadowed, his gaze so intense. Could it be I was alone, when his presence was so strong it was crying out from every stone?

I removed the door key and unlocked the map room door. Once I stepped inside, I was astonished at how the room looked now. All of the maps and charts had been removed from the walls and were folded neatly on the center table. I took a match from the box hanging on the wall, and lit all the lamps. That familiar golden glow cast circles of light on the bare walls. I took one of the lamps off its hook and held it out before me as I walked about the blank room. My heart beat so loudly I could barely hear my own footsteps.

With no maps or charts hiding it, I found the door in the wall rather easily. It had a flat black iron latch similar to my own bedchamber door, with a brass escutcheon underneath it. I held my breath. This was it! There was something behind this door Jonah wanted me to find. Half-crying and half-smiling, I held out the little key and inserted it into the lock.

Click.

Oh my goodness, it worked. I lifted the iron latch with a scraping sound and pulled the door towards me. An exotic spicy smell came from within, like I stood at the threshold of an Egyptian temple. I held up my lamp as I tentatively stepped into a tiny storeroom only a few feet wide.

It took me a moment to realize what I was seeing.

Crates. The little storeroom was filled with wooden crates. I counted half a dozen, each about three feet long, stacked in quite the haphazard manner about the room. They were shipping crates, the kind I had seen hundreds of times stacked on the docks ready for a ship's launch. I could smell the lumber. With my lamp providing a tiny circle of glowing light, I leaned forward into the gloom and read a single word upon the crates that caused my heart to choke in my throat:

Phoenix

The *Phoenix*? My father's ship, the *Phoenix*? I blinked, hardly able to believe it. But it was true. I'd seen so many of these crates loading onto his ship each time he left. They must have come from the real *Phoenix*. I reached forward and ran my fingers over the wooden letters. It was like touching my father's own coffin.

Yet, I was a hundred miles from Kennebunkport. How did they get here? Had Jonah sent away for them? A hundred questions crowded my dazed mind.

One of the crates close to me looked as if its lid had been pried open. Oh, what was inside? I set the lamp down and, with my good arm, shoved the flat wooden lid to the side. It creaked and scraped across the wood, suddenly tipped, and clattered to the floor in a rush of dust and wood shavings. Coughing, I picked up the lamp and passed it over the crate.

What was within could have shone with a light all its own. Astonished, I gazed over a large spread of gleaming golden coins, each an identical twin to those now lying at the bottom of the ocean.

"It's the coins," I whispered aloud.

I set the lamp down and reached in. My fingers brushed against their textured metal surfaces. I'd recognize the feel of them anywhere, and suddenly I was standing back in my old foyer at Kennebunkport, turning them about in my hands, marveling at their antiquated beauty. I grasped a handful, and then grasped another handful. For the love of all that was holy, this entire chest was brimming with gold coins!

I gulped. I suddenly stood up and let the coins fall in a tinkling pile back into the crate. Then I burst into a sob of joy as I realized I was surrounded by crates. There were five more!

Upon moving to another crate, I discovered its lid had also been opened. A shove, the light passing over, and I'd found a box containing the finest English silver services I'd ever seen, each piece crafted with astonishing attention to detail. Teapots, coffee pots, bowls, plates, trays, cups, sugar bowls. It was like moonlight had been captured in metal.

A third crate revealed what I could only dare to imagine - cases of jewelry, each piece more exquisitely made than the next. Carved cameos, ropes of pearls, long diamond earrings, jeweled rings as large as chocolates, shimmering tiaras, enormous gold porcelain brooches. A queen's trousseau richer in splendor than a fairy tale.

The other three crates contained items no less amazing in quantity and exquisite luxury - Indian silks and satins, Asian porcelain sets carved with dragons and cranes, and a crate so scented with exotic spices I couldn't believe what I found - papery rolls of cinnamon, sacks of vanilla bean pods, and tiny carved wooden chests filled with exotic pink salts and black peppercorns.

I got to my feet and held my lamp over this most wondrous of treasure rooms. What in the name of heaven had Jonah left me? He must have known of this ... He must have known.

A glint of light revealed an envelope on the floor. I began to weep as I picked it up. Yes, it was Jonah's wonderful scrawl across the front, and it was addressed to me. With my heart overflowing, I opened it and lifted out a letter. My love reached across the stars and spoke to me for the last time.

My dearest darling Harriet,

I can picture that lovely little frown on your face right now, as you must be so put out with me. Don't be cross with either the reverend or the doctor, either. They were only keeping my secret at my request. You have every right to be miffed, my dear, for I never told you of this treasure.

It has sat in this little storeroom for many years. Yet, I had to know Harriet, that your love for me was real, regardless of any money I'd provide. I'm only too glad to bequeath you my unique legacy.

Captain Sumner Tate — your father — stopped here on the island ten years ago. My father made sure one of his crewmembers was looked after, due to illness. Doctor Gravitch was sent for and helped heal the patient. He was Mr. Edmund Percy, if I recall the name correctly.

In return for saving Mr. Percy's life, Captain Tate gave my father the bounty of gold, silver, and jewels in this room. The captain lamented to my brother and I that he had no sons, but only a daughter, and she wouldn't be worth such a dowry.

Ah, but my love, you are worth more than a room of treasures. Your father didn't know it, but I feel I'm only giving back to you what was rightfully yours to begin with.

May this treasure comfort you and provide the home and legacy you could not without it. It's your gift to enjoy, Harriet.

I hope you do so every day of your life.

With all my earthly and heavenly love,

Jonah

I folded the letter, wet with my tears. Be at peace, Father. I know now why I've felt your presence within this fog since the moment I set foot on this island. I cannot believe that you were here, but you did come to Herrick Island after all. And it's time for you to rest at last.

Soon, Mrs. Quinn would bid me to come down to dinner, and I'd be more than happy to tell the Wenthams their future would no longer involve Herrick Island. Then tonight, I'd write to my grandmother and beseech her to come to Fogbound Manor. Out of a shipwreck and a funeral, I'd received a new legacy of love, treasure, and freedom.

I pressed Jonah's letter against my heart. Oh, my dearest. You are not just missed. You are ached for. I understand why you didn't tell me about my father and the treasure. But you shouldn't have feared my heart would be cold to you. No mechanical being am I. I have created a new clock, one shaped of our love, that counts the hours until we are together.

Until then, I will stay here, with your ghost and your home. You promised me I'd come here and find something real.

I did, and it's more than I ever imagined.

* * *

www.ingramcontent.com/pod-product-compliance
Lightning Source LLC
Chambersburg PA
CBHW060906250626
47159CB00008B/2890